My
Sister's
Ex

My
Sister's
Ex

a novel

Cydney Rax

THREE RIVERS PRESS
NEW YORK

For my sister Adrienne (P.S. This book is NOT about you).

Copyright © 2009 by Cydney Rax

Published in the United States by Three Rivers Press, an imprint of the
Crown Publishing Group, a division of Random House, Inc., New York.

www.crownpublishing.com

Three Rivers Press and the Tugboat design are registered trademarks of
Random House, Inc.

Library of Congress Cataloging-in-Publication Data available upon request.

ISBN 978-0-307-45440-9

Printed in the United States of America

Design by Maria Elias

1 3 5 7 9 10 8 6 4 2

First Edition

Sisters are probably the most competitive relationship
within the family, but once the sisters are grown,
it becomes the strongest relationship.

—*Margaret Mead*

We are caught in an inescapable network of mutuality,
tied in a single garment of destiny. Whatever affects
one directly, affects all indirectly.

—*Dr. Martin Luther King Jr.*

RACHEL

Where I'm Going

My cell phone rings like it's screaming for help. I smile when caller ID indicates it's Jeff. Like a dying flower that craves water and sunlight, I yearn to hear the man's voice.

Maybe Jeff's having second thoughts. I know I am.

Perched comfortably on the couch of my living room, I quickly answer the call. "Hey, how's it going?" I ask, trying to sound extra sweet and sexy. Trying to make him remember what he used to love. But Jeff doesn't respond to my sensual, tender voice. He says nothing. At least not to me. Yet I hear him talking. The commotion of background noise and other voices. A conversation. I press my cell phone securely against my ear and listen in.

Jeff says, "Oh, shoot, sorry."

"Hmm, you must be thinking about Rachel. Why else would you mention her?"

"Yo, sorry about that. I promise not to mention her again . . . That is tacky since technically this can be considered our first date. Now, as I was trying to say before, would you like for me to order more wine?"

"Yeah, go ahead. I'm really in the mood to celebrate."

"I'm just glad I can share this moment with you, Marlene."

"Mmm, you have no idea how good that makes me feel inside."

Well, damn. Is that . . . *Marlene*'s voice? Where are they, and why is my half sister with my Jeff talking about ordering wine?

Jeff says, "So does that mean you wanna do this? You don't feel like you're . . . ?"

"Baby, it's not even necessary for me to explain the way I feel about you. I've been wanting you . . ." The clattering background drowns out Marlene's confession.

What the hell? Speak up, tramp. I want to shout so bad, scream straight into my phone so both these scumbags know I can hear them. Know that the *Cheaters* camera crew is all up in their faces. They're busted. Can't lie. Truth always cancels lies.

And then, I instantly understand what's going on. It's obvious Jeff didn't intentionally call me even though his phone accidentally did. This man isn't trying to talk to me!

I continue to eavesdrop on their conversation and hear Jeff say, "Your hair looks so pretty. You just got it done?"

What'd he say? A couple of hours ago I stunk up my and Marlene's bathroom and hovered over her big head so I could style this chick's hair. After she shampooed her own dark brown locks, she twisted my arm and sweet-talked me into flat-ironing them; I said okay, and, as an added bonus, I put those cute little crinkle waves in it so her hairdo would look long and wavy and have lots of body. If I had known the skank was—

"Yeah, um, Jeff, I'm so happy you like my new do. It *is* cute isn't it?"

The smile in Marlene's voice drips with pure ecstasy. I

can imagine her broadly grinning as if a nice hefty tax refund check just arrived in the mail. Smiling and profiling and looking like a sheer fool. That girl oughta be ashamed. I distinctly remember when she hopped out of the shower tonight, she twisted her dried-looking lips and told me she was going to church of all places. A lying Christian. The only place she's going to is hell. Jeff, too.

"Hey, baby, taste this," I hear Marlene say.

She calls him "baby"? Okay, who just kicked me in the gut? I reach down and clutch my belly, rubbing it to ease my pain.

"Mmm, it's good. Oooo, hey, don't do that," Jeff says, laughing. I stare at the phone, wishing it was a webcam so I could clearly see what they're up to.

What doesn't Jeff want her to do? What are they *doing*?

"Ooo, sss, mmm." Oh my God, I hope she's not sucking my honey's fingers in public. Marlene knows that's one of my favorite moves that I'd always use on my Jeff. I'd take two of my sweetie's thick fingers, lick my lips with saliva, and get down to business, slowly and seductively shoving his fingers deep inside my slippery mouth. Lightly kissing, licking, pecking on the tips. Then, using lots of tongue, I'd feverishly devour all his fingers as if they were a different, delicious, and engorged part of his body. I'd watch my honey squirm, his eyes roll deep in the back of his head until I could see the whites. And I'd hear him moan. "Awww ooo ohhh yeah, Rachel." Hearing him moan got me super hot, too, especially when he'd say my name; his voice alone could cause a pool of wetness to totally soak my panties. And I'd start smelling that smell that you smell when you're about to make love. A stinky yet erotic odor that adds to the nastiness of the moment. And I remember, whenever I kissed, licked, and sucked Jeff's fingers, he'd always return the favor. Always.

Uh-oh!

"Um, damn, Jeff," Marlene says. "Let's get out of here."

I stand up, panic-stricken, and yell at my cell phone.

"You unconscionable prick. Your stupid phone . . . no, your *smart* phone with its voice activation feature . . . Apparently it . . . How can a damn phone with no feelings expose you and tell me what you're not brave enough to tell me?"

I toss the phone on the carpet. I'm talking to Jeff but, of course, it's apparent he's too involved with my sister to hear my frantic outbursts. I am standing in the living room of my and Marlene's two-bedroom apartment. It's ten-thirty at night. I know one thing—that girl better be home within an hour. She has to be at work at seven-thirty tomorrow. She works at the bank. And if she's too drowsy to pay attention to what she's doing, she'll screw up big-time and count out the wrong amount of change to her customers, and then I can enjoy watching the skank get fired. Yeah, that'll be good for her. Get her nasty, scandalous, Mo'Nique-looking self fired so she can be broke. Then Jeff won't give a damn about her chubby cheeks, because he's always said he prefers women who have a job.

I know unflattering information about her:

1. She's big as hell and has to use lots of soap and water to smell halfway fresh.

2. She passes gas in her sleep; how romantic is that? I pray to God he never gets to find out that little detail. But then if he does, hopefully it'll be a deal-breaker.

3. She's a big-time sucker for anybody who gives her a compliment. A man can be sitting in a wheelchair at the corner of a crowded intersection holding a cardboard

sign on his lap, but if the loser gestures at my sister to roll down her car window and calls her "cute," the gullible dummy blushes like she was just propositioned by Barack Obama, and she'll fork over a few crinkled five-dollar bills. Someone needs to send Marlene a slow check real quick, because she is so naive it's embarrassing. For centuries men have told women everything they think we want to hear. Doesn't mean any of it is true.

I'm so upset I swallow this huge lump that's lodged in my throat; a lump so sore, harsh, and burning it feels like I've swallowed acid.

I bend down and pick up the phone, not wanting to miss anything else they're saying.

"It's getting late, Baby Doll."

"I'm not worried about that. I'm good."

"You wanna go hang at my crib?"

"Uhhh. Yeah, Jeff, that makes more sense."

Oh, God, no!

I hear silence. Giggles. More moans. I want to throw up. How can she claim to be a Christian and be in public practically screwing a man she's only been with a minute? Unless they've been slipping and sliding behind my back all the time Jeff and I were together.

I knew him first. He loved me, too. I got to experience ten months of being loved by a man who made me feel like I'd been born again. He'd still be mine, too, if I hadn't gotten scared. Hadn't run away from his love. Love and fear don't mix, do they? I had to learn that the hard way. And I *hate* hard. Hate it so much, because it means I could have learned the lesson but didn't. I failed. Failure equals losing. I hate losing and not knowing how to guarantee that I'm going to win, be successful, be truly happy.

And maybe that's why the relationship thing with Jeff got messed up. He blames me. I don't know who to blame or what to think. Especially now. I am in no condition to face my sister after hearing what I've heard. What is she thinking? Who is she trying to fool? How can someone twist her mouth to say she's going to church? She distinctly told me, "Rachel, Solomon's Temple is having something tonight, so I'm heading over there. I'll be home later, okay sweetie?"

"Oh, okay, shoot. I know it's last minute, but maybe I could go with you."

"What? For real? No, girl, you haven't been to church in a month of Sundays. Why do you want to join me tonight?"

"Well, you look so happy I want some of what you're getting," I said, laughing.

She laughed, too. Rolled her ugly cow-looking eyes, and didn't say anything else. So I left that one alone.

I really didn't care if I went to ST with her or not. Like she said, I hadn't attended church in months, since last autumn. The church has thousands of members, and I always felt like a number, never a person. I wasn't convinced the pastor and ministers could meet my needs, and smaller churches depend on their members too much. So I chose to stay home and watch "church" on television. But lately I haven't even been doing that.

So I wasn't serious about going with her at all. Shoot, in my mind my Friday night was already set, and I was happy as a singing little sparrow. Had a couple great DVDs to laugh at (one featuring Queen Latifah, the other starring Ben Stiller). I had some of that buttery and salty microwave popcorn, plus several ice-cold Capri Suns stashed in the freezer, waiting for me to place my lips around their itty-bitty orange straws. Hey, I was gonna kick back at the crib and, once again, try not to mentally torture myself for my recent decision to split with Jeff.

But now?

The wounds are so fresh it's like I've been hacked with a saw and am lying on the floor bleeding to death . . . again.

Yeah, I know I initiated the breakup, but don't think for a second that Jeff was the only one hurt. "What did you say?" Jeff asked the day I mustered up the courage to tell him "we" were over. Earlier I had asked him to meet me near our spot, a beautiful jogging trail in Memorial Park. In times past, we'd go there to do our power walks, or to talk, hold hands, and engage in some serious PDA, not caring if anyone saw us. But on that chilly January day, we sat next to each other at a picnic table that was partially damp, and I remember my pants felt cold, moist, and uncomfortable.

"Jeff, baby," I murmured, nervously rubbing my hands together. "I can't do the wedding thing right now."

"Right now? Does that mean you are getting cold feet? You need a little time to think? If so, that's not uncommon—"

"Jeff, I have thought carefully about it. It's all too much. Too soon. I'm flattered, but it bothers me that we've been dating less than a year. I feel there's so much more I ought to know about you. And to be honest, I don't feel at peace about taking this big of a step. I'm scared we're moving too fast."

"Rachel," he said with widened eyes, "you didn't think we were moving too fast when you said yes a few weeks ago."

"I know, Jeff, I know. I was so flattered that you asked that I got caught up in the moment. And, the ring, my God, that was an incredible surprise. But I haven't been able to sleep well the past few nights. Can't think straight. Marriage is a serious step. I don't want to make any wrong decisions . . . so I'm choosing to not do anything."

"So breaking up with me is not doing anything?"

"Call it what you want Jeff, but no, we're not getting married. We're just not."

No doubt, I was crazy about Jeff, but at times during our courtship, I would feel deep twinges of emotional pain. Jeff wouldn't always call me back when he promised he would. He'd have me waiting by the phone, picking it up, looking at it, making sure the volume was turned up as high as possible; sometimes I would neglect going to the restroom when I had to pee, just so I wouldn't miss the man's call. And I'd wait for him so long my mind started talking to me.

Where is he this evening? Why did he say he was going to do one thing and ended up doing something totally different? This isn't the first time, either. He has you waiting for hours sometimes. And the excuse is always about how he had to work. Nobody works that much. Jeez, the guy is his own boss. He can make time to call.

Bottom line is I never could completely turn my heart over to a man who I don't fully trust. And when my mind would ask me probing questions, I'd want to scream and yell and cover my ears with my hands trying to drown out undeniable warning signs. It's those nagging inner voices that most women who are dangerously in love frequently ignore. But when my mind advised me to cool things off between us, I listened. That's why I had to tell him even when it hurt.

"Do you mean you want to postpone everything? Give yourself more time?" Jeff softly asked me, obviously just to be sure I meant what I said.

"Um, I mean that I won't be marrying you anytime soon."

Even though I spoke firmly, I couldn't help notice how his face was stricken with frustration, a stunned gaze, as if he'd just been sacked by several 350-pound football players.

Strangely enough, I felt as frightened as Jeff looked. I never wanted to be responsible for someone else's sorrow. It's not that I didn't love him; I just didn't feel prepared to go the demanding distance that marital love requires. And as much as I felt he loved me, I wasn't sure Jeff was as ready for this big step as he believed he was.

"I–I don't understand."

"I know you don't understand now, but maybe you will later. I need time to discover who I am as a person, as a woman . . ." Jeff was staring at me in such an odd way that the remaining things I wanted to say skidded into silence. An uncomfortable feeling began to enlarge. The intensity felt like a ticking bomb.

"Are you sure about this?" he finally asked.

"Yes, I am, Jeff. But, no, I— . Look, don't make this any harder . . ."

"You're going to regret this. You know that, don't you?"

"Oh, honey, don't be mad."

"I'm not mad, Rachel. I'm happy. So completely happy that I now understand you never really loved me like you said you did. Telling me you loved me because you thought it was the thing you're supposed to say. Love isn't what you say, Rachel . . . it's what you do."

Love is what I do.

I *do*.

I messed up the chance to tell Jeff "I do."

Have you ever made a decision and instantly regretted it but felt too embarrassed to speak up? To back out? Listening to Jeff tell me off for breaking his heart was probably the most grueling thing I've ever experienced. Listening to the truth about myself, my indecisiveness, my inability to truly commit to something and see it through to the end. But hearing him rip me apart made me realize, Rachel, even if you could change your mind, don't. It's too late. The damage is done. He'll never believe that you honestly loved him. Never.

There I was feeling stupid and miserable and wondering if I could change my mind, undo my confusion. While I wrestled with my decision, Jeff suddenly hopped off his seat, kicked violently at some rocks, and laughed bitterly. "I'm glad I got the news you don't love me before you officially became Mrs. Williams. At least now I get to hold on to my fifty percent. You probably just wanted me for my money."

"Please, Jeff, don't say that." I turned around in my seat and stared. "It hurts, it's not true, and it's not nice."

"Why are you concerned about me being nice to you? I was *too* nice to you, Rachel! That's the problem. You complained you wanted a good black man, saying how hard it is to find a decent brother, and when the good Lord blessed you with our relationship, you still act like you can't love and appreciate me. Rachel, I thought you were the intelligent, mature, and classy type, but I see I was wrong."

"Jeff!" I screamed. "Please stop, please."

"No, no, no. Don't cry Rachel. Too late for crying. You made this decision, and for once I'm not going to try to talk you out of what you feel you have to do."

"Jeff, baby, please."

"Not your baby anymore, Rachel. You've relinquished your right to call me baby, to call me period, or to do anything with me. Did you think about all this before you made your decision?"

"Baby!" I screamed louder, not able to help myself. "Please stop, I can't stand listening to what you're saying. Don't you know you're hurting me?"

"Where's my ring?" he said. And the fact that he said it with immeasurable calmness is what hurt the most. As angry as Jeff was, I knew he still loved me, but how could he go from raging emotion to great calm within two seconds?

"W–what did you say?" I blinked.

"Don't act stupid, Rachel. I paid a grip for that piece of jewelry; hell, it could've been a down payment for a house . . . a house with a new woman who can appreciate a good, honest, decent man when she sees one. I can't believe I was ready to marry you, ready to waste my life with an immature ass—"

"Stop, stop, Jeff, you're talking crazy."

I was sniffing and snorting loudly. Gobs of yellowy milky snot spilled from my nose, sliding rapidly, almost resting inside my open mouth. I looked the most natural type of ugly, and I knew that wasn't making anything better. And right then, almost instantly, my regrets nagged at me like guilt pointing its finger whenever I do something wrong. I felt so confused, so hurt, so wounded. I didn't realize that making this kind of decision would affect me in a way I never imagined.

Foolish me.

While I continued to weep, Jeff resumed ranting and raving, actually screamed at me the way a ten-year-old boy screams at his little sister for losing his favorite video game.

I was standing up by then, shoulders shaking uncontrollably, and, wishing I could hide, I slowly backed away from Jeff. He rushed at me, grabbed my hand, and forcibly removed the engagement ring from my finger; he twisted and turned and pulled on the ring until it popped off, making my skin look bloodred. He peered angrily at the ring, then shoved it in his pocket.

Boy, was it beautiful: eighteen-carat white gold with sixteen exquisite diamonds. It always flashed brilliantly in the sunlight, partially blinding me whenever I stared at it with dreamy eyes. I went to bed wearing that ring, showered with it on, always gently stroked its beauty with my fingers. But I guess I should have loved the man more than the ring. And after Jeff snatched and concealed the jewelry, he stared at me with hateful, water-filled eyes. He looked like he wanted to say something else but abruptly turned and walked away from me.

I watched my now ex-fiancé's back grow smaller until a lonely distance was created between us. When I couldn't handle looking at him anymore, I fled to my car, trying to leave Memorial Park as fast as possible.

I got in my car and drove toward home, still weeping and mumbling, "Oh God, oh Jesus, please help me, I'm about to lose my mind. I'm sorry, I'm sorry, so sorry."

I felt so distraught and confused that I missed my exit driving south on I-59 toward Sugar Land. Every landmark flashed by me so fast. I quickly sped past a shopping complex called The Fountains, the Kim Son Restaurant, Borders bookstore. Further down the road and across the highway was the defunct Bill Heard Chevrolet. I drove with such speed I felt as if I were ascending toward a place I've never been.

And remembering the day that I broke up with him, I find myself here, alone in the apartment. I tightly hold the phone in my hand and listen to my ex romance my sister. I think deeply about my relationship with Jeffrey Williams. Why on earth would Marlene betray me by going out with Jeff? I wonder about where I have been, and try to figure out where I'm going.

MARLENE

The Jeffrey Williams Way

"Wooo, Jeff, be careful," I sweetly tell him as I stick a forkful of steak and mushrooms near his open mouth. The well-done meat is sizzling and dripping with savory brown juices.

"Mmm," Jeff moans, eating up everything off the fork. "That tastes sooo good, Marlene. More, more, more."

I giggle and continue feeding this starving man. "You like that, Jeffy Jeff?"

"I love it, girl, but I feel guilty. I should be feeding you. You're the one who deserves to be honored."

"Awww, that's so sweet. But it's cool. I love doing this; just don't let that meat burn your tongue. What on earth can I do with a burnt tongue, you know what I'm saying?" I hope Jeff understands my sense of humor and realizes it's also an attempt to show him I am a sensual woman. He's ever so polite, and I want to get him to be more than just a good friend to me. When I ran into him today at Walgreens during my lunch break, we caught up on the current happenings. He's still purchasing and renting out property all over Houston. I'm still doing the bank thing and am contemplating taking a night class at the University of Houston. All safe, simple info. But I was careful not to mention Rachel. She was like the big ole elephant standing in the itty-bitty room, and I wanted to keep it that way. Instead of bringing her up, I excitedly mentioned the fact that my boss promoted me to lead bank teller earlier today.

"Yep, Jeff, it's cool to be doing something different. I've been at the darned bank more than three years now, and they're just now recognizing a sista's skills."

"Well, congrats, Marlene. Hey, we ought to do something special. You wanna go out with me tonight? Do a little something something to celebrate your promotion?"

"Hey, I'm cool with that." Inside I was screaming with pure excitement over the fact that Jeff wanted to go out, but outwardly I feigned an expression that suggested I didn't give a care one way or the other. I feel it's important to show a little interest but never act too desperate. Although I've always liked him, it doesn't mean that he feels the same about me. Plus, I noticed that he didn't seem to be concerned about Rachel, which made me wonder about his motives. Is it an innocent dinner? Would Rachel even care if I spent time with her ex? I felt a teensy nervous about what she may think but was too thrilled about going out with him to even second-guess what I was doing at the time.

"Alrighty then, let's just meet up at seven or so," Jeff told me. "I would scoop you up, but I got to meet a couple potential tenants at one of my properties on the north side."

I really didn't believe him when he said he would pick me up. After all, I live with his ex. I'm not sure if he wants to face Rachel under those circumstances. And I am not ready to face her, either. How would I be able to explain our being together? Besides, if it turns out to be just dinner, there won't be any need to tell her anything.

So that's how we hooked up at a restaurant. Wasn't

planned at all. Yeah, I got real lucky. But before meeting Jeff for dinner, I needed to make a little pit stop at my church, Solomon's Temple. As a high-ranking member of the college scholarship committee, I'd taken home tons of papers a few days ago, prescreening applicant info that I insert into a nice fancy spreadsheet. As soon as I returned the scholarship applications back to ST's administrative office, I sped to the steak restaurant, eager to meet up with my sister's ex.

I went on about my merry little way, and, quite naturally, I wasn't about to tell Rachel where I was going and who I was meeting to celebrate my good news. That would've been like asking Flavor Flav to get a face-lift. Dude thinks he's fine just the way he is, so there's no need to insult him about the way his face looks. And that's how Rachel would've felt: insulted, pissed, hurt, wounded, every negative adjective in the dictionary.

But if things go the way I hope they will, I will have to figure out a nice way to get this girl to calm down and maybe grow used to the idea of a Jeffrey Williams and Marlene Draper hookup. I may be rushing things, but, shoot, when it comes to love, strange things happen. People fall in love at first sight. They end up with someone they hadn't counted on. So you can't help who you fall in love with. Rachel's twenty-two; she oughta know that. And just because things didn't work out between her and Jeff doesn't mean I'm not allowed to get to know him better, right? Show me the written rule that says she and I can never be attracted to the same guy. If Chance and Real both knowingly went on the *I Love New York* reality show to compete for the same woman, then it's also not unusual for me to be attracted to a guy Rachel's dated.

"Hey, baby, taste this," I say to Jeff. I gently press a forkful of veggies against his open mouth. I didn't feel as if I was overly flirting by calling Jeff "baby." In the South, that's just our standard friendly way of talking to people. Certain people.

"Mmm, it's good." He takes one bite but then glances closely at the food. "Ooo, hey, don't do that," Jeff says, laughing.

"What?"

"Um, I don't do broccoli. I like the cauliflower and carrots, but broccoli makes me break out."

"Oh, sorry. I'll have to remember that. You know I can throw down in the kitchen."

"I'm sure you can," he says, and eyes me up and down. "I've tasted your delicious cooking before."

"Oh, yeah?" I say, smiling into his eyes and ready to hear how we're connected in a way I didn't realize.

"Yep, Rachel would . . ." and his strong voice turns into a weak whisper. And I flinch at hearing her name again, but am determined not to let his conscience spoil our night.

"Hey, let's toast," I say, changing the subject.

"Damn, you're right. Sorry." He smiles and picks up his glass of wine, raising it high above our table. "To Marlene Draper. Congratulations on your promotion, the increase in salary, and to your fabulous new beginnings at Compass Bank."

" . . . and new beginnings for my life, *period*," I say with determination. "This promotion makes me feel like I can improve in other parts of my life. Including my love life, which hasn't been the most wonderful."

"Oh, yeah?" Jeff grins. "What's been going on?"

"I just haven't met the kind of guy who gets me excited to wake up in the morning, you know what I'm saying? But today, right now, I just feel encouraged about my future," I say and smile broadly. "You feel me?"

"I do understand. When good things happen, even if they are tiny, you feel hope about everything around you."

"I couldn't have said it better myself, Jeff."

We clink glasses. He starts to take a sip of his wine, but I clear my throat. "Excuse me."

"What?"

"We need to wrap our hands around each other, and I'm supposed to spill a little of my drink into your glass and vice versa."

"Huh?" Jeff frowns.

"Toasting is to ensure that there's no poison in our drinks. That we both trust each other enough to drink from the same glass. That way I know you aren't trying to kill me." I laugh.

"Woman, excuse me, but that sounds ridiculous. For all I know you could be trying to kill *me*," he says with seriousness. "Hey, I'm just trying to give major props to a sista that's getting her grind on. Listen! You drink out of your glass, I drink out of mine."

His defensiveness makes me eye him closely. Whatever. I'll do what he wants. This time!

"Okay chill out, Jeff. I was just trying to do it the right way."

"When you hang out with me we're going to do it the Jeffrey Williams way. Is that all right, sweetheart? Baby doll? Beautiful girl?"

And I smile and melt and melt again, and I agree to do things the Jeffrey Williams way.

While sitting there I feel self-conscious. What if someone who knows Rachel pops up in the restaurant? Would it be embarrassing? Would I try to act like everything is cool? I feel like people are looking at me, but I can't help how wonderful it feels to be around Jeff. He makes me laugh; he is very complimentary; and considering how busy he is with his job, the fact that he is using his time to celebrate with me means a lot.

As soon as we finish our delicious meal and freshen up in the lavatory, Jeff kindly pays the tab and walks me to my car, a pink Volkswagen Beetle with a cream-colored convertible top. It's the cutest little car that any confident and flirty woman can own. I feel on top of the world every time I drive the darned thing!

"Hey, nice ride. Is this new?" he says, closely examining its body.

"Yep, I traded in my SUV for something, you know, a little more flirty and a lot more fly. Plus, I've always wanted a convertible. Always wanted to drive something that makes people stare."

"I *knew* there was something I liked about you. You know, Rachel . . . oops, I meant to say, Marlene, I gotta drive you around in my newly purchased Mach 1. I paid cash for it a few weeks ago. Red body. Black stripes with hood pins and louvers. I named her Ella, and she's the most important thing to me in the world, beside my rental properties."

He was talking about his car, but I was silently fuming about how he's mentioned my sister several times in thirty minutes. I guess her being in the periphery of his mind is something that comes with the territory. Will I be able to deal with that?

"Hey, I'm game, baby boy. I love driving, especially on a beautiful Sunday afternoon when the weather is just right. Sun shining bright, no clouds in the sky. Ooo wee!" I laugh. I want him to think that his slipup calling me Rachel doesn't faze me.

"Sounds like a plan. Anyway, follow me and we'll go hang out at my crib. This here is my work ride," he says, sounding calm and confident. "I'm sure you remember my other car . . ." His voice drifts off. "As you can tell, I love cars." Jeff walks a few feet away and points at an all-white Honda sedan that is sitting directly under the parking lot lights. "It's a good five years old but well maintained. Main thing is it gets me from point A to point B."

I like how he's freely sharing with me some of the things he loves most in his life. He walks me back to my car again, then enters and starts his Honda, backs out, and blows his horn. I follow close behind him as he heads for his place.

While I'm alone driving in my Volkswagen, Blinky rings me up, but I'm not really in a Blinky mood right now.

"Hey, Daughter Number One, whatcha doing, whatcha doing?"

"Hi, Blinky," I say coolly. "I'm out and about. That's what I'm doing."

"Oh, well, don't forget to swing on by the crib Sunday. Around two o'clock."

"Dang, who told you?" I complain. Monday is Blinky's birthday, but the family is getting together to celebrate one day early.

"Y'all know you can't keep nothing from me. Shoot, I'm almost sixty, and I didn't reach this age by being dumb."

"No comment, Daddy. No comment."

"Are you trying to call your daddy dumb?"

"You say you're not dumb, but you don't know what 'no comment' means? Where's Mama?" I say, changing the subject.

"She's bent over a sink messing with some turnip greens, black-eyed peas, and corn on the cob, and she's about to get into some crawfish, getting them good and ready for ya."

"Oh, wow, crawfish, your favorite. Yep, I'll be at your little so-called surprise party."

"Good, darling, I can't wait to see ya. Now where's Rachel?"

"Um, probably at home. Playing flip TV. Sleeping for hours. You know Rachel."

"Damn shame. I hope she's not still depressed."

"If she is it would be all her fault for ending her relationship with a good man. Times are hard right now when it comes to men and women sticking together for the long haul. Everybody knows that. And finding a good man who'll treat you like a queen is like stumbling upon gas that's a dollar a gallon. Now, she's the real dumb one, Blinky."

"Hey, Pretty Girl, don't be talking smack about your younger sister. She needs you right now, needs you to be in her corner, not talking her down to people."

"Well, if she doesn't wanna get talked down, she's gotta stop with the dumb stuff. I mean, jeez, any strong, intelligent woman knows that. I've known so many women who kicked out their boyfriends and are now crying for them to come back. She should've thought about the consequences of her decision before regretting it a week later."

I guess my bad attitude is my way of justifying the fact that I've sneaked and gone out with her ex. If she didn't want him, isn't he free to find a woman who will?

"Pretty Girl, you're not acting too pretty right now. Humph, I didn't see you taking your own advice when you were down in the dumps after your failed relationships."

"Blinky, you can't compare me to Rachel, now can you? Nope, don't answer, because you can't. I hate when you do that." He always defends Rachel. I'm not sure why.

"You ain't any better than her, so get off your high horse."

"Blinky, she owes me two hundred dollars—"

"Ha," he laughs. "Girl, you better kiss that money goodbye. You know how Rachel is. Treat it like a gift instead of a loan. And how did we get on the subject of someone owing someone money?"

"Blinky, from six A.M. to six P.M., you're always taking her side, but she doesn't deserve it." I have always been overly sensitive about how my daddy defends my sister.

"Okay, Pretty Girl, I can hear you getting all upset. I'll back down," he says quietly. "But frankly I don't see how you two live in the same apartment with the attitude you got, Marlene."

"My attitude? Ha!"

"Why you yelling, huh?" Blinky asks, and I realize it's in my best interest to calm down. It wouldn't be cool to go to Jeff's place in a rotten mood.

"No, we're straight, Blinky," I say and dab at the corner of my eye with my finger. A twinge of guilt gnaws at me, since my daddy doesn't know I'm following behind my sister's ex, going over to hang out at his place. I attempt to keep my voice reassuring and strong. "For real, you shouldn't be overly worried. Everything is okay between us, and if it's not it will be. Nothing we haven't been through before."

"Your voice sho sounds funny." I don't say anything to him. He continues, "And where you going so late at night?"

"Blinky, how you know I'm in my car?"

"Daughter Number One, do I sound like I was born yesterday? I know things. I always know things."

My daddy has always been able to sense things about me and my life and has no qualms speaking his mind; he rarely backs down from putting me in my place. I guess he and I are alike when it comes to that. We don't mind facing what scares us.

One thing I've learned in my twenty-six years of living is that even if you are scared out of your mind, sometimes you gotta act on your fears. You gotta be brave enough to walk out on that long diving board and take the plunge. Because that's the only way you're going to get anywhere or gain anything worth having. Playing it safe doesn't belong anywhere in my life. And all that scared-acting stuff is not the right move for Marlene Draper. I guess I inherited that attitude from our daddy, Vaughn Draper, aka Blinky. I'm told he was given that nickname because as a baby, he blinked all the time like something was caught in his eye. The name stuck. Well, this man is not a baby; he is an experienced man who will take a risk even if it damn near kills him. And so far death has escaped him, because, in our family, living to see sixty is a major accomplishment. I plan to follow in his footsteps. Taking chances and living life in such a way that it helps me get what I want. And I want a chance to be with Jeff.

When Rachel and I were little girls, her mother, Brooke, would always try to make sure that her daughter was dressed in outfits that were newer and prettier and better tailored than mine. At first I didn't understand, and I hardly paid attention to Brooke's shenanigans. But as I got older, I started to retain certain events more and more.

I was eight; Rachel was four.

"See Rachel's new shoes, Marlene? Aren't they cute?" Then she'd stop and blankly stare at my shoes, which had holes in the bottoms and soles that were falling apart so you could see what color socks I had on. When Brooke would interrogate me like this, I'd blink my eyes several times trying to stop the tears from spilling and soaking my face. But I'd always nod my head in agreement with Miss Brooke only because she was my elder, even though I barely wanted to. "Yes, ma'am, Rachel's shoes are so pretty. I have some just like them at home. I'm wearing these old shoes now because I don't want to mess up my nice ones." Rachel's mom would smirk at me, and I'd turn away feeling ashamed. I'd glance down at my shoes and hope that when I got home, I'd really find a pretty new pair waiting on me.

And when I did arrive and the shoes I dreamed of wouldn't be there, I'd search our house, going from room to room looking for Blinky. That's when he was jobless and extra cash was scarce. Mom was going to school and her job didn't pay much. So Blinky spent a lot of time holed away in the dark den; the windows would be covered up with pages from an old copy of the *Alexandria News Weekly* (he was born in Louisiana). Blinky would be propped up on his La-Z-Boy with an unlit cigarette bobbing from his mouth. And he'd be wearing his usual sleeveless undershirt and some raggedy-looking slacks that had holes in them from countless accidental cigarette burns. I'd grab his big arm and crawl onto his lap, whining. One day I told him, "Daddy, Rachel got some new shoes. Where mine at? I want some, too."

"You can't have everything your sister has."

"Did you buy them for her?"

"I don't have any money. Brooke's 'friend' got them for her." I knew it meant another man who was sweet on Brooke and would try to impress her by giving Rachel presents. "Get away from me, Pretty Girl."

"Don't call me that. Miss Brooke says I'm ugly. Am I ugly, Blinky?"

"Pretty Girl, you're not ugly. Why do you think I call you Pretty Girl?"

I shrugged my shoulders, confused.

"Then why Miss Brooke say I'm ugly? She always says Rachel is prettier than me. And Rachel has nice pretty dresses, too . . . and shoes . . . She *is* prettier than me." It's like I discovered the truth on my own. And I loudly burst into tears and covered my face with my chubby fingers. Blinky patted me on the back. Then he reached in his pocket and handed me a crumpled five-dollar bill, which, at the time, felt like a hundred dollars. I couldn't buy a new pair of shoes with the money, but knowing he cared enough to stop me from crying managed to calm me down for a moment.

The next time I saw my little sister, Rachel, I flashed my five-dollar bill in her face and stuck out my tongue. She raced to her room and came back holding a couple of crinkled five-dollar bills, plus a quarter. I guess Brooke's friend gave her that money. I burned with jealousy, shut my eyes closed, and waited for my sister to disappear. But she never did.

Jeff turns into the driveway of his modest, one-story frame home. Within seconds, the garage door automatically opens. Jeff pulls in next to another car whose body is completely cloaked with a sheet of light blue fabric. He jumps out of his car and waits for me, then walks over to the covered vehicle.

"Even though I have a garage, I still gotta protect Ella with the indoor car cover; it's actually called WeatherShield fabric, and it's great at protecting my baby from nicks and scratches."

"Ahh, so she's special, huh?"

"You better believe it. It's a classic that I enjoy maintaining. Ella is the kind of car that everyone knows is mine whenever I take her out for a drive."

"Well, let me see her."

"Of course." Jeff grins at me and reaches in his pocket. He retrieves a set of keys and inserts a tiny key inside a lock that is attached to the car cover. The lock pops open, and Jeff completely pulls the fabric off his Mach 1.

"Hey, this is so cool."

I extend my hand toward the hood.

"Don't touch it. I got it waxed recently and . . ."

"Oh," I say, embarrassed. "Well, she looks wonderful, and I can't wait to ride with you, Jeff."

He quietly nods then rushes to refasten the cover again.

Jeff says, "C'mon, let's go inside." I follow Jeff as he unlocks the side door that leads to the house. We enter his place, first passing through a tiny room that has a washer and dryer, and then I find myself in the kitchen. Leftover dishes are sitting on his dinette table. I notice half-eaten sandwiches sitting on napkins, and bottles of soda with missing caps line the kitchen counter.

"Excuse the mess, beautiful. It's not usually like this. I haven't cleaned up in at least two months; been too busy hustling and trying to make that paper."

"Oh, no problem," I say with an encouraging smile, but inside I am disgusted. I am not very tidy myself, but it's only because I get so busy I don't always have time to straighten up. I do a halfway job of cleaning at least once a week, though, which is better than nothing. I am not sure if Jeff's excuse is the real reason, especially since he invited me over. Well, I'm no shrink, but I have an idea.

The signs of depression aren't that hard to figure out. Quiet as it's kept, men get depressed, too, and I've learned it takes a man much longer to get over a breakup than it does a woman. I mean, it's only been a couple of months since Rachel broke off the engagement. So it is possible that he still . . . no, I won't let my mind go there. I am not about to be anybody's rebound woman.

"Honey, you can be transparent with me. If you are a messy person I like to know these things up front." I laugh and say sheepishly, "So tell me. Is this the Jeffrey Williams way?"

"Baby Doll, you're going to find out what the Jeffrey

Williams way is." He winks, yet looks embarrassed. Blushing, I go pick up a dirty plate and fork and take both items to his kitchen. The stainless steel sink is filled with old, cloudy-looking dish water whose bubbles have long disappeared. I take a deep breath and pull out the plug, allowing the water to drain. After I replug the sink, I turn on the faucet and squirt out a glob of liquid detergent.

Dang, I must really be feeling this man, I'm thinking to myself.

"Hey, you don't have to do that. You're company."

"I am not company, Jeff. I mean, I am, but I want to be more than just a guest. You know what I'm saying?"

He grins and nods, and I do my thing, taking a rag and washing the plates and cups and utensils while listening to Jeff talk.

"Man, I'm out there on the streets hustling every day. From sunup to sundown I chase paper. I can make two grand to thirty grand fixing up and selling properties. So far I own six properties, and before it's over I want to own twelve."

"Why you own so many houses?"

"Trump is my inspiration. He started buying one property at a time. And that's what I'm doing. I just want to see how far I can go."

"Are you a slumlord?" I ask with a playful grin.

"No, baby, no, I know how to treat people. I am fair; just pay your rent on time, and we'll be best friends." He winks.

"Oh, so you have good tenants, huh?"

"Uh, yeah, they're fairly good. If they're not, I evict them. And I sue them if I have to."

Hearing Jeff talk about his work turns me on. I love a man about his business. And he sounds so strong and sure. He's got his own thing going, and that's good because my life is busy, too. I think we'll complement each other just fine.

"Only thing about me is I love money, but I don't trust banks."

"Oh, so you don't trust me?" I ask and snicker.

"Baby girl, you aren't the bank; you just work at the bank."

"I know . . . but why don't you trust them?"

"Their interest rates are a joke, and I just want to always be able to have access to my money anytime I want."

"That's what the ATM is for."

"Yeah, and ATM stands for Always Taking My Money."

"Jeff," I say, giggling. "That's so cruel."

"Cruel, but true. The fees for using an ATM are outrageous. Plus, in an emergency, the ATM's can be tied up, broken—shoot, some folks even steal those machines, load 'em up on the back of a big pickup and drive away."

"Nevertheless, you can still get your money, Jeff; it's not like your cash is only in one specific ATM."

"Look, Marlene, I know what I'm talking about. Even if you can get to an ATM and get a cash advance, the banks charge you interest on all the money that you owe on your credit card, not just the amount of the cash advance. It's highway robbery, bank-style. So my theory is never, ever trust a bank. And I love that I don't pay fines because I . . . I store my money in unconventional places."

"Oh, yeah, like where?"

"Only special people get to know special things about me."

"C'mon, Jeff, tell me," I plead, anxious to hear more.

He merely shakes his head. I soften up and decide to back off.

I proceed to vigorously scrub and rinse off plates and skillets and pots, then wipe down the counters so that everything looks and smells fresh. Then it hits me that doing housework does not look sexy. Not on a first date. So I toss aside the dish rag and slink over to the couch where Jeff is now seated. His big-screen TV is on, and the volume is turned up high. NBA game. Lakers versus Celtics. I hate basketball, because it seems like the same plays keep happening over and over again.

"Ooo!" I squeal and clap my hands like I'm deliriously happy. "Who's winning? Who's giving a beating and who's taking a beating?"

Jeff's eyes light up and he grins. "You love b-ball? Have a seat. I knew there was something I liked about you."

I giggle, sit next to Jeff, and toss back my hair with a flick of my hands. I can sense that Jeff is staring at me more than he's looking at the game. I pretend not to notice and continue grinning, trying to always look happy and act positive and drama-free.

The game is being replayed from when it first aired earlier. It lasts another hour, late into the night. Jeff and I chitchat while the TV is on. I gotta pretend like I know who the players are, but I don't recognize anybody on the court except Kobe, and that's only because he was in the news for the rape accusation. Otherwise, I wouldn't know that man if he passed me on the street. But I mentally take notes, pay all kinds of attention. I know men love women who are excellent listeners. And I want to do all I can so that Jeff will turn his mind to me, and keep his mind off Rachel.

During one of the commercial breaks, Jeff smiles and nudges me. "Tell me some of your sexy stories."

"Huh?"

"Every woman who has ever dealt with a man has a sexy story. Come on. Tell me." His grin is irresistible.

So, praying my honesty won't backfire, I stare at him and say, "Okay, a long time ago I was messing around with this guy named Too Damn Fine." I pause for a beat. "Jeff, why are you looking at me like that? That's what they called him."

"That's a nickname. Okay, keep going."

"Too Damn Fine loved to wear his do-rags underneath a big black-and-white fitted cap that he'd tilt to the side. You know, a hat like a fedora. Anyway, his jeans always fell below the waist so that you could see his boxers. And he loved wearing muscle tees to show off his you-know-what."

Jeff laughs. "Keep going."

"So, obviously I couldn't let the fam know I was interested in this guy. They would have tried to talk me out of it. And the more someone tells me I can't do something—."

"The more you eat Chinese food?"

"Shut up, you're so silly. That doesn't make any sense." I scream and laugh and lift my hand to pretend like I'm going to playfully punch him.

"Okay, keep going."

"Hey, I do love me some kung pao shrimp and pork egg foo young." I smirk and wink at Jeff. "Anyway, me and Too Damn Fine would have to sneak around just to be with each other. I'd go out of my way to dress in church clothes, but I'd also carry a big ole backpack with me so I could change into my fun gear as soon as I got into his car."

"Ooh, you're so scandalous."

"No, Jeff, don't call me that. I had to do what I had to do to be with the guy I loved. That's just how I roll."

"I see," he says, staring at me. "What kind of car did he drive?"

"Uh, a whatchamacallit. I remember it was an American car, black on black. The shocks were terrible, but he said he did that on purpose. He wanted people to notice him when he drove down the street. Real arrogant, just how I like 'em." I laugh. "Anyway, he, oh, I remember now. He drove a mean-looking Charger. I love sporty cars. And he liked driving with all the windows rolled down and would pump his music so loud you could hear him coming blocks away."

"Keep going, Little Mama."

I love that Jeff called me "Little Mama" and that he really seems to be listening to everything I tell him.

Jeff is going to be mine.

"He picks me up. I start removing my church clothes and put on a halter top and some shorts right there in the front seat while we're driving down Scott Street, right past Frenchy's Chicken. And he drives us to Hobby Airport. And we keep going until we reach the roof of one of the parking garages. And we climb onto the roof of his car and peer up at the sky to watch the airplanes fly over us. It was so romantic, so beautiful."

"Okay, but when does the sexy come in?"

"Don't interrupt. I'm not done yet."

"Yes, ma'am."

"So, oh my God, I'm almost embarrassed to tell you this. I don't want you to think I'm a freak."

"I swear to God, I won't think you're a freak."

I take a deep breath. "Okay, Too Damn Fine grabbed me around the waist and pulled me against his big ole chest, and we starting slobbering each other down, feeling on each other like two high schoolers. I heard the sounds of planes taking off; shoot, for all I know other travelers might have been parked near us, but I didn't care. Baby boy, when I felt Too Damn Fine's private parts poking against me, I lost it."

"Damn."

"That's what I was saying. I was rubbing my cheeks against this man's face, kissing him like I've never kissed a man before, and we had sex right there on that roof."

"Eww, Too Damn Fine had him a big-time freak."

"Jeff," I squeal, and this time, I actually punch him with my fist. He stares at me with tenderness, which surprises me. I am happy, though. He could have looked at me with disgust. He could have asked me to leave, told me I am not the woman for him. But it's cool I can tell him my sexiest secrets, and he still seems to be down for me. I like that about him.

"I always wondered about you, you know that, don't you?"

Feeling warm and self-conscious, I shift nervously in my seat but remain silent.

"I mean, it was a little while after I got with your sister."

"Do you regret choosing her over me?"

"What?" he spits out.

Oh, heck. It seems like I've made him mad, something I don't want to do. It's too soon to make the man mad.

"No, I mean I understand that you loved her from the beginning and that's cool, but I was thinking since you said you always wondered about me."

"What I meant, Little Mama, is that even though I met both of you at the same time, and yeah, I kind of hit it off so well with Rachel that we kind of did our thing from there, I never forgot about that night when you and I . . ."

Mmm. Jeff is talking about how all of us met. We were at a mutual friend's house. A woman named Gail who knew a million people decided to host a party during the NFL championships. There were approximately a dozen men in Gail's house and thirty-five women, and Jeff was one of the men. He was introduced to me first, and Rachel later. A couple of sparks passed between us, and we held a nice, brief, flirty conversation. Then he left me standing there so he could mingle. I guess, from a man's standpoint, there was so much eye candy in the house, why be tied down to one woman? Later on, he met Rachel, and they connected so strongly that he ended up talking to her for the rest of the day.

When I was ready to go home, that's when he found out that Rachel and I were half sisters. Jeff was nice and polite. He acted like he hadn't eyed me only hours before meeting

Rachel, but I let it go. How could I make claims on a guy I just met? Especially since he and Rachel went on to become a couple a month later. Once they started hanging out, I'd be very friendly with him. He'd act fun-loving with me, too. I felt a little hurt, but accepted that they were lovers. When they got engaged I even bought them a congratulatory gift. But I never forgot what might have happened between me and Jeff. And now that they've broken up, here's my chance to continue our initial, albeit short, encounter that had me wondering about him ever since that party. Maybe he wondered about me, too. Shoot, he might be my future husband. You just never know. I sure plan on finding out what the future holds for me and Mr. Jeffrey Williams.

— 3 —

RACHEL

You Gotta Protect Yourself

Marlene didn't come home until almost one in the morning. I seriously wonder what she could have been doing all that time. I pretended to be asleep when I heard her open the front door. We live in a split bedroom apartment, and she went straight to the left side of the unit and didn't come to my side to say good night, "Hey dog," nothing.

Sleazeballs usually feel too guilty to say anything. It's all good.

I'm sure I'll find out the truth one day. What the hell does she think she's doing?

Early this morning Marlene showers and leaves for work before I even have a chance to fully get up. I lie motionless in my bed so I can hear her in case she's whispering on her phone (she isn't). Listening to see if she prays to the Lord like she normally does every morning (she doesn't). Hmm. And I prick up my ears to notice if she's singing "My Sweet Lord," or if she's belting out "Sexual Healing." She sings neither. Thank God she didn't, because although the girl won't admit it, she's no Mary J. Blige, and she definitely wouldn't make the top thirty-two on *American Idol*.

So I am actually very relieved when Marlene finally pulls herself together and rushes out the door. As soon as she leaves I go directly to her room, fling open her door, and invite myself in. I sure do.

As usual, her bed is unmade. Typical. Fat and slobby. Why can't Jeff notice these little details? I go straight to her dirty clothes basket and carefully examine the pile of clothes.

Hmm, bingo. Her panties. Rather, a *thong*. Can you believe that mess? How can someone who's damn near two hundred pounds and built like a Minnesota Vikings linebacker squeeze her thunder thighs into an itty-bitty thong? That's like King Kong trying to wear shorts designed for a Barbie doll. Nasty. I can imagine that the crack of her ass swallows up the thong so much it's almost like she's strung dental floss up her butt. Ughhh!

My eyes dart about, and I spot a ruler sitting on her desk. I make a face and, using the ruler, carefully pick up her panties so I can take a closer look. They're purple (Marlene's favorite color) and see-through. Frowning, I lift the ruler up high over my head so I can inspect the evidence from every angle.

Unfortunately, the thong is so damned skimpy and stringy that I can't tell if there're any sex stains on them. She probably wore the thong on purpose, trying to be cute and sexy. If I don't find out if she had sex with Jeff this way, I certainly can find out another way. Just go ahead and call me Columbo, or Kojak, or any one of those Charlie's Angels (nineties version).

Doesn't matter. I will figure out this mystery so we can all come clean one day. Me, Marlene, and Jeff.

I reach back into the laundry basket and search through dirty clothes, trying to find the outfit she wore last night. A purple and lavender dress with a plunging neckline. When I saw Marlene twirling around in the dress last night, I didn't think anything strange.

I remember she asked, "You like this? You think a man would like it?"

"Why you asking me if a man would like it? I thought you were going to church."

"Men are at church, too, right, Rachel? Jeez, let me get out of here. I don't need all this drama over a simple question."

She left in a huff, and I figured there was someone at church she was trying to impress. Boy, was I ever wrong.

I glance in the woven wastebasket that is perched next to my sister's end table. There's nothing in there: no movie ticket stub, no receipts, no concrete evidence to explain where she was with Jeff.

The alarm on my watch goes off, so I know I have no time to be prying in Marlene's stuff. It's time for me to be somewhere, and, considering the circumstances, I am glad to be going out and getting away from the apartment.

A half hour later I am sitting in the front row of my women's self-defense class. My best friend in the world, Alita, comes in late. I can hear her clearing her throat. She's sitting right behind me, in the second row, where we normally sit. Today, though, I'm sitting in the front row.

"Hey, why are you up there?" I hear her whisper discreetly in my ear.

"I'll tell you about it during break."

"Damn."

My girl knows me like the back of her hand. We met five years ago at the iFest, one of Houston's annual international cultural festivals that are held downtown. Each year features a different country, and there are dozens of booths that sell colorful clothing, spicy food, and unique items that represent the country. I remember seeing her and doing a double take because she is a dead ringer for Halle Berry. Caramel-colored complexion, petite, bony, beautiful dark eyes, sculpted cheekbones, and that famous short precision haircut Rihanna wears these days. I couldn't resist saying hello to Alita and, of course, telling her she looks just like the famous actress.

"I know. I get that all the time. I wish I had her money, though, you know what I'm saying? Wouldn't mind having any of her exes', too, 'cause they all fine as hell and richer than all my exes put together."

"Me, too, girl."

We've been tight ever since. And although my girl is attractive and gets lots of attention, I call her Hardly Berry, just to make sure she doesn't get the big head.

The self-defense class was her idea. She believes women need to protect themselves and be strong in every area of their lives. I wasn't hearing it, didn't feel like sitting in on the classes, but she promised to buy me a ticket to the Kanye West concert if I signed up. I said cool.

So here we are. Our instructor, Floyd Manchester, is a big bulky white guy with puffy eyelids. He looks like he should be in bed asleep, but surprisingly he has a loud voice and lots of energy, and he loves teaching the self-defense class.

"If you ladies go hang out at the club, never, ever leave your drink unattended. If you have to go somewhere for a minute, order yourself a fresh, new drink. Dump the other. It only takes a second for a man to slip the date rape drug in your martini, and it's all over after that. You'll wind up passed out and naked before the night is over."

"But Floyd," says Monica Gordon, a petite white girl with an irritating high-pitched voice. "What if you don't drink alcohol?"

"Doesn't matter. Don't trust an unfamiliar man's sodas or even bottled water. If someone wants to do you harm, they'll use anything they can, even something as innocent looking as water."

Floyd continues the class by giving us warnings about how to secure our homes with double-bolt locks, and how we shouldn't let a guy in our house at the end of a first date.

"What if he asks for a kiss?" shouts Monica.

"Kiss him on the cheek outside your home, tell him good-bye, and watch him go to his car, get in, and drive away before you let yourself in your home. I've heard cases of women who naively let a man in because he claimed he has to pee, and the next morning the woman wakes up with bruises all over her body and her vagina sore and bleeding. You gotta protect yourself by not falling for everything a man says. I don't care if he looks like Denzel and Brad Pitt put together."

"Hmm, I'd love to see that," says Alita.

"Anyway, seriously, ladies, don't be so weak by a man's outward appearance; it's what's inside of him that counts," Floyd says with firmness. He then suggests we take a ten-minute break so we can use the ladies' room before we start practicing our self-defense moves.

Alita grabs my arm as soon as I stand up. "Okay, what happened? You're sitting in the front row and clapping just because Floyd says we're about to learn some new moves, and you weren't that enthusiastic about this topic two days ago."

"Two days ago my sister wasn't stepping out on a date with . . ."

"Who?"

"Jeff!"

"Noo!"

"Yes!"

"Well, have you called the bastard to see what's up? Oops, I probably shouldn't be calling him that, but in my opinion, only a bastard would try to push up on his ex's sister."

I describe how Jeff's cell phone accidentally dialed me

when he was out with Marlene, and how unbelievably angry I felt when I overheard their conversation.

"And girl, I don't know what to think, but, considering my circumstances, I figure paying close attention to these self-defense moves may come in hand."

"Oh, so now you want to kick a Negro's ass?"

"Stop grinning, Alita. This isn't funny at all. I just feel like I have to let out my aggressions, and learning how to kick ass is one good way to do it." Water rapidly springs in my eyes when I imagine those two being together. I remember when Jeff and I were dating. Jeff would come to the apartment, and Marlene would be super chatty. She'd joke around and playfully tease Jeff a few times, but I would be in on the fun, too. Playing, laughing, and shooting the breeze. I never remember their ever being alone together.

"But why *Marlene*?" I plead with Alita.

"Hmm, girl, who knows why some guys do what they do. All I'm concerned about is that my guy stays on the up-and-up." Alita has finally met her match in her current beau, Henry "Big Hen," who says he will kill for her. She's so happy in her relationship right now and is gunning for me to hit the jackpot, too. She really thought I messed up when I broke up with Jeff but has since respected my decision.

"Well, if Big Hen asks you to marry him . . ."

"I'll take my time and think carefully before giving him an answer."

"I wish I would have done that with Jeff."

"Why didn't you?"

"Alita, remember I told you how scared I was? I mean, of course I'm crazy about the guy, but to be his bride? I'm so young. I feel like I haven't lived enough life yet. I haven't yet come into a strong sense of self. I don't want to have any regrets."

"But life and love are about taking chances, girl."

"You don't have to preach to me. It's too late now, Alita, don't you think?"

"No, not really."

"If he's kicking it with Marlene, it *is* too late."

"You and Jeff need to have a conversation."

"I can't."

"You gotta. You need to let him know how you feel."

"He's still pissed at me."

"But do you know that for sure? Have you asked?"

"I doubt he'd answer if I call him."

"Sneak and call him using Marlene's cell. Then he'd answer."

"Ouch, that's unimaginable. Crazy. Dang, I can't stand this. How can Marlene do this to me? I would never, ever do anything like this to her. Why can't she understand how I feel?"

"Girl, you're a trip. She doesn't even know that you know, so . . . you're not making much sense."

Floyd returns to the classroom, so we'll have to continue our conversation later. He instructs everyone to stand up, and we move the tables and chairs out of the way so that the center of the room is clear and accessible. Floyd then asks all twelve women to stand in a circle so we can first do stretching exercises.

For the next thirty minutes, Floyd and his coteachers take us through a series of self-defense moves. How to block. How to stand and where to place our feet in preparation for an attack. They explain why it is important to yell and scream when you're being attacked. Floyd tells us, "The louder you yell, the more power and strength you give to your body."

"No! Stop! Stay back!" We yell these words so many

times my throat grows sore and begins to hurt. I have to stop and sip bottled water a few times.

And before we know it, class is over. I'm hot and sticky and want nothing more than to jump in the shower and clean the dirt off my body.

"Alita, is it all right if I come home with you? I don't want to be at my place with Marlene tonight."

"Sure, no problem."

"I think I'll just wear a pair of your shorts and a T-shirt when I go to bed."

"Jeez, Rachel. Are you sure you don't want to go home and pick up some overnight clothes? Are you *that* afraid to face your sister?"

"Girl, she's still at work so it's not like I'll run into her . . . I just don't want to be at the house anytime soon. I need to chill out with you. No telling what I'll do to her the next time I see the wench."

"For real? Have y'all had physical fights before?"

"Ha, I remember when were young, she'd sit her big butt on my back many times. She'd grab my hair and yank at it. She was so heavy I could barely breathe, felt like I was about to die. My mama would have to pull Marlene off me. And then I'd get beat with a belt because Mama felt I should have taken the closest thing to me and knocked the hell outta my sister. Not easy to do when it feels like the Empire State Building is sitting on top of you."

Alita chuckles. "Your mama is a trip."

"Oh, baby, you have no idea. Mama's like that because she had to be. But I think she's trying to do better. Man, I gotta talk to my mama. Tell you what, I know I have some old pjs over at her place, so that works out perfectly. I'll pay her a little visit and then meet you at your spot later."

Alita and I share a warm hug and go our separate ways.

When it comes to how I view myself, my life purpose, and who I am, things can get fairly complicated. Sometimes I don't know where I fit in. I'm not as bad as a sinner, yet I'm not pure enough to be a saint. My feelings get so twisted up that it's hard for me to say how I feel sometimes, but the one person who I think understands me is my mom, Brooke.

My mom lives way across town in Third Ward, near Texas Southern University, Houston's only HBU (Historically Black University). For early March, the temperature outside is an unusually pleasant seventy degrees. The sun shines with such brilliance that it makes me feel happy inside, good enough to drive with my windows rolled down. I pull up in front of my mom's two-story house and park my car on the street. I walk along the side of the house and use my key to open her side door. Seconds later I find Mama in the spacious yet cluttered living room. Three mismatched couches and two love seats, plus scratched-up wooden tables covered with vases holding fake roses, fill the space.

"Hey, Ma, don't do that." She's standing on a utility chair trying to hang curtains.

"Hey, Little Bit, what brings you over to this side of town?"

"I was missing my mama, that's what."

I walk over to her and hold out my hand to help her get off the little ladder. I close my eyes briefly and squeeze her in a tight hug. She smells like gardenias, and her skin feels as soft as flower petals. My mama is middle-aged perfection. Her flawless brown skin makes her look ten years younger. Her fine grade of hair is usually kept in a nice traditional style, but today it is flying about. I feel tempted to find a comb and help her look prettier.

"You've been working hard, Mama. Your hair is looking crazy."

"Oh, it's just hair."

"Mama, what's wrong? You always try to look good."

"Looking good all the time doesn't mean anything...
sometimes it's not the biggest priority."

I feel guilty. Sometimes I forget moms are human, with
tough issues they have to deal with. I wish that I would
remember to call her more, find out what she needs, and stop
unloading all my drama on her.

"Mama, let me finish hanging those curtains. I think you
should go put a comb to your hair. Or, if you want, I can style
it for you. I did Marlene's hair last night, flat-ironed it."

"Oh, yeah, what was the occasion?"

I can't help myself. "This trick had a hot date. You'll never
believe who it was with."

"Who, girl?"

"Jeff." I can barely say his name.

Mama's eyes widen. She looks taken aback, and she
walks away from me muttering things I can't hear.

"Yep, can you believe those two?" I say. "It must be some
kind of a joke."

"Stranger things have happened."

"Oh, Mama, you don't think . . ."

Mama stops walking and turns around to stare at me. "I
don't think; I know. I am living proof of strange things. You
have no idea."

"Is this what happened with you and Loretta?" Loretta is
Marlene's mama.

"I don't know what you're going through with Jeff and
Marlene. And I don't know how serious they are. All I can
say is, I hope she doesn't get pregnant by him."

Mama turns and walks away from me toward her bedroom. Right then, I know it isn't right for me to burden her
with my silly relationship problems. I can't share my hurt
when I know how much she's still hurting. So I quietly fin-

ish mounting the curtains, making sure they properly fit on the rods. When I'm done working, I traipse through the house and find her upstairs, napping in her bedroom, where it smells like bleach. I pinch my nose and give her a kiss on the cheek and drop a crisp twenty on her nightstand. I leave her house with more questions than when I came.

Later that night I swing by Alita's. I notice Big Hen's pickup parked in front of her town house. Not surprised. If she's not with me, she's always with her man.

The screen door to the town house is locked, but I can see directly into the living room. My cheeks turn red and warm the instant I spot Alita cozily sitting on Big Hen's lap. She's pressing her lips against his neck and cradling his head in her hands. I want to close my eyes, turn away, and leave unnoticed, but I can't help staring. Immediately I become even angrier at myself. That's exactly what Jeff and I used to do. He was so affectionate. He loved to play with my hair, gently grab my face in between his hands, and kiss my lips, my cheeks, my forehead. At times he made me feel so loved.

"Hey, you two," I yell, "can you stop your freaky porno show for a second and let a sista in the house?"

Alita hops off Big Hen's lap and races to open the door for me. Henry is right behind her, grinning.

"Hey, girl, I don't mean to interrupt." I giggle. "What's popping, Hen?"

"You got it," he says and winks. "Come on in, make yourself at home. So you'll be wearing my girl's clothes tonight, huh? I hope I don't get you two mixed up."

"Ha," I say and follow them inside the town house. "That shouldn't be too hard. I don't look like Hardly Berry. Plus, I will be sleeping downstairs. You two will have the entire upstairs to yourselves."

"No, girl, it's cool. I can spend some time with you, and

then I gotta rush up there and take care of my baby. But it'll be good to make him wait. Let him anticipate what's to come."

"Eww wee, that's a good thing. Make him wait, girlfriend," I say and grin at Alita.

"He's patient and understanding," Alita says with a satisfied look on her face. "And he pays the rent, hello!"

Alita and I high-five. Big Hen playfully sneers at us and rolls his eyes. He goes and plops on the couch, picks up his black Guitar Hero peripheral, and hangs the strap around his neck.

"You know something?" I gush to Alita. "I won't say this often, but I envy you and your guy."

"Well, that's cool, but successful relationships take hard work. You gotta learn to pick your fights," she says and nods at Big Hen. "Like, he is sweet as pie, but I can't count how many times he leaves his boxers and work clothes in piles all around the town house. I don't say anything. I just pick up his clothes and toss them in the laundry room. I ain't about to kick this good man out over some dirty underwear, you know what I'm saying?"

"You better not be that petty, Alita," Big Hen says. "You know how we do."

"I know, baby," Alita says and giggles at her man, who's now standing in the middle of the living room looking silly and belting out "You Really Got Me" while playing Guitar Hero.

Alita turns her attention back to me. "Yes, girl. When Hen and I stick to our agreement, we never go to bed mad. If we get upset we agree to talk about how we feel within thirty minutes. Then we have to get busy with the makeup sex, and everything's good after that."

"Do what works for you, girl."

"Yep, gotta do that," Alita responds. "I've had too many messed-up situations, and I learned how to set standards."

"Okay, but how did you get him to pay the rent? I know at first he was paying just half."

"Well, as of last month, he actually offered to pay it all. And I thought about it and was like, why the hell not? He's over here all the time using up water to take showers, eating up food, using toilet paper, and burning up electricity so he can play his video games. And my key ain't free, so if he wants to come and go he's gotta be willing to pay the price."

I can't help but think about my own situation. If I had been in my right mind I could be getting what she's getting. Cooling out with my guy, not experiencing any major drama, and still getting the best sex of my life. How stupid am I?

You really gotta be major stupid to let a good man slip away from you—a man who ends up in the arms of your sister.

Later that night, I can hear Alita's moans and her bed creaking above me while I toss and turn on her living room couch. I fall asleep dreaming about how to get Jeff back into my life.

4

RACHEL

Be a Real Woman

The next afternoon, *Alita* and I walk through my daddy's kitchen and open the door that leads to the backyard. We step outside and go stand underneath the covered patio. First thing we see is Blinky's lanky frame crouched over a dark blue oversized trash can. He's a light-skinned black man with piercing green eyes and brown and gray hair that he always tries to dye, but the gray comes back twice as fast. Just as I expect, Blinky's music is turned up so loud that I can hear the kitchen windows vibrating. I hear the words "Payback is a thing you gotta see ... Revenge ... I'm mad." I recognize that head-bobbing James Brown song anywhere. My daddy loves old-school music. I do, too. But it's tough to enjoy the rhythm when you've got the blues.

Sweet smells hit my nose as soon as I get to the backyard. All kinds of fresh fruit are arranged on a large utility table: oranges, lemons, pineapples, and pears. Blinky and Loretta are slicing up fruit and dumping it in the trash can. Oh, this party is about to get crunk for sure! Hypnotic music. Barbecue smelling delicious on the open pit. Trash can punch. And not a second too soon. I am going to need a nice stiff drink, considering what I am about to go through.

"Hey, Daughter Number Two!"

"Hi there, Daddy. How you doing? You look good," I say and look pointedly at him. I can feel Loretta's eyes burning a deep hole in me.

"Don't be rude," Blinky snaps. "Don't you see Loretta standing here?"

Even Stevie Wonder would notice this Amazon woman. Loretta is taller than my dad by two inches. Her skin's yellow tone perfectly matches her long, fiery red hair, which today is wrapped up in a colorful scarf. Loretta is one of the few black women I know born with that hair color.

I manage a stiff smile and say hi to Blinky's woman. She waves, throws back a fake smile, and continues chopping up slices of mouth-watering watermelon.

"Hey, you want to make the Kool-Aid for the punch? Grab the packets and the sugar on that table over there. You, too," Loretta rudely says to Alita. "Y'all not guests. You're family, so get to work."

I grit my teeth and decide to cooperate. The last person anyone wants to argue with is Loretta, Ms. Queen Bee.

Alita, cool as a bag of ice chips, smiles sweetly and starts measuring cups of sugar.

"What are you thinking about, young lady?" I quietly ask her.

"Girl, you don't wanna know. Just be happy I've got your back, sis."

"I am very happy. I don't take a true friend for granted. God knows there're enough backstabbers around."

And just then Marlene walks in. Alone. I almost want to smile, but not at her. No. I want to grin about the fact that she is alone. Manless. At my daddy's party. Just like me.

"Hey, everybody," she says in a loud voice brimming with joy. Okay, her voice is sounding a little too perky. Maybe she just got out of church and is still feeling fresh from the praise and worship, or maybe there's another reason why she's acting so buoyant.

Marlene is holding a large rectangular glass container covered with aluminum foil.

Oh, I can figure out why she's grinning. Big girl is about to eat.

"What you got there, Marlene?" says butt-kissing Loretta. "Don't tell me it's your famous yummy potato salad."

"Yes, Mama. You know I had to put my foot in it, throw together my magical cooking skills."

"Hmm, when did she manage to make that? She wasn't even at home last night," I softly mutter. Marlene, Daddy, and Loretta give me a puzzled look, but I ignore them.

Reason why I know Marlene didn't come home is because I had Alita call our apartment several times. I told her to do a star sixty-seven. No answer. My sister's been gone two nights in a row. I could have slept in my own bed instead of enduring back pain trying to crash on Alita's couch.

"Where were you, Daughter Number One? Shoot, I called you for over two hours, and you never answered my calls. That's not like you, Pretty Girl."

I flinch when Blinky calls her Pretty Girl. Not just flinch but my shoulders tighten up to the point that I feel a sharp ache streak through my body. That's what happens when I get stressed. But I ignore my pain and tear open red Kool-Aid packets and empty them. Then I pour in gallon after gallon of bottled water that's lined up next to the pitchers. I do all this like I'm really gung ho about making Kool-Aid. It's like no matter how horrible or angry you feel inside, you have to learn how to control your emotions. You can't let your enemy know something is bothering you, or else they may think they're more powerful than you.

"Mmmm," I say with a giant, fake smile. "I *love* your potato salad. Make sure and save me some." This is my first time talking to the skank since Friday evening, when she got me to style her stupid hair.

Marlene sighs really loud like she's irritated by my voice and announces, "Hey, everybody, there's someone I want you to, um, meet, if you want to think of it that way." She throws back her head and giggles, then disappears from the patio. She quickly steps back inside the house through the sliding glass door.

"Girl, close the door all the way so flies won't get in the house," I bark, even though I'm sure Marlene can't hear me. Alita and I lock eyes and smile. Alita moves one hand and positions it to her right side like she's one of Charlie's Angels. I laugh. She is forcing me to remember the self-defense moves that we've learned.

My laughing ceases when Marlene walks back through the door. She's leading Jeff by the hand. My ex is the color of gingerbread. His lips are thick, wide, and smooth, somewhat like J.J. Walker's from *Good Times*. Lips that thick are perfect for sensuous, hour-long kissing. I notice that he appears calm, not nervous as hell like he should be looking.

"Is that Jeff? We ain't seen you in a bit, dude. How are you doing?"

I can't believe my daddy is acting nice and hospitable like this. Doesn't he remember Jeff used to come to family functions with me?

"I'm doing as well as can be expected."

What's that supposed to mean? I lock eyes with Alita. She looks as confused as I am.

"Actually," Jeff speaks up as if reading my mind, "lately things have been going surprisingly well. Like I have a sudden burst of new energy."

Marlene is standing next to Jeff with her head held high. She's grinning, for God's sake. Like she's proud she's outdoing me. She always tried to outdo me when we were younger.

I remember when we'd go to family reunions. Although there would be dozens of cousins running around screaming and having fun, doing relay races, and playing team-oriented games like kickball, I would always be the one she wanted to beat. It would strike me as strange that I was the perceived enemy instead of all my rowdy, bragging, loud-talking older cousins who were from out of town and across the way.

Jeff finally gives me direct eye contact. "Rachel, what's up? Hey, Alita."

"Yo, Jeff, come give me a hug." That's Alita. She may talk about him behind his back, but she is one to act civilized when the situation warrants it.

"Alita?" I whisper.

"Shhh, I know what I'm doing," she whispers back and steps up to Jeff and offers him a hug.

Jeff wraps his arms around Alita but curiously eyes me while he embraces my friend. The way he stares at makes me feel warm and gooey. I miss feeling his arms slide tight around my waist, gripping me close and pulling me near so I can rest against his warm body. I yearn for that wonderful feeling of security. There's nobody to blame but myself.

Marlene coughs loudly then physically pries Alita and Jeff apart.

"That's enough," she tells them, irritated.

"Watch that, sista," Alita says, and walks away.

"No, you watch it . . . *sista*."

"She's gotta be kidding," Alita says and resumes helping me make the punch.

"Well, I just wanted y'all to see a familiar face, and I will let you get back to doing what you do. I'm going back inside the house," Marlene explains.

Right then, with the music thumping and pulsating, I hear James Brown scream, "I don't know karate, but I know ka-razy."

" 'Yes, we do,' " Blinky sings along and starts busting a move, swaying his skinny hips and wailing his long arms. " 'Yeah, hey, woo.' " He looks and sounds like an old fool.

"Blinky really can get down, huh? He should audition for *So You Think You Can Dance*," I say sarcastically. "Get it. You *think* you can dance?"

"I heard what you said. You so smart, you get up here and dance," Blinky says, and playfully grabs my arm. "Do the Soulja Boy, c'mon."

"Blinky, will you stop it? I don't feel like dancing."

"Daughter Number Two, you better stop pouting, forget about your ex, and dance like the boy doesn't exist. Show this man you can have fun with or without him. That your life goes on."

Alita looks at Blinky and openly frowns. She knows my daddy's past with women, that he hasn't always been on his best behavior and hasn't always treated them with respect. Blinky should not even go there. He seems faker than a Chanel knock-off purse.

Blinky continues to reach out for me, grabbing my hands and trying to get me to bust a move.

"Life don't depend on Jeff," he chants.

"Blinky!" I scream and look around the backyard feeling embarrassed. "Don't be saying stuff like that."

"What? You think we don't know what you're thinking? You don't have to tell us you feel bad. We can see how sad you are, Daughter Number Two."

"Oh, God, I'm about to do something else. I can't stand

listening to this," I groan. "Some people are missing a sensitivity chip."

The James Brown song is on repeat. Same old words. Same old screaming.

Blinky continues popping his bony fingers and rocking his hips back and forth. All he needs is a wig, and I swear he'd bring the Godfather of Soul back from the grave.

" 'I'm mad. I want revenge. The big payback,' " Blinky keeps singing and dancing. Looking at him makes me even more upset. Even though it is his birthday, I want him to act more sympathetic to me.

Just then some more of my kinfolks pour out from the house and spill to the backyard through the sliding glass door. A couple of great-aunts shuffle in holding thick white Bibles under their arms; they've come here straight from church. Some adult and teen cousins run outside making noise, followed by Blinky's fine-ass cousin Uncle Scooter. Then Perry, my daddy's only sister, walks into the backyard closely behind her two kids, Braylon and Kiki, who are seven and four, respectively.

"Hi, Auntie Perry."

"How's my favorite niece?" She grins and kisses me warmly on the cheek.

Loretta looks at Perry like she can't believe she favors me over her precious Marlene.

"Hey, Alita," Perry says, and looks her over. "I see you got some little bumps on your forehead. Are those sex bumps?" She laughs. "I hope you're really putting it on your man."

Alita just smiles and shakes her head.

"Okay, first things first," says Aunt Perry. "Pour me a drink. I don't care which one of ya'll do it, just hook a sister up."

"We're not done yet," Blinky says. "We got plenty of beer in the cooler."

"Hook me up with some punch first. I don't care that it's not done," she says, staring at me.

I immediately grab an eight-ounce Styrofoam cup from a stack that's sitting on a nearby table.

"Girl, you must be buggin'. Get me a twenty-ounce cup or one of those oversized cups from out the house. I gots to get my drink on. My big bro is turning sixty so . . . Hey, 'The Payback.' " Perry starts singing, popping her fingers and doing the bump with Blinky. For her to be over forty you wouldn't think she'd be this wild. But ever since she gave birth to her kids after being infertile throughout her twenties and thirties, she's been enjoying her life to the fullest. She's a firm believer in the "life begins at forty" theory.

I decide to help her out and get one of those Taco Bell supersize cups from the house.

"C'mon, Alita," I say to my friend, who nods and follows me inside.

Marlene is in the kitchen next to the refrigerator, running her mouth to Jeff. She's squirming and fanning herself. She looks like she's about to turn away from him, but when she sees me and Alita approaching, she turns her back to us and faces Jeff.

I stand right beside Marlene with my hands squarely on my hips, a big power move that always make me feel confident and unshakable.

Even from inside the house I can hear the Godfather of Soul scream, "Give me some hits, I want some hits."

Alita clears her throat. "Hey, what's going on? Why are you guys in here? The party's outside."

"The party is wherever we are," Marlene says sweetly and stares at Jeff. He smiles back down at her. I don't like for him to look her in her eyes like that.

"Oh, God, give me a freaking-ass break," I say.

"Speak up. What did you say?" She sounds shocked.

"Marlene, aren't I free to talk?" I ask, eyeballing her.

"Nothing's free, Rachel. E–e–everything has a price." Although she's trying to be bold and strong, Marlene looks and sounds nervous. I think she's just trying to show off in front of my ex.

"Whatever, Marlene. You've got a lot of . . ." and I stop speaking.

"Are you finished? Anything you need to say, be a *real* woman and say it to my face." She is still squirming and bouncing up and down on her feet looking crazy.

"What's wrong with *that real* woman?" Alita asks out loud to no one in particular.

"Marlene has to go to the ladies' room," Jeff explains. "Or, should I say, the real woman's room," he jokes. He looks at her like she needs to go ahead and take care of her business before she accidentally wets herself.

"BRB," she says real loud and threateningly rolls her eyes at me.

Finally, with the skank now leaving the room, here's my chance to do a one-on-one with Jeff. Something I should have been done before now but was too afraid. It's hard to admit that you think you've made a mistake. But sometimes, even if it's risky, you gotta express deep-set feelings.

Alita nervously clears her throat. "I guess it's a good time for me to go back outside now," she says. "The food's probably ready and I'm star—."

"No, you're my girl, don't leave. I need you to stay here with me."

"Okay, girl. I got you."

I turn to face my ex. "Hey, Jeff. I really wish I would've known you're into drilling horizontally."

"What you talking about?"

"You and Marlene."

"Again, what you trying to say?" He has the nerve to look bewildered.

"Oh, God. I hate it when men play dumb."

"Not playing dumb, Rachel."

"Oh, then your dumbness comes naturally?"

"Wait, wait, wait. What's with the smart attitude? You're the one who rejected me."

"And how many times do I have to hear about that, Jeff? Ten more? A hundred more times? Don't forget, you—you were rushing things, and, believe it or not, I got scared and confused. I loved our relationship and the way it felt, but you were telling me things I hadn't thought of at that point."

"Such as?"

"How many kids you wanted to have. I believe you want three."

"At least."

"Well, good luck getting three kids out of *that* one," I angrily snap.

"Wait, wait, hold up. Why are you making me and Marlene married? I don't want to marry every woman I date . . ." He pauses. "I just wanted to marry you."

I squirm and can barely look him in the eye. "Jeff, I already feel bad."

"Not trying to make you feel bad. It's just that when you dumped me—."

"I didn't dump you."

"When you dumped me," he continues, "I felt numb, mad, hurt." His eyes widen, and his voice is filled with awe. "I even stopped doing my real estate for a minute. Couldn't think, eat . . . could barely breathe."

I just stare at him, astounded that he can admit his

moments of weakness to me, something that he didn't always do in the past.

"But after a couple weeks of that mess, I said, hey, the sun still rises and sets. I guess Rachel Merrell isn't big enough to keep the earth from moving forward. And if planet Earth hasn't stopped because of Rachel . . . then maybe I shouldn't stop, either."

"Okay," I say and swallow with nervous anticipation.

"And I got rid of all your photos, *our* photos, our silly little photos that we'd take . . . us making faces, having a good time together, chilling and living our lives."

"Okay, okay, okay."

"What? You don't want to hear all that? Well, all that is what you've brought me to. All that brings us to today, here. Right now."

And I feel a combination of regret and extreme anger. It's like he's blaming me. Accusing me of doing things that have caused him to do things. To be here. With her.

"Long story short, Rachel, I'm going on with my life." He looks pointedly at me. I can hear the words inside his head. *You need to move on with your life.*

But how can I? How on earth can I act like what he's doing is all right with me? Okay, maybe the fact that he's accepted an invite to a family barbecue shouldn't be such a big freaking deal. But it is, especially since he's with my sister, someone who craves male attention.

It's not like this hasn't happened before, in an indirect way. I would meet a gorgeous, charming guy who had the gift of gab. I'd bring him to our apartment. He'd be all over me, would barely say hello to my sister. She'd dress provocatively, usually wearing something that would show her cleavage. And when my man still wouldn't notice her, she'd storm out of the room, the tension thick and suffocating.

And the next time I'd see her, she'd bring home some strange man she'd met at a mall or something. He'd be tall, skinny, and gorgeous. He'd be all over her, too. He wouldn't even notice me. And that's when I remembered my sister likes to compete. Maybe that's what she's doing with Jeff. Showing me a thing or two. And, cross my fingers hope to die, when she's done showing me whatever she's showing me, she'll get bored and go on to the next plaything.

"Jeff, how long do you think you'll be dating her?"

"If I'm lucky, I will date Marlene for a long time, longer than the time you and I were together."

"But Jeff," I say, feeling hurt. "You once told me I was the only chip in the bag. And the fact that you could move on so soon . . ."

"A man has a right to move on, Rachel."

"Yeah, but do you have to be so Brad Pitt–ish?"

"Hey, at least Pitt got to walk down the aisle the first time."

"But he still cheated on his wife. Does that make it any better?"

Instead of answering, he whips his sunglasses off his head, puts them on, and folds his arms.

"I really look like Pitt now, huh? Really cool man."

"Jeff, stop grinning," I complain, frustrated. "I'm trying to be serious and I hate when you act silly."

"Is that why you dumped me? I'm too immature?" he asks and presses his thumb up against his nose. I can see clear inside his nostrils. He looks like he has a snout.

"Ha, this is crazy. I'm trying to hold a mature conversation with you."

He removes his sunglasses, and his silly expression turns sober.

"Rachel, to be honest, I have no idea what's going to

happen. Last time I made plans about my future ... every single thing blew up in my face."

I wince.

"But for now, for today, I am going with the flow. Having a good time. Your sister is kind of wild and unpredictable. I like that about her."

"Okay, I don't want to hear you talking about ..." I can't stand saying her name right now. In spite of me and him having a much-needed talk, I still don't know why she's doing this to me. How far is this going to go? And even though I initiated the breakup, this severely hurts me.

It feels like two people have swung their heads back and butted me right on my forehead, punching me so hard that I see a bright array of stars and it feels like something is squeezing my head. People you love the most can inflict the most damage. They hurt you so bad you wonder what the true definition of love is. Does true love hurt? Because in some ways, I still love Jeff, and all I feel sometimes is hurt.

Just then Marlene dashes back into the kitchen.

"Sorry, being in the bathroom took longer than I expected. What's going on here? What ya'll doing?"

Lie first and tell the truth later.

"For your information, I was talking to Alita," I say, nodding at my friend who quietly stood by all that time. "I don't care to talk to him. I will leave you and your new boyfriend alone." I say that so she won't know that what she's doing truly bothers me. But I doubt she believes me.

I start to say something else to her, but my Aunt Perry staggers in from the backyard through the sliding glass door and peers curiously at me.

"It takes that damn long to get my cup?"

"Oops, sorry Auntie. I forgot."

" 'Oops, I forgot,' " she mocks. "Naw, girl, how can you forget about me? You know how I am." She lets out a loud and drawn-out belch that sounds disgusting.

"Yuck," I say. "That stinks. You've been out there drinking bottles of beer, haven't you?"

"Yep, I sure was," she says and belches again while she's talking. Then her face turns green, and she dashes to the sink and pukes. I hear her throat contracting. You can smell every greasy thing she ate for breakfast. I want to throw up, too.

Perry turns on the spigot and rinses out the sink using a small rubber hose.

Jeff grins and says, "Beer before liquor, never been sicker. Liquor before beer, you're in the clear."

"Shut up, fool," Aunt Perry snaps. "Hey." She scrutinizes him closely. "What are you doing here? You and my niece back together now? When's the wedding?"

"Ain't gonna be no wedding," jumps in Marlene. She has the nerve to yank Jeff by the arm. We're now all gathered next to the kitchen sink facing the breakfast table.

"He with you?" Aunt Perry asks. "Is that how we do things now?"

"You got a problem with that?" Marlene says.

"You're the one with the problem, girl. I can't believe your stupid ass. You got a lotta damned nerve walking up in your daddy's house with that man on your arm. Can't you even p–pretend to respect your sister?"

Marlene gasps and stares rudely at Aunt Perry.

"Damn shame, girl, you were not raised right. But with your mama's ways, what do I expect? I never did like her ass. Miss Loretta—the Woman Who Can Suck Dick Betta. That's what they used to say about her back in the day!"

"What did you say about my mama?" Marlene asks, standing in front of Aunt Perry.

Marlene always tries to defend her mom, even though

my mama told me she dated Blinky first. Loretta and Brooke were best friends years ago, before Marlene or I was born. Even though Brooke was ten years older than Loretta, they got along famously. But their relationship changed when the two women fought over Blinky. Now the ladies can't stand each other half the time.

"Girl, don't act like you don't know what I'm talking about," says Aunt Perry.

"No, you don't know what *you're* talking about," Marlene cries out.

"I think I know about this more than you. I was alive at that time and you weren't. So like I said before, Loretta is the Freak Who's Always in Heat."

"Stop saying that stuff about my mama," Marlene shrieks.

"She told it like it was, that's what Perry did." Brooke, my mother, suddenly waltzes in the kitchen. She must've just gotten here. I doubt she was invited, but formal invitations never keep her from showing up.

Mama continues what Perry started: "Yep, that's her, all right. Miss Loretta—the Whore Whose Tongue Is a Dick Wetter."

"Eww, I can't stand y'all. How can you sit up here and diss my mama? She's not even here to defend herself."

"Believe me, honey, whores and man stealers can't defend themselves."

"Oh, there you go, Brooke. You still can't get over the fact that Blinky picked my mama over you. That was, what, twenty-something years ago. Get a life, loser." Marlene laughs like something is funny, but I'll show her what's funny. I cock my fist and punch Marlene square in her forehead. Her head snaps back, and she lets out an eerie wail. My knuckles are now burning and that pisses me off.

"Don't you talk to my mother like that, you idiot." I yell at her so loud everyone grows quiet. Jeff runs up to me and grabs my arm, and I reluctantly push him off me.

"Leave me alone. You have nothing to do with this. You need to run after *her,* since she's the one who brought you to this party."

"Rachel, please. We should talk. Even though you're mad, I hate seeing you and Marlene act like this. You shouldn't be hitting your sister. Apologize."

"Nooo," Marlene butts in. "Let her dumb butt stay dumb. I'm fine. Thanks for being concerned, since no one else is."

Face red, my mama forcefully takes me by the hand and leads me to the family room. Alita follows behind us asking, "You need anything, sis? Need a glass of ice water or trash can punch?"

"She doesn't need that. She needs to watch who she's hitting, though, I know that much," says Marlene, hollering after us and following us into the family room.

Aunt Perry, who is right behind me, Mama, and Alita, says, "You gotta watch your temper, Rachel. You may be pissed, hell, I'm pissed for you, but you don't need things to escalate where you catch yourself a case."

"Yep, I'm gonna file assault charges on you, Rachel, you hear me?" Marlene screams. I look toward the kitchen, but she's standing several feet behind me, apparently listening in.

"Girl, get your fat ass out this room. Nobody's talking to you, and nobody's going to sue anybody," screams my mama. "Dare you to make me mad." And, like a wise woman, Marlene twirls her big butt around, clamps her mouth shut, and disappears.

"Dang," Mama complains. "She is one of the nosiest people, I swear."

"It's cool, Mama," I say. "I didn't mean to go off on her, but she's crossing a line when she says things about you in front of your face. I won't stand for it."

"Well, thanks for defending me. That girl needs to watch herself."

"She'll be all right. She just wants an apology. But don't worry about her, okay?"

"Oh, she's not the one I'm worried about."

"You worried about me, Mama?"

"I don't want you to go through the shit I went through, Lord knows. It's like some doggone déjà vu."

"Ain't that the truth," says Aunt Perry. "I remember like it was yesterday. Shame."

"It's getting crazy," I say. "None of this makes any sense. How did we get like this? I know I shouldn't be swinging at her—."

"You did more than swing," Alita murmurs.

"I know, it wasn't cool," I admit. "But she started this. I'm really shocked that she brought my ex to this party. That was pretty bold. Is Marlene that much like her mother?"

My mama's eyes are blazing from ancient traumatizing memories. She looks how I feel. Sad. Frustrated. And I know even though things have calmed down a notch, it's gonna be later rather than sooner before this mess blows over.

The more I think about myself and my mama and the hurt we've been through, the more I know the battle has just begun. I head back to the kitchen to finish the fight that Marlene (and Loretta before her) was stupid enough to start.

5

MARLENE

The Best Woman Will Always Win

One memory I have that'll never be erased is the time I got jumped by five girls. We all attended the same elementary school. I was in fifth grade, the new and different, yet intriguing, chick. At first this close-knit group of girls would gather around me, eager to befriend the new kid on the block—they'd chat me up, scoot their desks close to mine so we could giggle and talk in class; they'd save a special seat for me in the lunchroom; and I'd get dragged by the arm so we all could hang together on the playground. It felt great to be accepted, to be "in" for a change. I am not sure why they took to me. All I knew was I loved having lots of friends, girls who laughed and high-fived me when I cracked a good joke, and girls who hated the same teachers I came to hate.

But then the good times changed. About four weeks after I began attending the new school, a stuffy nose, harsh cough, and watery eyes kept me from going to classes three days in a row. School policy was if you're sick stay your sick butt at home and don't come back till you're well. When my health improved my mother sent me back to school, which ended up being the very next Monday. My excitement about returning grew into puzzlement the minute my friends pretended like they didn't see me when I waved hello. They wrinkled their noses and moved their desks far away from mine when I sat down. Instead of laughing with me, they laughed at me. Threw back their heads and giggled and slapped their knees at the girl with the flabby arms and thick waist. I stared straight ahead when I realized the girls that I learned to like plain ole didn't like me anymore. I ate lunch by myself at a long, dirty lunch table, and during recess, when we congregated on the playground, the playing turned ugly.

"You think you something, don't you, Marlene?"

"What are you talking about?"

"I'm talking about the fact that you an uppity girl—you think you better than us."

"That's not true. No, I don't."

"Stop lying. You think you the shit but you ain't all that. You're too stupid to know that no one likes you for real."

"Why are you talking to me like this? I thought you were my friend!"

"No one gave you permission to talk."

"But I just—."

"Shut up, bitch." Whop! One girl repeatedly smacked me in the face with her open hand. Another jumped and twisted my arm behind my back, yelling "Get her!" Another kicked me in the stomach like my belly was a soccer ball. She laughed hysterically the second I started wheezing. Then a slew of hands all came at my face, fists balled up, socking me in the jaw. I felt like a piñata. I closed my eyes, yanked my arm, and swung my fists, trying my best to defend myself. I wanted to swing hard enough so I could make contact with a nose, a jaw, an eye. I wanted so bad to inflict pain on those girls. And I also wanted to win the fight. I intended to show them they couldn't love me one day and hate me the next and think I'd go along with their games. Even though it was one against five and the odds were against me, I still had to win. I desperately yearned to come out on top even though my future looked dismal.

Later I learned that what the girls did to me they did to every new girl who came to our school. Stupid, silly, immature mind games. Girls bullying girls. Kind of like the Lindsay Lohan movie *Mean Girls*, except in my case, the meanness started at an earlier age.

Fast forward to now: the new kind of playground fight.

It's several minutes after Rachel delivered a blow to my head.

After Rachel and her mama leave the kitchen, Jeff carefully examines my wound. I wince when he brushes his finger across the swelling. He opens the freezer door and shakes some ice cubes out of the tray. He grabs a napkin off the counter and wraps it around the ice, and applies it to my forehead.

"I can't believe Rachel. She was wrong, so wrong," he says.

"Yes, she was." I blink and can feel hot water spring in my eyes.

"Don't cry," Jeff softly says. "I know it hurts, but it won't hurt forever," he reassures me.

"I hope not."

"I *know* not. Physical wounds heal quicker than any other wounds."

Right then Rachel, Alita, Aunt Perry, and Brooke bounce back into the kitchen like they're boxers in a ring. We're clustered by the refrigerator.

Rachel plants her hands on her hips. "And another thing," she says as if we were in the midst of a conversation. "I am tired of your mama talking shit about me to Blinky."

"Rachel, hush," I say with a dismissive wave of the hand, like her words are stupid. "Leave my mama out of it. You're frustrated and using her to start messing with me, and she isn't the issue."

"Then what is, bitch? School me."

"I am not about to go there with you, girl."

"But what if I want you to?"

"Rachel, grow up and stop acting stupid."

"You're the stupid one."

That does it.

"Oh, so I'm the stupid one? A woman who gives up a perfectly good man and gets mad when he moves on is about as dumb as George W. Bush—."

And that's when she shoves me so hard I nearly lose my balance. I have to rest my hand against the fridge to keep from hitting the floor. Suddenly all eyes are on me. I morph into a scared little girl surrounded by her former so-called friends. I feel insecure, like I don't know if I should defend myself, or make excuses, or play the innocent role. But in spite of being uncertain, I know I have to raise my fist and swing hard. Raise back my fist and swing again. So what if my sister says idiot things like "Christians don't fight." During moments like this, I let Rachel antagonize me all she wants. Just because you believe in God doesn't mean you have to be somebody's fool. Like you don't hurt, don't have feelings, or don't feel like defending yourself sometimes because you're too impatient to wait on the Lord to defend you.

So when meddlesome Perry throws in her two cents by calling me a "pathetic hypocrite," whop, I make sure my sister's favorite aunt gets smacked, too. And Alita being in the room is another potential fist that's going to come after me sooner or later, so let me get this girl before she gets me. And Rachel, well, she's the ringleader, the girl-fight instigator who has power and influence over all the other girls. And it's weird because it shouldn't be this way; the bigger sister should gang up on the younger one. But these strange kinds of things have happened between me and Rachel ever since we were young.

And I see our conflicts won't end just because we're getting older.

"Who the hell you think you are trying to take a swing at me?" Aunt Perry says. "Girl, don't you know I'll whoop your ass? You ain't too big for me to take an extension cord to you."

"Marlene, have you lost your mind?" Alita joins in, looking amazed.

"Hey, everybody, time out. This is wrong and it's nuts." Jeff speaks up. He physically separates me and Rachel and gives us all incredulous looks. All these women pushing and shoving and for what? I can't even remember how things got started. But that's how it is sometimes when raw emotions simmer underneath the surface.

It's just like a volcano. You hear it bubbling, you see clouds of smoke billowing, and you know something dangerous and explosive is about to happen. I can only guess that the volcano erupting between my sister and me is going to expose some things that have been buried and hidden for far too long.

"Rachel," Jeff says angrily, "you ought to be ashamed of yourself."

She opens her mouth to speak, but not a single word comes out.

"All of you need to chill out before something else happens that you regret," he continues scolding. The other ladies are breathing hard and their reddened faces glimmer with shame.

"Marlene, will you come with me?" Jeff pleads with me, and I instantly follow him. We walk through Blinky's kitchen, dining room, then through the foyer and out the front door.

Blinky lives in the hood, and the hood never sleeps. There're always people around watching to see who's coming and going. Normally, when I am outside the house, I wave and talk to the teenage guys who are always loafing around and sitting on the curb of the house next door, but today I pretend like they're invisible because I hope they aren't staring at my forehead.

Jeff scrambles down the front walk until he's standing next to Ella and opens the passenger door. I quickly slide in and look straight ahead until he bounds around to the other side of the car and settles in on the driver's side.

"I love a woman with fire, but damn, Little Mama, do you gotta get into it with your entire family all at once?"

"Jeff, you saw how instigating they can be. They all hate me, team up on me. Nothing I do is ever right. They always side with Rachel. You see how they let her hit me? I have to fight, or else they'll run over me even more."

"Slow your roll, Little Mama. It's cool. We just gotta chill. Y'all can't be wilding out at your own daddy's birthday party. That's not righteous."

I flinch when he says "righteous." What if he thinks I'm a hypocrite? Where is the sisterly love I'm supposed to be showing? I barely want to think about the fact that Rachel and I are related, let alone act like I deeply love the girl.

"Jeff, you're right. I'm sorry. Things went way too far. But she's an expert at pushing my buttons and getting me all twisted up inside."

"Don't let her. You're older. Be the example."

"I know. I should. But I can't. I won't. She always gets what she wants. I've always had to struggle."

"Marlene, you know it's not true. I think you're being paranoid."

"Oh, yeah? Well, what about the fact that one time she was chosen to be in a back-to-school fashion show that was sponsored by the mall? I am the one who thought of applying first and suggested that we try out together. But instead of picking me, the judges picked her hands down. Can you believe that?" I ask, blinking back tears.

"First of all, you sound like you're in elementary school, like a little kid that's mad because someone stole her favorite toy."

"I'm not a kid—."

"And secondly, you know good and well Rachel doesn't get everything she wants. If she got to be in that fashion show, it's only because she got lucky."

"What are you saying?"

"No doubt, Rachel is a pretty woman . . . but so are you."

"You're just saying that." I sniff and eye him suspiciously. Jeff knows just what to say to make me feel so good inside.

"Anyone can see that you believe you're attractive. You wear pretty clothes, your hair looks good, and you strut around like you're on a darned catwalk sometimes. Like you're the runner-up of a beauty contest."

"That's the problem. I'm always the runner-up, and Rachel is usually the winner."

"Again, you're exaggerating, Marlene. And nine times out of ten, when folks exaggerate—"

"No, Jeff, really. I could tell you some things. But it hurts too much to think about. All I know is for once in my life, I aim to get exactly what I want. I want to win." I eye him seriously and pray he can see my determination and sense my deep-rooted desire.

He grins at me almost like he's reading between the lines and is flattered.

"Let's chill out here for a sec. Give peeps time to cool down, 'kay?"

I nod and close my eyes for a few minutes and try to relax.

"Hey, you. You look gorgeous when you're asleep," he whispers.

My eyes pop open. I can't help but blush. Jeff makes me feel like a little girl sometimes. Like he notices me and I am special.

"I'm not asleep," I murmur.

"Hey, then if you're awake, I want to show you something." He gives me a mischievous look and picks up a small key ring with a Ford emblem. He inserts a key into the glove compartment. Seconds later he retrieves a fat roll of cash about the size of some balled-up socks. A crisp hundred-dollar bill is on top.

"Remember when I told you I don't trust banks?"

"Yeah."

"I felt like I had to take control of my destiny. Kind of like what you ought to do in your own family situation."

"Explain."

"You feel like folks pick on you."

"They go overboard whenever issues pop up."

"And you don't like that, right?"

"Not at all."

"Because?"

"Because if my family were to just calm down, or mind their own business, we wouldn't get into these altercations as much."

"Right, but when you do get into the drama, it makes you feel like you're losing."

I smile brightly at him. "Precisely. And I don't like to lose."

"Because you're a winner. You like to be in control of your destiny."

"Yeah, of course, but what does this have to do with your bankroll?"

"My mistrust of banks has forced me to make certain decisions to ensure my own security, financial security."

I just stare at him, then at his bankroll, then at him again.

"Oh, you're one of those, huh? You'd rather take a risk of stashing cash in the car than depositing it in the bank."

"Yep, I know where my money is at all times. No one makes mistakes and gives my money to anyone else, and I don't have to worry about all those ridiculous fees."

"Okay," I say and shrug. "But that doesn't really have anything to do with me."

"Listen, Marlene. You should take control of your own life and stop letting the family bully you and cause you to feel bad because you make decisions they don't like."

"Yeah, I'd love to do that, but I'm kind of outnumbered. There's power in numbers, ya know what I'm saying?"

"But there's also power in high self-esteem. Know who you are, what you want, stand your ground no matter what. You don't have to physically fight back, just be strong about who you are, what you believe in. They'll have no choice but to leave you alone."

"That sounds good, but do you really think it would work out for me?"

"You won't know unless you try. I think I know what you want." He smiles as if suggesting that he knows I want *him*. "But," he continues, "you gotta change the way you go about stating what you want. That's what you have to work on.

"Yep," he says, thumbing through his cash. "I had to empower myself when it comes to money, and you gotta empower yourself when it comes to relationships." It sounds like Jeff's shuffling two decks of cards; that's how much cash he has.

"Um, that sure looks like a lot of . . ."

"I have almost twenty grand . . . but I don't have quite that much in my work ride. This here is just one of my stashes."

"Hmm, isn't it dangerous to leave your money in your cars?"

"I dare anybody to try to put their hand on my dough. I don't play that. Anyone who knows Jeffrey Williams knows: don't mess with my money, my car, or my woman."

I feel warm inside and start fanning myself.

"You hot?"

I laugh.

"You look beautiful when you laugh, Marlene. You should laugh all the time."

I want to do whatever I can to get him to stay as sweet and supportive as he is.

"Look Jeff," I say, blushing, "I'm going to try to do that, I promise. Thank you for bringing me out here, away from the drama. I don't know how I find myself in the midst of craziness sometimes. I'm not looking for trouble, but trouble always finds me."

"Okay, there you go being unreasonable again."

"Why you say that?"

"You are too smart a woman not to know that me and you—us, together, that combination—equals drama. High-octane drama. Right?"

"Um, well, yeah, but—."

"I already know you and Rachel aren't always on the same page when it comes to things like who pays what bills, which one should help Blinky when he's in a pinch. Y'all clash a lot—."

"Yet we live together. I know. Makes no sense. But my crazy daddy insists that we get along. That we try to make our relationship work no matter what. That's his dream. I think he feels guilty."

It's not often that I talk about what my father did, how his actions have caused a strain in the family. As the story goes, Blinky has always been a ladies' man, the ultimate mack daddy. Women would do all kinds of things to capture

Blinky's attention. So my mama, Loretta, and Rachel's mama, Brooke, were just two of his main squeezes back then. I guess they were considered his coveted first string. When times were good, my mama and Brooke would each get a portion of his cash, some great sex and lots of attention, and he'd take 'em out to a movie, dancing, bowling, or the skating rink.

In addition to my mama and Brooke, Blinky dealt with his benchwarming wannabes. Women who wished they could command his attention but weren't important enough to earn a permanent spot. The most he'd do is "one night 'em" and call it a day.

Aunt Perry enjoys disclosing family history and all the scandals. And the way Aunt Perry tells it, long before Blinky came into the picture Brooke and Loretta were PICs (partners-in-crime). They'd schedule hair appointments together, buy groceries and share the same shopping cart. They'd trade cute purses and even cuter shoes, and go hang out at the club every Thursday night. One time, my mama had to skip their ladies' night out because she had to study for an exam at the local college, but Brooke got her caught up on the happenings at the club real quick. Brooke told this story to Aunt Perry. Then Aunt Perry, known for proudly revealing family scandals, relayed the gossip to me. I've heard what happened so many times, it's like the voices are in my head.

Hey, Loretta.

Hey, girl, what you know good?

I met somebody.

Oh, yeah. He cute?

Oh, girl, he's better than Billy Dee Williams and Sidney Poitier put together.

Mmm, so when am I gonna meet your new cutie pie?

You don't even have to worry about that. You'll meet him real soon.

Once Brooke started seeing Blinky, my mama said that Brooke lost her "woman power." Loretta claimed Brooke began doing things a real woman wouldn't do.

Hey, Loretta.

Yeah, girl, what's up?

Do me a favor. I got to work late today. Can my best friend pick up my main man from the Greyhound station? He's coming in from Louisiana, and I don't want him waiting around downtown for me. I'll give you gas money later.

Aw, girl, you don't even have to worry about it. Blinky's cool with me. I don't mind picking him up. Save your gas money.

That's a true-blue friend for you.

That's what friends are for.

And when Brooke began experiencing problems in her relationship, guess who she'd tell?

Loretta, I can't tell you how sick I am of his shit. I cook for the man, wash and iron his clothes, clean the nasty-ass house, drive him here and there and take him to buy his six-pack, carton of cigarettes, and a bag of weed, and this is what he does to me?

What he do, Brooke?

Well, after a long hard day, you know me, I'm looking to get busy up under the sheets. Well, the sorry Negro can't even get it up for me anymore. Says he's too tired and don't feel like doing this and that. We used to fuck every night and all of a sudden he's sooo tired? Tired from what? He barely lets me kiss him, let alone get on top and ride him the way he likes me to ride him. He's been spending a long time in the bathroom putting on fancy dress shirts, spraying himself with skunk-smelling cologne, and is barely home for dinner anymore. Loretta, he must got another woman. What else could it be?

Brooke, you tripping. Nobody in they right mind would want Blinky.

They may not be in they right mind, but you better believe some women out there want my man. That's what women do; they always want somebody else's man and don't care who they hurt to get the man. Sneaking conniving bitches gonna get tired of acting foul one day.

Mmm-mmm, girl. I hear ya. That's a damn shame.

Even though the info was very juicy, I can't believe my aunt was so willing to divulge all the drama that went down between Loretta, Brooke, and Blinky. And once my daddy realized I knew about his history with my mama and Brooke, he tried to play it off by changing the subject so that the topic was me and Rachel. He'd say that even though those two women are catty we don't have to be like our mothers. He'd try to make us believe that although we're sisters, we can be each other's best friend. Maybe he's attempting to repair what happened between my mama and Brooke, by insisting that his daughters, the product of his affairs, experience a solid and close relationship no matter what.

But what Blinky says conflicts with the advice my mama gives. She feels it's her motherly duty to explain how things can get between some men and women. That the storybook ending may come about through a non-storybook way. And how the best woman will always win. The best woman is the woman who ends up with the man. My mama would repeatedly pull me aside and make these statements, but she would never explain the meaning behind her words. So these days, I ignore her sometimes and listen to her at other times.

In response to Jeff's comments that me and Rachel aren't always on the same page, I remark, "My daddy thinks that most sisters are bound to argue once in a while. He may let us fuss here and there, but he won't tolerate it for long. Even though I think he feels guilty about breaking up my mama and Brooke's friendship, he won't let it be an excuse as far as me and Rachel goes. He used to force us to make up when we were little."

"How'd you feel about that?" Jeff asks.

"I didn't know any better back then."

"And now?"

"Now I know I have a choice. But it's all about making the right choice . . . for me."

Jeff spends the next ten minutes trying to loosen me up by imitating Chris Rock. He's really good at doing that chipmunk facial expression that Rock seems to have. I laugh hysterically and as the wetness of my tears of laughter stains my cheeks, I begin to feel much calmer and it feels great to relax.

"You hungry?" He stares at me with a hopeful grin.

"I could eat," I say.

"Good. I'll go fix you a plate."

"No, it's cool. I'm ready to go back inside and face the wolves."

"Let's roll."

I am so pleased that Jeff is by my side. His kind and supportive words are my protective covering, and I mentally embrace his strength.

When we return to the house, I notice that the kitchen has emptied of the troublemakers. But I see my little cousins are chasing each other and running around in circles, screaming and laughing like they've lost their minds.

"Quit running before somebody gets hurt and busts their head."

"Okay, Ms. 'Lene," says Kiki.

"And who left the refrigerator open?"

"Braylon," Kiki says.

"Boy, please close the refrigerator door. You're going to make the food spoil."

"Shut up," yells Braylon. "If it spoils you won't eat it all up, fatty."

"Watch your mouth before I tell your mother."

He quickly hushes up and presses his back against the refrigerator door so that it closes.

Jeff nods at me to follow him back outside to the jungle.

" 'The big payback.' " Both Rachel and Aunt Perry are doing the bump. They're snapping their fingers then waving their hands to the beat of the music.

"That song is still on?" I say, frowning. "Jeez, can't ya'll find something else to play?"

"Nope." Perry shrugs and does some foolish dance move that causes Blinky to holler and clap his hands like he's a little kid instead of sixty.

"You sure don't act your age," I say to my daddy.

"Daughter Number One, how would you know how a sixty-year-old acts, huh?"

"She doesn't have the—" Alita, who's positioned next to my sister, quickly clamps her hand over Rachel's mouth. They're standing in front of a table loaded with food. There's crawfish, ears of corn, greens, and black-eyed peas. Racks of beef ribs and stacks of cooked hamburgers that had been smoking on a huge grill and filling up the entire yard with that delicious, smoky aroma.

Rachel leers at us the second we arrive outside. After she gives me an evil glare, her eyes get stuck on Jeff and sag at the corners. I see wetness even from where I stand. Either she's about to cry, or the smoke from the pit is irritating her pupils.

"I don't feel like dancing anymore," she whines and stops dancing so she can take a seat. Alita quietly sits next to her.

"Well, we can get back to grubbing, no problem," says Auntie Perry. She plunks down at the picnic table that's big enough to seat twelve people.

"Oww," Rachel cries out and vigorously rubs the corners of her eyes from all the thick smoke. She abruptly stops rubbing and gives Jeff a hurt look as if she expects him to come ease her pain, but he looks away.

"You hungry? Don't just stand there. Fix my daughter a plate." My mama grins at Jeff then winks at me. I wish she'd knock it off.

"Is there room at the table?" I ask.

"Nope," says Auntie Perry.

"Yep," says my mama. "You two look so cute together, like Janet Jackson and her cute little rapper boyfriend. I can't remember his name, but ya'll know who I'm talking about. Forty Cents!"

"Forty? Dang, Mama, that's embarrassing. You don't know what you're talking about."

"Um, is he Nickelback?"

"Mama, *please* stop it."

"Okay, fine, but like I said, y'all look good. So come sit here next to me and Blinky. I saved y'all a seat."

"But will there be enough room for—" Alita shoves Rachel in the gut and interrupts her smart comment. I like that. Alita is Rachel's friend, but she's no fool. That girl ain't gonna let anything else stupid go down, that's for sure. I almost feel bad for slapping her earlier.

Jeff fixes my plate for me while I settle into my seat.

"Daddy, is there any more potato salad? I don't see it."

"Um, no," Loretta says, rolling her eyes at Rachel, who suddenly stares directly at the food in front of her.

"Your potato salad messed up, sweetie," says Aunt Perry. "I heard you spent a lot of time preparing that food, but I guess no one will ever know what it tasted like."

"Why not?" I say, confused. "What are you talking about, Auntie Perry?"

"She's talking about how your potato salad accidentally dropped on the grass. It got dirt and ants on it so we had to dump everything in the trash," Blinky explains.

"How did that happen? Jeez, ya'll are so pathetic," I complain.

"Your sister is the one . . . " Mama replies. "She 'accidentally' let it slip to the ground when she was trying to carry it, and I don't know why she'd do that, since you'd already put the dish on the darned table, I swear to God."

"Okay, Loretta, hush your mouth," Blinky interrupts. "It's over and done with. Now Daughter Number One, if you hadn't been gone so long, maybe you could've kept guard over your little potato salad. You missed a lot being gone. We said grace, and you know how I like for you to say the grace."

I blush. "I know, Daddy. Sorry. It won't happen again."

Blinky laughs. "As long as I can remember when you girls were little—"

"Marlene has never been little," says Brooke.

"Don't start!" barks Loretta.

"You started it, think about that, why don't cha?" replies Brooke, staring at my mama.

"Could you all please stop it?" Uncle Scooter looks up from his plate just to say that, then starts ripping apart some barbecue with his teeth. The rest of us settle down.

"Anyway," Blinky pipes up. "As I was saying, when the girls were younger, I'd have Pretty Girl say the grace. And Rachel would be so cute. She'd always want everyone to hold hands. And she'd wait for me to say, 'Hold your little sister's hand.' She loved that . . . loved for everyone to be in unity."

Rachel looks puzzled. "I don't remember all that."

"Well, it's true. You remember it, don't you, Pretty Girl?"

I nod and blush, feeling embarrassed by Blinky's bout of nostalgia.

But as he gets on a roll bringing up our childhood antics, everyone calms down and begins swapping family stories and telling jokes raw enough to make a black man's face turn blue. After a moment I manage to relax, and I actually end up having a good time, especially after Rachel and Alita decide to leave early. Rachel hands Daddy a postdated check and makes him promise not to cash it for another week.

He says okay, thanks her for coming, and gives her a tight hug good-bye.

Jeff and I hang around for another half-hour, then he drops me off at home. Rachel comes through our front door well after dark. By then I've retreated to my room. I stay up late, entertaining myself by watching several romantic comedies until one in the morning. And when I finally grow tired of looking at the TV, I slide under the covers and dwell on the day's events before falling into a deep sleep.

Take your little sister's hand.

I wake up in a sweat, quickly jumping out of the bed with the bottom of the sheets twisted around my ankles. I manage to run a few steps from the bed and end up collapsing on the carpeted floor. Then I realize I had a disturbing dream, and I can feel my heart beating wildly inside my chest.

Hearing Blinky's voice in my dream feels strange. It's as if he's standing in the room with me, sternly telling me what to do.

Like when I was in fifth grade and Rachel was in first. We had to walk six blocks to the elementary school in Third Ward. The buildings we passed were old and dilapidated, with missing bricks and broken-out windows. Stray dogs barked at us and bared their sharp teeth. Rachel stopped walking. Frozen from fear. Her bottom lip quivered; her little legs shook.

"I'm s–scared."

"That dog's not thinking about you. C'mon girl. We gonna be late." And I saw Blinky ride past us, sitting in the passenger side of some strange woman's car. He rolled down the window and yelled, "Take your little sister's hand."

I instantly obeyed and squeezed Rachel's tiny fingers in mine. Her hand felt soft and warm, and I could tell she was happy and relieved that I reached out and touched her.

"Now raise it toward the sky." Blinky's command sounded silly, but I raised her soft little hand high in the air until our daddy smiled and nodded; satisfied, he waved at us. Then he and his woman quickly drove off until I couldn't see the car anymore. He often left us girls to fend for ourselves. We'd rush to school as fast as we could, hoping to make it before the bell rang. Today six blocks is like walking through my apartment twelve times, but back then it felt like Rachel and I were trying to reach the moon.

Take your little sister's hand and raise it toward the sky.

I shudder and retrieve the sheets from the floor. Even though my heartbeat feels steadier, I'm still afraid. Especially since Rachel's emotions are so raw regarding me and Jeff. And to know that she sleeps on the other side of the living room freaks me out. Who knows what kinds of things she contemplates in her room? And who can predict what she's capable of doing? I don't trust her. No, I take that back. Sometimes she surprises me and does things I don't expect. Nice things. Thoughtful gestures. But I doubt I'll see any of that sisterly niceness oozing out of her anytime soon.

6

RACHEL

Unfinished Business

The morning following Blinky's birthday party leaves me feeling no different than I felt the day before. I wake up furious. My jaw is rigid with frustration and helplessness. I want answers, and, thanks to that James Brown song that keeps playing in my head, I'm seeking something even more important than answers, too.

I quickly dash out of the bed and rush through the living area until I reach my sister's bedroom door. Of course, it's closed, so I softly tap on her door, then twist the knob and step in and flick on the overhead light. A sky blue blanket covers a round lump spread out on her queen-sized bed.

"Wake up, Marlene."

She doesn't say anything.

I walk over to her and nudge her hard, pushing against her shoulders so that she rocks back and forth.

"Did you hear me? Get your butt up right now."

"Huh? What time is it?"

"Yep, you overslept again."

She sits up in bed and vigorously rubs her eyes. I can see a purple bruise on her forehead. I really hate that I had to resort to physical altercations with her, and seeing that mark makes me feel worse. Yet I need to speak my mind.

"This is going too far, Marlene. Why are you willing to mess up your job over a man?"

"Rachel, please. First of all, I took a vacation day today, so I haven't overslept, but then again, I have slept a little too long because Jeff and I are supposed to be meeting at Waffle House. So actually I should be thanking you for my little wake-up call." She giggles quietly.

Waffle House? I am crazy about Waffle House and haven't been able to bring myself to go to the place since Jeff and I parted ways. We used to eat there every other Saturday, braving the crowds to order coffee, hash browns, scrambled eggs, bacon, and a huge waffle. I can't believe he'd take her to a place he used to take me. What's wrong with IHOP? Or even Whataburger?

"I don't even believe what I'm hearing. Why are you doing this?"

"Doing what, Rachel? Living my life and trying to make myself happy?"

"Marlene, tell me something: how well do you know Jeff?"

"What? I know him pretty good, but, of course, our relationship is still fresh, so I'm spending time getting to know him."

"Ugh, this is so ridiculous."

"What, Rachel? Why are you even asking me these kinds of questions?" She sounds irritated and makes a move toward her closet, which is bursting with all kinds of beautiful outfits. "You act like you don't know how things go. It's obvious I need time to learn more about the man."

"He does not want you, Marlene."

She angrily snatches a floral print baby-doll dress off a hanger. I remember when she bought it, not even a couple weeks ago. She interrupted me watching a DVD just to ask me how it looked on her. I told her it looked great. I lied. She looked like a Cabbage Patch Kid on steroids.

"Rachel, don't even try it."

"Marlene, can't you realize that Jeff is only going out with you to get back at me? That's what people do. Remember our mothers?"

"Of course, dummy—"

"I'm not dumb, and I wish you'd stop calling me that."

"Look, Rachel, regardless of what I call you, you are not going to convince me that Jeff isn't feeling me." She pauses, then blurts out, "Dang, jealousy is written all over your face. I don't blame you for being envious. You messed up big-time, but it's too late now. And I refuse to suffer in my love life because you made a bad decision."

"You're making a bad decision," I shout. "There are things you—"

"I don't wanna hear it!" she shouts back.

And I shut up. Let the know-it-all bitch learn things the hard way. She's hardheaded, and if it takes her falling flat on her stupid face to realize a thing or two, then let her fall. I don't care anymore. I know Jeff still cares about me.

"Little sister, just count your losses and go fish for another man in that big dating pool that's out there. And if you luck out, you can find someone as good as Mr. Williams. How about that?"

That's it! I've had enough!

I stand directly in her face, not caring how loudly I yell or how crazy I sound.

"You are such a fool, Marlene. This man is not really into you. You'll see."

"You're a jealous hater."

"No, I'm not."

"You are. Don't blame me because you couldn't hold on to your man."

"Ah, did you hear what you just said? You said 'your' man. You know Jeff and I still have some unfinished business."

"You finished your business with him when you told the dude you wanted out."

"But Marlene, common sense would tell you that I haven't completely gotten over him." I don't like admitting this, but it's important that she knows the truth. "After we broke up, you'd ask me how I was doing. I'd tell you that I miss Jeff."

"If you really missed him, you would have tried to repair your relationship with him back then. And you didn't. So that window of opportunity is now closed. Shut tight. Locked."

I just look at her like she's a candidate for the insane asylum, because that's how she's behaving. Sometimes I wonder if women are genetically predisposed to screw up, to lose our minds over a man.

"Fuck you, Marlene. Because that's all you're going to be good for to Jeff."

"You's a rude SOB!"

"Oh so now you're cussing, too?"

" 'SOB' is an acronym. Acronyms aren't cuss words."

"Well, ain't that a B, you MF?" I say, trying to be smart.

"Whatever, Rachel. He's an ex. You made him an ex. And you'll be better off when you start acting like an ex."

"Marlene, that is so stupid. Do you know how stupid you sound? This entire issue is about integrity, which I know you can't even spell or define."

"I'm the one with an associate's degree, remember?" She's rubbing that in my face because I enrolled at San Jacinto Community College for one semester but didn't return. I got a low grade in algebra and felt so depressed I didn't want to take any classes.

"A lot of stupid people have degrees, remember?"

She knows I'm referring to her mama. Loretta has a bachelor's degree, but no one is impressed because it's from the great University of Phoenix. Okay, so everyone isn't bright enough to graduate from Harvard, but at least show some effort, no matter what college you attend. Loretta, poor thing, paid cash for other people to write her papers. That figures. But her shortchanged education didn't stop her from getting a job as an assistant counseling and crisis manager down at the women's center. For the life of me I can't figure out how anybody could hire a woman who still hangs panty hose to dry on her front porch. She's fifty and wears miniskirts and sequined blouses with pink and yellow plastic bangles hanging on her arms, like, a total of ten or twelve. Her arms are too thick to pull off a fashionable and respectful look, but you can't tell that to Loretta. This woman feels she can do whatever she wants, and if it annoys you? "Your problem!"

Selfish, selfish, selfish.

Like mother, like daughter.

"Okay, joke's over now, Marlene. You really can't be this cruel, insensitive, and selfish. Can you?"

"As long as Jeff doesn't mind, why should I?"

"I can't believe you'd take my leftovers."

"Shoot, sometimes leftovers taste good."

"When I give you a taste of your own medicine, I wonder what you'll say then."

"If that's your way of threatening me, bring it on, Sis. Bring it on."

I have been pleading with Marlene a good twenty minutes. It's apparent she's too stubborn to change her mind. So I gotta change my strategy. I leave her room and glance at my watch. It's only eight A.M. That leaves me enough time to do what I want to do. I rush to my closet and select an off-white chiffon puff-sleeved blouse and a black pencil skirt that falls just above my knees. And I reach up to my top shelf and pull out a pair of BCBGirls black peep-toe pumps, then find some sheer panty hose. I get dressed as fast as possible, finger-comb my hair, and grab my work uniform plus a pair of comfortable flats that I can change into later.

It's only by a sheer miracle that I am able to leave the apartment before Marlene. As I depart my bedroom and pass through the living area, I can hear the shower running. Thank God Marlene loves to take long, hot showers. And that's why, if I'm smart, I always take my shower the night before, because if I try to take one after she gets out, the water runs miserably cold. But she doesn't care. She claims long showers are her "therapy." Well, this girl needs to stay in that shower for the next few weeks.

Drown, bitch, drown. It seems like something tragic will have to happen to get my sister to wake up.

Meanwhile, I am not opposed to using some different techniques to get what I want. So I sneak out of the house, hop in my car, and drive out of the apartment complex until I hit Highway 6 South. It's amazing how one day you tell yourself you'll never go a certain place ever again, but the next day circumstances cause you to retract your words. Minutes later I pull up into the parking lot of Waffle House, which is adjacent to an Advance Auto Parts. I recognize Ella right away. Jeff's precious car is parked at an angle taking up two whole spaces so that no one else can get too close. The way he dotes on his car burns me up. Yet I gotta do what I gotta do. My heart beats wildly, and a line of sweat develops on my forehead. I feel as nervous as the day I knew I would tell Jeff no to getting married.

I step out of my car and begin walking toward the

restaurant. As usual, it's crowded. Waitresses are taking orders and barking them to the cooks. The cooks pour coffee, crack egg shells, and spoon pancake batter onto the waffle maker. Customers are eating breakfast and chatting loudly as this Monday morning's activities begin.

Jeff is sitting by himself in the corner of the restaurant. His PDA is firmly pressed against his ear. He's vigorously nodding his head, and I see his lips moving, like he's talking to someone. I quickly slide into the seat in front of him and rest my hands on the table. He looks up, his eyes enlarge, and he talks loud.

"Hey, man, I gotta do something real quick. I'll hit you back this afternoon," he says and hangs up. "Rachel? What are you doing here?"

"Jeff, we need to talk."

"Oh, yeah? Is that why you're here? So you can talk?"

"Yes, Jeff, yes."

"Why can't you just pick up the phone? Call a brother?"

"I'm scared you won't answer my calls."

"You're scared I won't answer your calls?"

"Please stop repeating everything I say. I'm nervous enough as it is."

He smirks, and his facial expression makes me feel like I'm swimming against a tide. His inability to take me seriously makes this hard.

"How'd you know I was here, Rachel?"

"My sister said you two were meeting. Jeff, why are you doing this, honey? I mean, what are you trying to prove?"

His eyes flicker with amusement. I guess he can see through my questions. He closely examines my blouse and starts sniffing the air. He knows my fragrance. Donna Karan Cashmere Mist. I remember whenever I'd wear it he'd sink his nose into my neck and inhale my seductive scent. Then his lips would press against my skin. I'd close my eyes, lost in the magic of his touch. We'd end up kissing and rubbing our hands all over each other. In a matter of minutes we'd peel off each other's clothes. And he'd kiss me everywhere, sucking the hungriest parts of my body until he completed the job, while I twisted and jerked, screaming out his name and cradling his head in my hands. I'm beginning to question why I was so afraid of his love. I can't bear for Marlene to have what I used to have.

"All I'm saying is"—I clear my throat to explain—"whatever it is you two call yourselves doing, it's happening way too fast. Jeff, haven't you learned the effects of doing things, important things, too quickly?"

"Baby girl, I'm out here every day on my hustle. And decisions about my houses must be made at a moment's notice—"

"Okay Jeff, but relationships aren't like purchasing houses—"

"I got to keep things moving. Whether it comes to business or relationships, keep it moving."

"Relationships need more time, Jeff . . . all I'm saying."

"But that's the point. Life is too short to take our sweet little time trying to decide what we want out of it. I have to get mine 'cause I have a goal. My game plan is to add three more houses this year, and the year is nearly half over. I plan to make some money so I can wine and dine my woman. And I want to travel with my lady, Rachel. Remember that?"

I flinch. Nod.

"Remember how we'd look through those cruise catalogs, flip through the travel section of the Sunday *Chronicle*? And we'd point out the places we wanted to go, and wonder what it would be like to eat outside at a café in Paris. We'd imagine touring Egypt from the Nile River, or spend time making love in a Norwegian villa. Just getting away from it all and really experiencing life?"

"I know Jeff, I know. I was there."

"Right. You *were* there. I thought it would be me and you. Forever, Rachel. Building our lives together as one. You'd work at the clinic. And I'd be the hustling real estate guy. We'd start popping out babies, little Jeffreys and Rachels, every couple of years until we had two girls and two boys. And we'd raise our kids together, live in a two-story brick house in a gated community, and everyone would have a passport, so together we could explore the real world and experience things we've never imagined."

I really wish he'd stop. It's like he's rubbing it in. Making me remember his finer qualities. Recall his passion and ambitions. I think about the fact that, yeah, he wasn't allergic to hard work. No, he wasn't interested in obtaining a college degree, but it was okay. Jeff would say true education comes from the streets. That he could live and die by the streets and learn everything he needs to know to successfully make it in life. And he convinced me that we could live "the Jeffrey Williams way." He'd remind me that he loved me enough to make me his wife, and that it was an honor for him to even ask me for my hand in marriage. Because statistics indicate that almost 42 percent of African American women will never get married. They're destined to spend their entire lives alone, manless. Sure, they can make a baby with a man, but it won't be the same as being a true, strong, two-parent family. So I was beating the odds, he told me. I lucked out when I met him. A man devoted enough to me to place his ring on my finger.

I glance down at my left hand. I must admit it has never looked so barren. I want to choke with grief, but I know now is not the time.

"I–I don't know what to say, Jeff."

He stares at me with sad eyes for a moment. Then he reaches his hand into his pants pocket.

"Say yes, Rachel."

"What?"

"Say y-e-s."

And he pulls out my ring. And I gasp and stare at the ring, then at Jeff.

"I–I don't understand," I say, barely above a whisper.

And his eyes tell me what I need to know, what I've always known.

"I lo—."

"What the hell are you doing here?" I hear Marlene's irritating voice pound into the back of my head. Jeff discreetly places his hand in his pocket and feigns an innocent look.

"Don't worry, Marlene," I inform her. She *did* end up wearing that baby-doll dress. "Waffle House hasn't run out of food. Yet."

"Girl, you better get out of my seat with your sneaky self. That's the last time I tell you about me and Jeff's plans."

"I know all about his plans, believe me." I stand up. His eyes penetrate through me, and I'm too stunned to look at him again. All I can think about is my engagement ring shining in his big hand.

"You're too desperate, Rachel. I mean, really, why do you insist on continually embarrassing yourself? Just leave, okay? Go!"

And I do just that. I go. I wonder what would have happened if Marlene hadn't shown up. Was Jeff trying to tell me he still loves me? That he's never gotten over me? That he truly still wants me after all this time? I can hardly breathe just thinking about it. But the fact that he's still at *our* restaurant, ready to eat breakfast with my sister, with *my* ring in his pocket, makes me believe he's confused about which woman he really wants.

7

RACHEL

Something Better Exists for You

You *know how things* can be when you're too upset to drive, yet you know you have to? So picture me in my car, driving down a busy street, my car swerving in and out of my lane, like I'm drunk.

I am holding my Samsung PDA in my right hand and trying to clutch the steering wheel in my left hand. I need to text Alita because I am sure she's not reachable by phone. She works as a cashier at Wal-Mart, and they discourage employees from taking calls while on the clock, but that doesn't stop us from texting each other all day.

"*Call when u get time,*" I furiously type on the keyboard and push send.

Two seconds later: "*He's driving me crazy,*" I type, then I push send again.

Five seconds later, I click the keys once more, "*He asked me 2 marry him again.*"

And ten seconds later my cell phone starts playing Rihanna's "Don't Stop the Music," which is Alita's ring tone.

"I assume your text is referring to your ex. Am I right, or am I on crack?"

"You're not on crack, Hardly Berry."

"Girl, uh no, this is crazy. What is Jeff doing? Is he

serious? What happened? Tell me everything in two minutes."

I explain to her how Marlene and Jeff were meeting for breakfast, but I got there before her. That he presents me with the ring I love and asks me to say yes.

"Wow! Did you say yes, no, or you'll think about it?"

"Girl, I was so shocked I didn't know what to say."

"I'd love to hear what Marlene would've done if you had told him yes," Alita replies and starts cackling.

"Dang, she's such a fool. I told her he isn't serious." I feel a little proud of myself which causes the tension in my shoulders to lessen, yet thoughts of their eating breakfast together bugs me.

"Man, so you think Jeff still loves you?"

"I think he still cares for me, of course—not to brag, but he truly cared for me. But I guess my shocking him by not being ready for marriage was more than he could take."

"And maybe he's had time to think . . ."

"And maybe he's going to break up with Marlene!" I exclaim with glee.

"But technically, Rachel, they aren't going together, right? It's only been a few dates."

"Well, the way Marlene tells it they are practically a couple, but I'm starting to think this is more my sister than him. You know what I mean? I think she wants him so bad that she's willing it to happen."

"Oh, Jesus, this is getting so juicy, but the store manager is starting to give me the evil eye."

"I understand. See ya—."

"Wait, don't hang up, Rachel. We need to talk some more about your crazy love life. Are you about to go to work?"

I respond, "I have to be at work at the clinic by 10:30. I always like to get there at least twenty minutes early, so I can scope out the waiting room and predict what type of day I'll have. I hope I have a great day considering what I've already been through."

"Look, sweetie, try to stop thinking about this stuff for a minute, get yourself safely to work, and we can get together this afternoon. I have to get back on my register before my boss's eyeballs pop out from staring at me so hard."

"Ugh, okay. I'll holler at you later."

So with my girl not being able to talk to me right now, I know I must deal with the stress of this situation on my own. And instantly I feel my shoulders start to tense up again. One thing I love doing when stressed is slide a mix CD in my car's player and just meditate and listen to songs. Music is powerful and able to affect my moods. The song that does the trick for me is "Me, Myself and I" by my hometown girl Beyoncé. I remember seeing her perform the song at the Houston Livestock Show and Rodeo a few years ago. Talk about female empowerment. Jeff used to be my best friend, and although Alita is my girl, I know I gotta step up my game and be my own friend, like the song suggests.

I quietly sing to myself and resist biting my fingernails. Thankfully, my cell rings, and I gladly answer.

"Hey, Mama, how's it going? You doing all right?"

"I called to check on you, Little Bit. You need anything?"

I laugh. "That's the question of the century, Mama. I don't even know where to begin. I feel so confused this morning. About Jeff, and me, and Marlene. He still has strong feelings for me, and I don't know how to handle it."

"If he has those kinds of feelings for you, what's he doing with Marlene?"

"That's what I'm trying to figure out . . . because no way he can truly care about me and her. I sense he still wants me but is too scared to outright admit it."

"Does your sister know?"

"You know, I think that if he hired a helicopter to post a banner across the sky that said 'Jeff Loves Rachel,' she'd swear it was a different Jeff."

"Not *her* Jeff, huh." Mama laughs.

"Exactly. I can't talk any sense into her," I say, and a chill runs over me. "It's like she's lost her mind, Mama. And the way she's acting is affecting how I respond to what's going on."

"Well, take this from an old woman. It's going to be tough dealing with that shit right now, but it gets better, or at least it can if you do things the right way." She pauses. "If I had done things the right way, my life would've turned out different, for sure."

"Oh, Mama, here you go again. I wish you wouldn't talk like that."

"Girl, you know how guilty I feel, how bad I feel thinking back on decisions I've made, foolishness that could have been avoided. Shoot, as old as I am I still don't do things right. Sometimes being bad feels too much fun." She cackles. It feels so good to hear her laugh.

"Well, I guess Marlene is having a ton of fun right now, huh? She's beyond bad, Mama. She and Jeff went out this morning," I say, and my voice breaks. "She got all dressed up just to go to a Waffle House. It seems like she's changing, and I've never seen this side of her." I imagine how Jeff must feel. Sitting across the table with my sister. My ring burning a hole in his pocket. He better hope it doesn't fall out.

"Meeting a certain type of man can do that to you . . . make you do things you never done before . . . if you let it. Your sister's in for a rude awakening, though."

"You think Loretta can talk some sense into her?"

"Ha! That's like asking a whore to keep her legs closed for the rest of her life. Ain't gonna happen."

"Sad."

"Yep. But you'll learn how to take your focus off what Marlene is up to and go on with what you need to be doing. You got a good job."

"Yeah, right. I'm on my way to work now, Mama, and you don't know how bad I wish I can call in sick."

"Don't do that. Remember when you and Jeff broke up and you took off for three days? They can see right through that 'I have a fever of 110' mess."

I giggle at the memory. "Oh, well, I guess I'll put on a brave front. Good thing is I'll get to hook up with Alita this afternoon. She'll help me through this."

"Make sure she stays the real type of friend that a woman needs. I know you want to tell your best friend all your business, but you gotta be careful."

"Mama, I know. You've already told me. And I put Alita through the friend tests that you told me to do." Mama taught me that loyalty and dependability are important traits of true friendship. Alita and I don't date each other's exes, we won't borrow money from each other, and she and I are there for each other during any family, health, or relationship crisis. We don't throw each other under a bus just to make ourselves look good.

"Alita passed the test?"

"The girl earned straight As on your tests. I trust her."

"Lucky you. Humph! Loretta was such a cool-ass friend when we were younger, before we had babies. We'd crank up our beat-up car and go joy-riding, flirting with men, hanging out at the Miller Outdoor Theatre dancing to music, just having the time of our lives. I was more of a party-girl, and she would tag along and try to keep up. So much fun. But our fun didn't last."

I grow quiet and ponder the hurtful events my mama

has had to endure because of Loretta. I remember hearing them on the phone a couple years ago, arguing at one o'clock in the morning. Loretta was so mad I could hear her shrill voice coming out of the speaker:

Is Blinky around?

Loretta, I don't know why you call my house to see where Blinky is. He is no concern of mine.

You better not be lying, Brooke. It only takes five minutes for me to drive over to your house.

Even if I was fucking Blinky, I'm not stupid enough to do it in my own house. Hell, we know how to go to a fancy hotel and enjoy ourselves.

Are you saying you are with him?

I'm not saying anything to you, Loretta. Why would you expect me to help you out? Give you info to help your relationship? I didn't see you trying to help me twenty-something years ago.

Get over it, Brooke. I was the better woman so—

And you better hope he ain't out there lining up the next better woman; you'll find yourself in the same situation I'm in.

They went back and forth, throwing out accusations and yelling insults. Listening to them was disturbing. I couldn't sleep, and I didn't like how Loretta was a pro at causing my mama to get bent out of shape. And now here I am, almost going through the same situation, all over a man.

It's one thing to learn that the one who betrays you is your best friend. Sure, that's unbelievable and it hurts, but it's a whole other ball game when the traitor is your room-mate/sister/supposed-to-be-family member. There's nothing worse than when your own sibling betrays you.

"Mama, I hear what you're saying. But what I don't understand is how two women can start off as best friends, being close and trusting each other, to ending up enemies and not able to be in the same room together without arguing and getting into a fight."

"Are you scared that's what's going to happen with you and Marlene?"

"To be honest, sometimes I don't want to see us get to that point. And other times I just don't care. I've gone to bed the past few nights imagining myself torturing this girl in her sleep. Grabbing the first thing I can find and knocking some sense into her."

Mama laughs hysterically, and I feel slightly guilty at disclosing my true feelings.

"It sounds funny, Mama, but when I entertain those thoughts, it bothers me. I don't want to turn into some kind of out-of-control monster, yet I wouldn't be able to stand it if she continues to pursue a serious relationship with my ex."

"Little Bit, let me ask you something. If you found out Jeff was dating an entirely different chick, would you mind as much? Or is it just because he's dating your sister?"

"Mama, he–he's not dating her, okay, don't say that. He's playing a game. I–I know he is."

"How you know that?"

"If we seriously sat down together, and I told him he's my heart and I want him back, he'd dump her like an old pot of chitlins."

"I wouldn't be so sure. Jeff loves his chitlins."

"And chitlins always stink; they never smell good. But seriously, Mama, I know Jeff still loves me, and I think I'm going to give it some time. He's going through a little phase where he's trying to make me jealous, that's all."

"You really sure about your little theory?"

"Of course I am. Think about it. Like you said, he could be dating any other woman right now, but he's spending time with Marlene, okay? Not dating like you said, but he's spending time with her because she is the closest thing to me, even though, technically, she and I are like night and day. But still, it's like he has me when he has her, in some odd way. So, I think I don't have to worry about them anymore. I am confident that once I ignore them, Jeff will see he can't push my buttons; he'll no longer mess around with her and return to his right mind."

"When are men ever in their right mind?"

"You gotta give them some time, sometimes a lot of time, and cross your fingers that one day they'll come to their senses."

"Ha, if that's the case, my fingers need surgery. I've been crossing my fingers for so long it's like I have four fingers instead of eight."

"Mama, you know you're not right," I say teasingly.

"I'm just telling the truth about my situation. But I want to see you happy. Hopefully things will work out exactly the way you want, Little Bit."

"Speaking of work, I'm just pulling into the clinic's parking lot, and I see an empty space that's waiting on me. Then I gotta hurry up and go to the bathroom and fix my face, and do the job thing so I can earn my little paycheck. I'll call you soon as I get off work."

Mama hears me out and softly tells me how much she loves me, that I'm her reason for living. I feel embarrassed by her display of emotion and just murmur, "Thanks for calling, Mama." I quickly hang up and concentrate on parking my car.

Moments later I am in the ladies' restroom splashing lukewarm water on my face. I reapply some mascara and lip gloss, then thoroughly wash my hands so I can go to the lab and face my coworkers, plus the endless line of patients.

And for the next several hours, I make sure my voice is authoritative, yet friendly and positive, as I call out patients' names. After I introduce myself, I collect their urine samples and prick folks with needles. The small waiting area is cramped and crowded.

I stand with a clipboard in my hand and loudly say, "Duane McGraw."

This big and tall guy stands up, then rocks back and forth on his feet. He's so big and bulky he looks like a high-rise building swaying in the wind.

"That's Duane *Anthony* McGraw," the big guy states.

I shrug my shoulders and ignore his arrogant pose.

"Come on and have a seat."

He takes his time getting to me, like he enjoys walking in slow motion. I concentrate on preparing my equipment and take a deep, measured breath.

"How is your day going, sir?" I say, trying to be professional.

"Couldn't be better. You haven't heard the news?"

I gaze at him and feel startled by his odd question.

"Can you roll up your sleeve for me, sir?"

I clean his skin with a cotton ball soaked with alcohol and ask him to ball his humongous hand into a tight fist.

"Yes, indeed, old boy made that move. Got engaged. The team is throwing me an engagement party."

"The team?" I ask. I prick his skin with a needle and begin to draw his blood.

He winces and closes his eyes and begins to whimper like I'm stoning him to death.

"Hey," a teenager within earshot says. "That's that tight end Duane Anthony McGraw; they call him Dam for short. He has some sweet moves."

I inspect my patient more closely. He's got a big, wide ring on his left finger. I notice an NFL emblem on a thick gold chain that is wrapped about his neck.

"Well, congratulations. Sorry, I know exactly who you are, but I haven't had time to look at the news today," I lie. "Must be nice. Is your wife-to-be excited?"

"She cried when I said yes."

I draw enough blood to fill the bottle and secure the adapter cap.

"Are you saying that she asked you to marry her?"

"That's exactly what I'm saying."

"That's a trip. What made you say yes?"

I continue collecting blood samples and want to burst out laughing every time this big man grunts and twists in his seat. He looks like a little kid. I should offer him a green lollipop.

"My girl, she is down for me, you know what I'm saying? Even though she knows a lot of women are after me because of who I am, Vanessa doesn't trip out. She knows when it's all said and done, I'm the one who will be in her bed every night. I'm going to pay every single bill, and as long as I'm in her face giving her attention, I'm going to honor her."

I'm the type that reads between the lines. You can't only pay attention to what a man says; you have to listen for what he doesn't say.

"Excuse me for being blunt, but does this mean you feel you have a right to cheat on Vanessa as long as you don't disrespect her to her face?"

"You can take that how you want. Bottom line is she is going to have my last name, not any other woman. Quiet as it's kept, that's how a lot of men out here feel. Real talk. At the end of the day, a woman's gotta be confident she's number one. Once a woman is clear on her position with her man, everything else falls into place."

I finish my work with Mr. Football Playa and think about what he says for the rest of the afternoon. Think of how his relationship philosophy factors into the hesitancies I experienced when it came to me and Jeff. Sometimes I felt like the majestic queen; other times I felt like a mere mortal.

During my break Alita calls, as promised. "Hey, Ms. Phlebotomist, how's work?"

"Girl, same old, same old, but I swear to God, some folks know they don't need to be getting married."

"What you talking about, Rachel?"

"There was this so-called famous athlete that came into the clinic. He was talking about how he's engaged to this woman. But he practically said he will still cheat on her. That he may step out on her, but she's still his number one."

"Well, Big Hen better not cheat on me. That's why we aren't getting married. I'm scared marriage would mess it up. And I do not plan on becoming a divorce statistic."

"I don't blame you," I tell her. "Just think, if Jeff and I got married, I wonder where we'd be five years down the road." I shudder. "What if we got married and were very happy and he woke up one morning and told me he was leaving me for another woman . . ."

"And the woman turned out to be Marlene."

"Girl, I'm telling you, not only would there be a quick-ass divorce, there'd be two funerals, you hear me?"

"I hear you, girl. Anyway, I hope you're coping all right today."

"Yeah, I'm cool. I just can't stop thinking about why Jeff still carries my ring in his pocket."

"That's some messed-up stuff. First of all, he was wrong to take back the ring. Everyone knows a woman never returns the ring."

"Apparently I don't know what everyone else knows, or else I would have fought him for it. Or maybe I felt he deserved to have it, under the circumstances. That's probably why I'm in this predicament in the first place. I need clarity for my life so I can make the best decisions. I get so angry with myself, Alita, I swear to God. I wish I can go back in time, undo some things."

"Everyone makes mistakes, Rachel. Even Marlene."

"You think so?" I ask, feeling hopeful for the first time since the day began. "You think she's making a mistake?"

"Your sister is delusional. She is chasing a hopeless dream. You just gotta wait this out and watch her fairy tale morph into a nightmare."

"Great, then maybe I can carefully revisit my relationship with Jeff. I'll do everything I can to make sure things stay on point this time. If I had been brave enough to face the issues I had with him in the first place, maybe we wouldn't be going through this."

"Which issues?"

"Certain things about him disturbed me. I wasn't sure I could trust him one hundred percent. That's the main reason why I broke up with him. If I am to be with a man for the rest of my life, I want everything to line up perfectly."

"Um, Rachel. That's kind of what I wanted to talk to you about when we were on the phone earlier."

"Okay, go ahead." I am devouring a Club Lite sandwich that a coworker picked up for me from Jason's Deli. Imagine toasted whole grain stuffed with smoked turkey breast and ham, a strip of lettuce, tomato slice, and Swiss cheese. I keep a bottle of Grey Poupon at work and had slapped a spoonful underneath the lettuce. Just the way Jeff likes his sandwiches.

"Even though you are convinced you still care about him, I think it's only because he's with your sister. And I think you should consider using your energies in other ways besides Jeff, because he's not the only man in the world. And as soon as you let go of trying to get him back and consider dating others, you will find out someone or something better exists for you. Something much better."

"Better than Jeffrey Williams?"

"Even better than Big Hen."

"That's easy for you to say, Alita."

"True, but you know it hasn't always been this way."

Boy, do I know. I remember how Alita would call me on a daily basis; she'd complain for hours about the men she was dating. It's not that they were all bad; they just never clicked with her the way she wanted. And after a while she'd get tired, kick the guy to the curb, and begin that vicious dating cycle over again. But one day she heard Bishop T. D. Jakes say that if you find someone who possesses 80 percent of the qualities you're seeking in a partner, then you're doing good. It's true many women make up a long and detailed wish list of what they want in a husband. But Jakes said get rid of the lists, because no human being can possibly fulfill all the things jotted on them.

"So do you really think that you'll never be with any other man besides Big Hen for the rest of your life?"

"I may be twenty-three, but I'm smart enough to realize there are no guarantees. All I can do is enjoy our relationship and do what I can to make sure it's successful. That means not wasting time fussing at my man about petty things. And I try not to go to extremes where my emotions are way off balance. Things like that can run a man out of your life."

"Damn, Alita, why didn't you tell me this good stuff a couple months ago?"

"Hello, Miss Thing, you weren't ready to *listen* when I told you this good stuff. To be honest, you rarely listen to my advice, but that's what I love about you."

I don't see how anyone can love me right about now. But

I'm glad that Alita cares for me even when I don't seem worthy of love.

"Hey, sis, I know how you can be, so I won't hound you. Just let me know when you're ready to listen to my specific suggestion of how to get over Jeff. You're going to have to be totally focused to do what I think you should do."

I tell my best friend that I will get with her when the time is right. I leave work around seven and decide to pick up some carryout from Olive Garden on the way home.

After I leave the restaurant, first thing I see when I open my apartment door is big-head Marlene. She's standing in the center of the living room with a wooden broom tightly clutched between her fingers. She's singing out of tune to a ballad that's blasting on the CD player. And she's twirling around with the broom as if it's a human being. Her eyes are closed, and a small smile forms on her lips. I watch her for a moment and shake my head. Like many times in the past, even though I grow upset with my sister, I still cave in sometimes and end up talking to her.

When I can't take watching her dance with the broom anymore, I tell her, "You look so crazy."

Marlene's eyes pop open, and the broom crashes to the floor. She rushes to lower the volume of the music.

"Girl, don't be sneaking in here on me like that. I wasn't doing anything," she says nervously, her face red. "I just need to sweep the kitchen, but got sidetracked."

"Oh, okay, I see," I say and tote my Olive Garden sack over to the kitchen table.

"Hey, what's in the bag?" she asks, licking her lips.

"Why are you asking? Don't you have a hot date tonight?" I say sarcastically.

"Girl, he called and told me . . ."

"He called and said what?"

"Um, that food smells so good. I love those salads and yummy tasting breadsticks. You know good and well that Olive Garden is one of my favorite places to go eat."

"Then I suggest you get up and drive yourself over to your favorite restaurant and get you some carryout. Or why not have your sweetie do it for you? He used to do it for me all the time."

"Rachel, stop being so nasty and sarcastic. Jeez, by the way, I am going to ladies' meeting tonight at the church. You want to go with me?"

"Marlene, you must be losing your mind. Why would I want to go to church with you?"

"I was just asking . . . no need to raise your voice."

I am so disgusted with her that I grab my bag and head for my bedroom. I feel like she should apologize to me, but she's acting like we've officially made up and now are best buddies. Frustrated, I set my dinner on the TV tray and turn on my HDTV. There's nothing on that seems even halfway entertaining, so I flip through my collection of movies, neatly organized by genre in DVD racks. Action, drama, comedies, romance, and horror.

"Fuck romance," I say to myself. "I don't have a man. Screw comedy, because there's nothing funny happening right now. Forget action, because it looks like Rachel Merrell won't be getting any action anytime soon. Hmm, that leaves horror and drama. Drama will have to do, because that's all I seem to be experiencing these days."

Even though the winter holiday is months away, I decide to settle down and watch *This Christmas*, an engaging African American film that stars Loretta Devine, Idris Elba, and Chris Brown, among others. One of my favorite parts is when the two older Whitfield sisters engage in an all-out brawl one night and start cussing each other out and pulling each other's weaves right in front of their mother's house. I envision myself as actress Regina King beating the hell out of Marlene.

The movie has barely begun when I hear a frantic knock on my bedroom door.

"Who is it?"

"Don't be dumb, who else would it be?"

"What do you want?"

"Rachel, come here, please," Marlene yells. "Loretta is on the phone crying."

"What does that have to do with me?"

"It's about Blinky!"

I hop up out of the bed, open the door, and run as fast as I can. I find Marlene pacing across the living room and folding her arm under her big set of boobs. She looks gorgeous as usual.

"What happened? Put Loretta on speaker," I say, and Marlene nods.

"Mama, did Blinky hit you in the jaw again?"

"What do you mean, 'again'?" I ask, looking surprised. "He never hits her!"

"Girl, you are so naive it's not funny," Marlene says and rolls her eyes. She hesitates, then whispers to me, "He's done it once before, but Loretta didn't want you to know, because she thought you'd run and tell Brooke. I feel it's something you should know, because I don't know how to handle Loretta when she gets this upset. We need to convince her not to press charges." She speaks in a normal tone and says, "Mama, where is Blinky right now?"

"I dunno and I don't care," Loretta's shrill voice rings out through the speaker phone. "He ran out of here like a little fucking coward. I'm going to kill his ass. He oughta know better than to be putting his hands on me."

I'm sure she feels hurt and embarrassed because she makes her living counseling women going through domestic crises. But I'm so surprised that a woman as strong as Loretta would allow Blinky to go off on her like that. I wonder what happened to cause Blinky to lose his temper to that degree.

"Well, did you hit him back?" I ask.

"Is that Rachel? Girl, he socked me in my eye so hard I couldn't even see him good enough to hit him back. But I could smell that evil liquor on his breath," Loretta yells through the phone.

"Ya'll need to use better judgment when it comes to partying and drinking," I say in a huff. "Can't always blame bad behavior on the tequila."

"I hope you aren't trying to lecture me, young lady. I'm not trying to hear all that right now."

I clamp my mouth shut and nod, but it's not like Loretta can see me.

"Rachel, can you act a teensy bit more understanding?" Marlene begs me, looking perturbed. I know it's because although she wants my input about this situation, she still wants to be in control, the older sister who makes the final decision when it comes to family matters.

"I understand that a man shouldn't hit a woman... unless he's prepared to get locked up. Blinky ought to be ashamed. But Loretta knows how he is."

"Don't talk about me like I'm not here," she screams.

"Okay, Loretta. I'm sorry for being blunt, but you know Daddy either acts real silly or gets depressed and mean when he's in that partying mood and has too much to drink. I'm not trying to excuse his behavior. He's wrong, point-blank. But next time this happens, don't let him overdo it."

"What did you say? You're saying it's *my* fault?"

"No, Loretta—."

"Look, girl. You are not making my eye feel any better. I am in pain, you hear me? I feel like calling the police."

"No! Don't bring the police into this. Too many black men are overcrowding the county jail already over stupid stuff."

"Rachel, this is crazy," Marlene finally jumps in. "This is not the time, nor the place. Our daddy hit our mama in her face. That's serious. We need to figure out how to support my mother. This is about being down for the family."

"Oh, hell no, you'd better not talk about being down for our family," I shout, fuming when I think of her audacity. All I can envision is her and Jeff. I continue, "Why now, Marlene? Why didn't you feel this way about 'family' a few days ago? You are one of the biggest hypocrites I've ever met."

"Marlene, ignore Rachel. Sometimes she can be so insensitive . . . just like her mama."

"Loretta, leave my mama out of this. At least she isn't crying the blues because some man jumped her," I snap, knowing my words sound harsh, but I feel way too agitated to behave kind and gentle to Loretta. "True, Blinky shouldn't be raising his hand at you, but Loretta, sometimes you are a difficult woman to deal with. Only so much a man can take."

"And what would you know about having a man, Rachel?" Loretta screeches again. I can picture her face contorted in a glob of ugly frustration. I realize this must be very challenging for her. She's the woman who always has answers for other women and their relationship problems. I wonder what great idea she'll come up with to fix this mess. "You don't know what you're talking about, young lady. I'd look like a fool trying to listen to advice from you. You couldn't even hold on to your fiancé—"

"I'm not listening to you. Did you hear me? You don't

matter to me." I drown her out and cover my ears with my hands. If she wants me to feel sorry for her, she should think about the horrible things she's done to my mama.

"Rachel, stop acting so childish. That is my mother you're talking to. We're *sisters.*" Tears are spilling from Marlene's cow-eyes, a sight that's about as rare as seeing Amish people hanging out at the shopping mall.

"We're sisters? Since when?" I squeal, uncovering my ears. "Because ever since you stepped out with my ex, 'sister' is not the word I think of when it comes to you."

"Nothing can come between us, Rachel," she murmurs with a dazed look. "You may allow yourself to be mad about the Jeff situation, but you don't have to be. We could work this out."

"I don't want to hear anything you have to say, Marlene. I just don't. I've got bigger fish to fry. Plus, my food is getting cold, and I'm going to have to start the movie over again because of you. So you handle the family business, Sis!"

I swing around and storm away to my room. My legs feel like anchor weights. I grab the doorknob to close the door but decide to leave it slightly ajar. I halfheartedly resume watching the movie, but none of the characters' dialogue makes me laugh. Instead I want to cry. I have never fought as much with my sister as I've fought with her this past weekend. The yelling, the insults, the mean glares and uncomfortable tension. I don't like how things are developing between us. And even though my "sister" feels we can work it out, I cannot figure out how to make the situation better.

8

MARLENE

What Kind of Woman Am I?

Sometimes I don't understand my sister. Sure, she may be upset right now, but when it comes to family crises, everyone normally sets aside any differences and handles issues accordingly. Rachel may talk smack about Loretta, but she can't deny that my mama did not hesitate to help out years ago when the family went through a little crisis.

I was in middle school; Rachel was still in elementary. One humid, hot summer, Brooke practically experienced a nervous breakdown worrying about Blinky. Even though she didn't have to, Loretta took Rachel in and treated her like her own. The family thought Brooke should go away and stay at some mental institution where she could be examined. She stopped eating regularly, lost about fifteen pounds, had trouble sleeping through the night, and it was clear she wasn't interested in raising her daughter during that time. Rachel came to live with us for about a month after her mama was diagnosed with having major depression. That isn't a real long time, but it was long enough for Rachel to miss her mommy so much that she started calling Loretta "Mama." She'd curl up on Loretta's lap every night and would let my mama comb and braid her hair, give her a bubble bath, and teach her fun stuff like how to paint her tiny fingernails. Rachel's memory may go blank about that time in our lives, but I definitely haven't forgotten.

"Okay, tell me what happened," I say now to Loretta, holding the phone to my ear. I shut my bedroom door and sit comfortably on the floor right next to my bed.

"Naw, you know how Blinky is. He gets to drinking. His boys came over and he likes to show off. Talking loud, calling me a crazy bitch in front of everybody, and then laughing like he's making some type of hilarious joke at my expense."

"Okay, well, that figures; he was drunk, Loretta."

"My thing is, if you want to drink, then you better be responsible for your actions. But he kept pushing my buttons."

"Well, if you know Blinky gets that way maybe you should have left the house."

"Oh, here you go repeating what your sister said."

Although I'd never admit it to Rachel's face, my sister does make a good point.

I take a deep breath. "Mama, how many times have you talked to young women who go to the club, they have too much to drink, then chose to leave with a man they barely know? You said a stiff drink and a stiff dick don't mix very well. All I'm trying to say is that women, and that includes you, need to be more accountable—"

"I warned Blinky to knock it off a hundred times. I tried to leave the room. He came after me, laughing and getting aggressive with me in spite of me trying to calm his crazy ass down. Yet you're blaming me, Marlene? I know I taught you better than that."

"What you taught me," I state, raising my voice, "is that the better woman always gets the man." I can't help myself and continue, "And sometimes in order to be the better woman you have to assess the situation and walk away before crazy things get started. Because this is the second time it's happened."

"I know you are not trying to lecture me; I am the mother, did you forget that?" Her voice raises an octave. "Who the hell you think you are, Marlene? I will come over there and knock the shit out of you? So what's up?"

"Oh, and what's that going to prove, Loretta? That we all are big and bad and full of hell and can whip each other's butts if we have to?" Even though it's in the past, I can't help recall the way my sister and aunt instigated a fight with me during Blinky's party. It was upsetting to be treated that way. I was always advised to fight my own battles and never back down from a challenge. Still, it would have been nice if my mama had been there for me, the way Brooke was for Rachel.

"Mama, why didn't you defend me that day?" I ask in a soft voice. "The day at Blinky's party when everyone clowned on me."

"What? Oh!," she remarks obviously remembering. "Girl, I had no idea it was happening at the time. Hello? I was busy outside, the music was so loud I couldn't hear shit."

"Still," I mumble, "I wish you would've been there . . . wish you had a sixth sense that told you that your only daughter was in trouble only a few freaking yards away."

Loretta, undoubtedly feeling guilty, doesn't like what I just said and starts defending herself and yelling again, but I cut in. "Mama, listen. I'm already stressed enough as it is. Rachel's acting crazy and that makes me act crazy. And now our parents are acting crazy. It's embarrassing. So unreal. I need comfort, Mama; someone who understands me, not people who judge me and treat me harshly."

"Your ass needs to be shaken around like a bag of microwave popcorn so you get some good sense, because few people understand it when you act like a fool," she shrieks so loud I swear the speaker phone is about to break. I know Loretta's yelling because she think she's always right and can't stand to hear the truth. She's expecting me to feel sorry for her and probably wants me to call my daddy and tell him a thing or two. My mom may be twice my age, but there are times she acts my age. And when Mama gets mad at me, she gets so upset that, sooner or later, she sounds like a fool; that's why she's talking about the microwave popcorn mess. I know she hates for me to go on and on and on, but sometimes I can't help but express what I think. Most of the women in my family are strong like that. We try not to keep our emotions hidden inside, where they threaten to boil over. No doubt, we are blunt, but at the same time we try to be honest and truthful. And yes, truth hurts and can uncover ugly things. Things you sometimes wish you never knew. Which reminds me, I need some spiritual nourishment, and I can't wait to go to church tonight.

Using a softer voice, I tell Loretta, "Look, Mama, I apologize if you don't like what I'm saying, but it's not the best time for me. I feel for you, believe me I do. Blinky was wrong, wrong, wrong. Maybe you should just leave the man altogether, yet I know how much you care about my daddy."

"It's about time," she remarks, sounding much calmer. "You seem much better, more understanding. I am crazy about your daddy. I just don't like the crazy things that go down every blue moon—"

"Mama, I gotta go—," I interrupt, feeling the need to cut her off. "Just try to stay out of Blinky's way. Even though you're upset, I wouldn't try to hit him back or anything like that. He could go ballistic, y'all could get to fighting, and I know you don't want to end up like a couple of your clients who've served a lengthy jail sentence." I hang up after quickly saying good-bye. I say a prayer that she comes to her right mind and takes time to clearly think about the situation. I pray she doesn't hold a grudge against me. I have my mother's back, but sometimes a daughter takes the role of a mother when needed, and this is one of those times.

I spend the next twenty minutes finding something cute to wear to church. I love dressing the part: wearing clothes that have vibrant colors and complement my figure. Even though I'm a big girl I feel I have no reason to hide. I am proud of my voluptuous arms, luscious thighs, my juicy booty, and curvy hips.

By the time I arrive at the church complex, I notice a calmness inside of me that feels like a warm blanket spreading over my soul. That's what church tends to do to me. Gives me the center and balance that I lack. But I feel even more elated when I see Jeff's name light up on my cell phone screen just as I'm removing my car key from the ignition.

"Hi there, Baby Doll, you miss me?"

"Um." I giggle. I decide to stay inside my ride and chitchat. "Jeff, babe, where have you been? Not that I was worried. I just expected to hear from you by now."

"Working hard, making that cheddar for you."

"Oh, yeah? You're out there making more money, huh? Well, you still could have called."

"I *am* calling, Beautiful Girl. You know I can't get through the day without hearing your precious sweet voice several times."

"Mmm," I say, helplessly giggling, "That sounds so good to me, it truly does."

"What ya doing right now?"

"Well, I just got to Solomon's Temple but I'm still in my car. They're having their weekly women's service tonight and—"

"Well, it's a good thing you haven't got out of the car yet. What are you wearing?"

"Why do you ask?"

"Does it look good? Is your outfit something that can easily fall off your body?"

"Jeff," I shriek, blushing as if someone can hear our conversation. "You're so nasty."

"Aww, woman, don't even go there trying to play that innocent church girl role. I already know you got some freak in you."

I instantly regret telling him about Too Damn Fine. I don't want Jeff to think I'm easy. I especially want to watch myself since Rachel thinks that the only reason Jeff is interested in me is because of sex. I have way more to offer a man besides that.

"Jeff, stop talking so naughty. Service will begin soon. I'm about to go in the building and find me a seat, but it's good to hear from you."

"No, you're not about to go in the building. The only building I want you to go to is mine. Can you meet me at one of my properties? I just bought it today. That's why you haven't heard from me. I was closing on a deal. I'm so excited."

"Um, shoot, I dunno—"

"Beautiful Girl, c'mon on. You're a part of my life now. A big part."

Mmm, wow. "Hmm, well, um . . ."

"Rachel always loved riding with me and seeing the properties . . ."

I wince and glance at the well-lit, two-story stone building. I sit in my car and watch dozens of women strut in four-inch heels; they're sporting gorgeous outfits with Bibles clutched under their arms. Outwardly, they look just like me, yet I don't feel like being one of them right now.

Starting my ignition, I ask Jeff for directions to his newly acquired house.

With excitement peppered in his voice, he tells me how to find a street that sounds unfamiliar located off I-10 East. We continue holding a conversation while I drive.

"Hey, I had a talk with your sister . . . right before I called you."

"Oh, yeah, about what?"

"You saw her at the restaurant this morning."

"What about it?"

"Did she mention anything to you about our conversation?"

"Not really. I know she's still upset about me and you."

"Well, I read her the riot act. That's probably why she's even more upset."

"Oh, did you? What happened?"

"Marlene, I'll be honest. I still have the engagement ring that I bought her. And I just happened to have it with me, in the jacket of my pocket. And I was reaching in my pocket to get something else, and I accidentally bring out the ring."

"Hmm," I say. "That must've been awkward, right?"

He laughs. "Damn, *awkward* isn't the word. She misunderstood. I read it in her face, her body language."

"You mean she thinks you still want her?"

"Exactly."

"But you don't?"

"I want to spend time with you, Beautiful Girl."

"Oh, Jeff. I'm so happy to hear you say that."

"Hey, it's not like I hate Rachel. I will always care about her . . . like a sister, but not like a wife. Not anymore."

"So does this mean your conscience is clear, Jeff? I mean, do you truly feel okay about us seeing each another?"

"Marlene, I have no doubts about seeing you, no hesitation.

I think we're all adults here . . . and I'd love nothing more than being around you. I think you can help me move on with my life, and make things better."

Good Lord, I think listening to him is better than listening to Pastor Solomon. For a man to be this real, this vulnerable, I just feel overwhelmed. Rachel truly messed up letting this refreshingly honest and decent man go.

"That's all I needed to know, Jeff," I say, smiling.

Jeff changes the subject and continues instructing me about which exit I should take and what streets to look for as I get closer to where he's located.

"Okay, you're almost there," Jeff says. "I see your car now. See me?" He flashes the headlights and hangs up. I feel excited as I drive toward the end of the street that's filled with one-story homes that look like they're in mediocre condition. I spot his ride and park directly across the street behind him.

I continue to sit behind the wheel of my car and wait a minute or two, but when he doesn't get out of his car, I open my door and wait for him, standing on the driver's side. He smiles at me from inside of Ella, looking like he just got off the phone. Rachel always said that Jeff was constantly on the phone, and his monthly cell bill runs into the hundreds.

"Hey there, Beautiful Girl," Jeff says and gets out of the car. "You look breathtaking tonight. Thanks for coming. I know how much you love church."

I smile and blush. "You're going to get me in trouble."

"Why? They do roll call or something?"

"No, silly. It's just that, I—I've never done anything like this before . . ."

"Damn, you make a brother feel special."

"I'm only treating you how you make me feel."

"Got it." He winks. "I like that."

"Is this the house?" I ask, changing the subject.

He nods and leads me toward a one-story frame house that's an obvious fixer-upper. The outside is in desperate need of a paint job, and slabs of wood cover several missing window panes.

"C'mere, girl." He brings me inside, grinning wickedly. A rush of heat pours through my veins, and I feel my heart beat violently against my chest.

Surprisingly, he kisses me on the cheek and stares deep into my eyes. I stare back intensely and feel warmth surge through me again.

"You're mine," he whispers and kisses me again, first cupping my face in his hands, then moving in to press his thick lips squarely on mine.

How could Rachel give this up? I shut my eyes and concentrate on returning his sweet kisses with as much passion as I can. I want him to know under no uncertain terms that I am very much into him. He wraps his arms around my shoulders and squeezes tight, aggressively pulling me against his warm chest. Oh my God. My nipples are as hard as walnuts. Can he actually feel them?

Feeling self-conscious about my body, I gasp when he finally stops kissing me.

"Question. Am I too much woman for you?"

"Huh?"

"You know, Rachel has a very different . . . um, bone structure than me."

"Are you calling yourself fat?"

"No, I wouldn't say that—"

"Marlene," Jeff says, "calm down. If I'm not able to wrap my arms around you, then you're too big."

He then throws his arms around me and squeezes. I am so happy to be with him. How can something that feels this good be wrong? It's not like I get to experience this much love and affection every day of the year. And it feels so good to be loved. Not that Jeff deeply loves me, but I hope he will in time. The fact that he cared about my sister enough to propose to her tells me he isn't afraid of love and commitment. And that's just the kind of man I'm looking for.

He takes me by the hand and leads me into a large bedroom. When he flicks on the light, I stop in my tracks.

"What's a bed doing here?"

"They left some of the furniture so . . . I think I got a helluva deal."

"Oh."

"I'm going to charge seven hundred a month for this baby. Plus utilities. I gotta place ads in the newspaper at the end of this week."

"I'm really glad for you, Jeff. You seem like you're really goal oriented and know how to make things happen."

"Thanks, babe. This is my whole life, you know what I'm saying? I want to line up properties and then when everything is situated, which means I want to hire a property management firm to collect rents and stuff, I'll start focusing on other areas of my life. Like, I can't wait to travel, go to Europe, overseas."

"That costs a lot of money."

"Don't worry about that. I got you."

I can't help but grin, because it sounds like I'm part of his future. Right now I feel I'm living inside a wonderful dream. A handsome, hard-working, goal-oriented man wants me to be part of his life. How can I not want to do things the Jeffrey Williams way?

Jeff stares deeply into my eyes, connecting with me in a way that I haven't experienced before.

"Remember when we first met? When I first laid eyes on your gorgeous self?"

I groan and nod, furiously blushing from the wonderful attention he gives to me. Jeff pushes me against the bed with his hands until I'm forced to sit down. He lifts one hand to move my hair to the side of my face and slowly rubs his nose against my cheeks.

"I wanted you then, like I want you now." He kisses me tenderly and pushes his tongue deep into in my mouth.

"Jeff." I gasp coming up for air. "No, I can—"

"Shhh," he whispers and kisses me on the lips again, silencing my concerns. "Just relax, baby. Pretend like I'm your ex, Too Damn Fine."

"Are you going to pretend like I'm—"

"Shhh, you talk too much."

He pushes me on the bed, rubs his hands across my breasts. I'm sure by now he knows my nipples are solid, hard, an indication of my feelings for him. It's too late to turn back now. He lifts up the hem of my dress. His hands sizzle and sparkle with passion. He strokes his fingertips across my nipples. I am torn between letting him rub me some more, and telling him I'm trying not to be that kind of girl.

But what kind of girl am I if I say I am down for Jeff, yet I don't want him to make love to me? What kind of signal would that send?

I take his hand and pull it up to my chin. He laughs, caresses my chin for a quick moment, then places his entire hand on top of my breast. I sigh, moan, squirm underneath his large hand, which feels hot yet soothing.

Relax, I say to myself. It could be worse. As big as my breasts are, I can't blame the man for wanting to get a good squeeze. At least he's with me. Not with Rachel. Not with anyone else. I'm tripping out big time. I gotta enjoy this man's company and know that I am the chosen one. I do what I have to do to be with the man I love.

An hour later, when it's all over and Jeff and I are wiping each other's sweat off our skin, I am trembling with insecurity. Have I made a mistake? Will he put me in the same category as the average woman? Is God disappointed with me for not being the best woman I can be? Jeez, I haven't even waited a few months, let alone a few weeks, before I decide to lay with this guy. Jeff is smiling and talking nonstop while I quietly get dressed. Hmm, he doesn't look like he's disappointed in me. Us. I wonder if this will be the last time I see him.

"Hey, Beautiful Girl," he says, his face shining with after-glow pleasure. "Thanks for coming by to see me. I know you probably got things to do and so do I. So please, call me as soon as you get home so I'll know that you're okay."

I am speechless. I can only nod. Although Jeff walks me to my car and grabs my keys to open my door, his gestures fail to lift my solemn mood. I wonder what would have happened if I had chosen to go to church instead of agreeing to come see him.

On my way home, parts of me ache to call Jeff. Listen to the sound of his voice. See if I can predict our future based on the things he tells me in the minutes after we have sex. But I stay strong, not giving in to my soul's desire, and I drive home with a variety of thoughts to keep me company.

It's almost eleven when I step back inside the apartment.

Rachel is sitting in the living room, in the dark. The TV is on and the flickering light barely illuminates the room.

She reaches over to flick on the lamp when I enter the apartment.

"Don't!" I say.

"How was church?" she asks.

I want to sniff myself . . . is Jeff on me right now?

"Um." I sigh heavily. "I wish I knew."

"Huh? Didn't you go?"

"No!"

"Then where were you all this time?"

"I was, shoot, I am so tired, and I got to get up in the morning. Need to get ready for tomorrow."

"You're not answering my question, Marlene."

"I–I was with him."

"Oh."

I stand in the middle of the room like I'm waiting for her to toss a hundred more questions at me.

"Did you have fun?"

Shocked, I reply, "It was um, it was cool . . ."

"You don't sound too convincing."

"Rachel, I want to ask you something, but don't think anything of it. It's just hypothetical."

She laughs, but she replies, "Sure."

With the light from the TV flickering and the volume turned low, I say, "How long did you wait before having sex?"

She's quiet, thoughtful. "I assume you're talking about having sex with Jeff, because you already know about when I lost my virginity."

"Um."

"Don't answer." She stands up, flicks on the light, stares at me with an unbelievably hurt expression etched on her face. She scrunches up her nose, starts sniffing, then stops.

"Did you have sex with him, Marlene? Please tell me you didn't."

When I remain quiet, she screams and dashes madly from the room, sobbing and covering her mouth with her hands.

I head for my room, stop dead in my tracks, return toward Rachel's room, but end up in the bathroom. I lock the door behind me, remove my clothes, and firmly twist the shower knob. A blast of water streams from the shower, a fountain of rain that soothes and relaxes my soul.

The noise from the shower is loud, but not deafening enough to drown out my sister's exasperated yelling right outside the door.

"How can you do this? You're so stupid, so cruel. I've told you I don't know how many times how I feel, and you just go on like you can't hear or don't care? How can you let a man come between us? How can you stand to look yourself in the mirror, Marlene? Huh? Say something. I know you hear me."

I hear her, but I'm too busy, standing naked in the shower, washing all traces of Jeff from every place his fingers explored my body.

I shower for as long as possible and am relieved when I no longer hear Rachel screaming at me through the door. Yet, when I finish cleaning my body and am thoroughly dry and have applied lotion to my skin, I slip my arms through the sleeves of my robe and go look for my sister.

Rachel's sitting on the couch, one leg lodged under her thigh. The TV is turned off. It's so quiet. Eerie. She's staring into space; a dead, cold look fills her vacant eyes.

"Little Bit," I begin.

"Don't talk to me."

"I can't help but talk to you, Rachel. Just hear me out."

"Nothing you can say will make any difference. I can't even stand to look at you."

"Sweetie, please."

"Enough with your little pet names. Save those gestures for your fucking *boy*friend, and the boyfriend that you're *fuck*ing."

She yells so loud I jump back in surprise. This has gone too far.

"Rachel Merrell, be quiet and listen to me for a minute. You need to get a grip—"

"I'll grip your—"

"Stop it. Wait. Please hear me out."

"Go ahead."

"To me you're acting so. . . I have rights, too, ya know. Believe it or not, it's not all about Rachel Merrell. And I am not going to live my life getting your permission to live, to breathe, to be."

She folds her arms slowly and glares at me.

"I want to be honest with you, Sis," I say in a gentle, more controlled voice. "That's the only thing I can promise you right now. I won't tell you everything you think you want to hear; I'll be true to myself and tell you the reality."

"Oh, really. And why do you think I want to hear it?"

"Because you've asked me a hundred questions all last weekend, you ask questions every day. So you can't tell me you don't want to hear this, Sis, unless you are lying to yourself. Now, can you handle the truth, or do you never want me to speak to you ever again?"

Unbelievably, she stares into space, face stony, for a full fifteen minutes, and when she finally decides to answer, all she says is "Truth."

I remember the first time Rachel and Jeff made love. They had the nerve to do it in our apartment on a Tuesday night. Reason why I remember is because I went to a revival service that evening. We had a glorious time at church. I got home quite late, almost midnight. You can tell how good church is by how late you get home.

So I here I was, happy and singing, but I toned it down once I reached our front door; I quietly entered the apartment because, shoot, I didn't want to disturb Rachel. I got undressed, hopped into bed. I tried to fall asleep. But I had trouble getting comfortable in bed. Too many strange sounds kept me awake. Moans. Groans. Grunts. And I could hear the headboard steadily banging against the wall. Tap, tap, tap. Tap, tap, tap.

I thought, What the heck is all that noise? I assumed the noise came from someone else's apartment. But then I heard this wail, "Ooohhh, Jeff, oh baby, oh baby."

I started blushing like I was the one having loud sex late at night. But an hour later, still awake, I sat up in bed craning my neck to listen. Tap, tap, tap. Tap, tap, tap. That poor wall really took a beating. I couldn't believe my sister could last that long. I never lasted that long. And Jeff obviously could last that long. Moments later, I quietly got out of bed. I left my room and kept going till I was outside Rachel's door. I heard Jeff say, "Ohhhh Rachel, your pussy tastes so good and feels wet. You like that? You want some more?"

She screamed, "Don't talk, keep licking." Then she purred like a cat. They had pillow talk conversations. Made wild animal sounds. Alternately screeching, moaning, and laughing. I felt silly, nosy, and jealous. When I started yawning and bobbing my head like a drug addict, I knew it was time to go. I got back in bed, finally fell asleep. I felt real groggy when I woke up that morning, like Rachel wasn't the only one Jeff kept up all night.

That morning, I slid out of bed to go take my shower. I passed by my sister, who was busy in the kitchen. She was cracking some eggs, frying sausage patties, and stirring a pot of grits. She looked relaxed, incredibly peaceful. She served me my breakfast like I was her houseguest. Rachel waited till that night to tell me about the great time she had with Jeff. I listened to her go on and on about the fantastic sex that she said she could get used to having. I never told her I heard them going at it all night. But when I told Loretta about what Rachel told me, she said, "A real woman never gives all the details about what her man does to her in bed. That's dangerous."

So tonight when Rachel claims she wants to hear the truth, I ask her, "Do you want hear the whole truth and nothing but the truth?"

"Marlene, stop being so difficult and tell me."

I softly reply, "We were kissing and stuff, making out, and I let him put it in me, barely. Actually it was good, but it wasn't what I thought it would be." I pause and blankly stare at her.

"I don't want to hear any more."

"But you said you want the truth."

"Just because I say that doesn't mean it's what I really want."

"Okay, Rachel. Now that you know what we've done, what do you want? Do you want me to be happy, Rachel?"

She stares at me. "Sure, I do . . . It's just that . . . I don't like how you're going about it."

"Tell me something. Do you think you'll be okay with me and him in time?"

"Marlene, I think you don't realize what you're doing. He wants me back, did you know that?"

"Did you know that he was accidentally carrying your ring in his pocket?"

"What did you say?"

"Yes, he told me. Tonight. Told me how you assumed he still loves you, but he said that he only cares for you . . . like you're his sister."

"Jeff said that?"

"Yes, Rachel, yes."

"I don't believe it."

"You want to call him?"

She covers her ears with her hands. I run and pick up my cell. Come back waving it in her face. "We can call him now, Rachel. Nip this in the bud."

"Marlene, please don't do that."

"You can't handle the truth. You say you want it, but you cannot and will not be able to deal."

"The truth is, I can deal with him. If he truly forgot about the ring, which I seriously doubt, then I can deal with that. It's an honest mistake. But you," she says, staring at me, "you are a whole different matter."

"Well, what about—"

"Hold up, I'm not done, Marlene. Remember when I dated that guy named Obie?"

I nod.

"And I introduced you to him. And he couldn't take his eyes off you. And it made me upset?"

"Yeah, you actually threw my cell phone in the bathtub because you found out he'd called me."

"Right. He called you. And you got so arrogant. You thought it meant he truly wanted you. In a way that he didn't want me."

"Yeah, right."

"But when I told him to lay off, he never talked to you again. He apologized to me. He said he had a temporary lapse in judgment."

"Yes," I whisper. "I remember."

"Jeff is Obie part two. I doubt that Jeff accidentally was carrying my ring. He's just telling you that to cover his ass. But regardless of all that, I know his judgment when it comes to you is questionable."

"You're still jealous, I see," I tell her in a trembling voice.

"I feel what I feel, Marlene. And if it takes you getting

hurt to believe that I'm telling the truth, to find out I'm not as jealous as you think I am, so be it. Have you ever considered I may be trying to protect you? That I'm not totally jealous of you? That what you say is jealousy might be sisterly concern?"

"Not that I haven't thought about it. I can't imagine it, Rachel. But what I'm building with Jeff right now isn't my imagination. It's real. You want me to call him? You want to see for yourself?"

She sighs, defeated. "I care about you more than you can understand, Marlene."

"You're just saying that."

"Much more than you'll ever know."

9

RACHEL

Have You Thought About Online Dating?

"*Hey,* Miss Hardly Berry!"

It's a few weekends later in early April. I have just arrived at our self-defense training and have taken a seat near the back of the room. It is a few minutes before the session begins, and my fellow classmates are lingering about, clutching containers of coffee in their hands and catching up on what everyone did the past week. My girl Alita is sitting next to me brimming with joy, a wonderful glow emanating from her face.

"Wow, whatever you have, can you give some of it to me?" I tell her.

"Hey, you can have what I have, but are you willing to do what it takes to get it?"

"Girl, stop talking in riddles. Speak plain English to me."

"Sometimes I'm not even sure you'd understand English."

"Ha, Alita, are you trying to call me dumb?" I laugh.

She grins and nods.

"That's cold-blooded, girl. Anyway, what's popping? How's Big Hen?"

"Ooo, he is amazing, just a-ma-zing. For instance, last night was our regular date night and we had a ball. We hung out at Dave and Buster's, the one off the Katy Freeway. Girl, we drank beer after beer and had some so-so-tasting appetizers, but it was still fun. Then we played tons of games and earned a lot of tickets. I beat my man at Skee-Ball; he was pissed and pouting and I kept kissing him every time I got a high score, which made him even madder. It was so funny. We had a great time just being together and acting silly."

"Hmm, wow, I wish I could have gone with ya'll."

"Oh, yeah, so what did you do last night?"

"Don't even ask, girl. I just stayed home, looked at some bootleg movies that I've already seen two or three times. I was bored out of my skull, Alita."

"I wish I would've known you had nothing better to do. We could have scooped you up."

"That would've been cool to hang out with you, but to be honest, I can't imagine having fun by tagging along with you and your man."

"Then we need to change that, by helping you to get a good man so you can hang out, have fun, and start living again."

I laugh. "Hmm, you're so right. Hook a sista up."

"What?" She gasps, eyes enlarged. "I can't believe those words have come from your mouth. Have you finally given up on getting Jeff back?"

"Shhh," I tell her and feel self-conscious. "I don't want to think about it, talk about it. I am coming to terms with everything. At least I don't do what I did a week ago, which was go to bed at night and envision myself throwing a brick at his window."

"Girl, you are not James Brown, so let this big payback stuff go. Jeff's not worth it. You have too much going for you to lose sleep over what he's doing."

"I know, you're right, but it's . . . it's easier said than done.

But I'm getting there. Then again, one day I may not care if I ever see his face again."

"That would be an improvement. Keep up the good work, girl. Predict your excellent future . . . give yourself something good to look forward to. Oops, hush. Here comes Floyd. Class is about to start. We'll talk again during break."

We sit down and receive an hour's worth of lecturing about how to secure your home from intruders, and how to always be aware of your surroundings when you're walking to and from your vehicle.

"And you young folks are big on Facebook. Putting all your personal information online is never a good thing. It's very easy for a pervert to copy and paste all your info and set up another profile to perpetrate someone. What you want to do is remove opportunity for someone to harm you or steal your identity."

"Hmm, that's something to think about," I remark to myself.

"Another thing," Floyd says. "Make sure and keep your shades drawn. You'd be surprised at how people can see through your windows at night."

"Aww, snap," Alita says aloud.

"Ooh, looks like you're remembering a time when you forgot to close the shades, huh?" I tease, holding a side conversation with my friend.

"Girl, sometimes Big Hen does that shit on purpose. I think he gets off knowing that people can possibly be watching us. You know he sleeps with no underwear."

"Yuck, spare me."

"You know Rachel, it's been too long since you've had some. I can just tell. We need to help you get a man ASAP."

"Ladies, can you please stop the side conversations and

pay attention? You should be taking notes on some of these risk reduction strategies."

"Yes, sir," Alita says and picks up an ink pen and starts writing. She scribbles notes then passes them to me.

I read her beautiful, neat handwriting. Her letters are big and wide, which tells me that she's filled with confidence. "Have you thought about online dating?"

I pick up my pencil and scribble back, "Hell no!!!!!"

She laughs, writes again. "Just try it one time, and I'll never bother you about it again."

I scratch out the first part of her sentence and a few other words so that the sentence now reads, "never bother you again." I make a silly face, cross out the word "you" and write down "me."

She picks up the paper and bursts out laughing so loud that everyone turns and gives us annoyed looks.

"Okay, ladies," Floyd states. "I think it's time we took a ten-minute break. And after that, let's be ready to practice some moves."

Alita and I race to the ladies' room since there's only one available stall.

"Okay, Hardly Berry, what were you talking about some online dating for?"

"I believe it would be good for you to get back out there, date around, and allow some gorgeous chocolate hunk help renew your self-esteem."

"I think my self-esteem is intact."

"Not that you should totally depend on a guy to make yourself feel good." I hear her laugh while she's sitting in the stall. "That's what Big Hen says he likes about me. He knows if he were to tell me something derogatory about myself, it wouldn't bother me one bit because I think more of myself than anyone else does."

"A woman who has confidence is considered sexy. I know, I know," I say wistfully. Maybe she's right about mustering up the nerve to date around. If I take a risk instead of playing it safe, who knows what kind of man I could meet.

Alita emerges from the stall to splash water on her hands and hold them under the eco-friendly dryer. I enter the empty stall and continue talking to her. "Well, I don't know much about online dating. But it sounds kind of risky. What if I meet an insane person?"

"You don't have to go online to meet crazy people, believe me. Remember Stanley Hudson, my ex who I caught wearing my underwear one night? Man, I couldn't get rid of him fast enough. And from the outside he looked so straitlaced."

"Humph, he liked lace, all right," I say, and we laugh together. I wash and dry my hands, and we slothfully walk down the hallway so we can delay our return to class.

"London is a pro at online dating," Alita tells me.

"Oh yeah?" I say. London is Alita's twenty-one-year-old cousin. She's so attractive she could easily work as a fashion model. She constantly smiles, is all big-hair, and has blemish-free skin and a sleek body that exudes sex appeal. Round tits, curvy hips, London struts around like she knows she has it going on. She's the type of girl that all the guys want to date, but they'd be too intimidated by her because they'd assume she already has a man.

Alita and I stop by the vending machine. I insert a dollar fifteen worth of change and wait for my ice-cold strawberry soda to come flying out.

"Alita, I am no London by any stretch of the imagination."

"Girl, what are you talking about? You don't have to be drop-dead gorgeous to get attention from men on the Net. All you gotta do is breathe."

"Scary," I say, and my mood turns serious. "I would want

to meet someone who shares the same interests as me, you know. Someone who has some standards, to make sure we're compatible, all that."

"Are you saying you'll consider going online to find your dream situation?"

"You make it sound so good, so tempting, but I want to think about it first. I have a final unresolved issue with Mr. W."

"Unbelievable that you'd still take time to deal with him. But who am I to rush someone else's heart? All I'm saying is when your heart is ready for change, you'll know it."

Alita and I return to class. Floyd has everyone stand in a circle. We prepare ourselves by first doing a series of stretches; then we proceed to practice some new moves. Learning how to block, to breathe, to kick someone on the shins, and to gouge eyeballs. And toward the end of the session he begins talking about Tasers. He informs us that even policemen get tasered so they can learn the effects, and how much it hurts to have electricity run through your body.

"I was reluctant to get tasered, but I had to go through it, face the unknown, in order to effectively do my job. Suffice it to say, the fact that I am standing before you today lets you know how strong my body is."

We laugh and shake our heads.

"But at the time," Floyd continues, "being tasered wasn't funny. A big man like me was rolling on the ground. Screaming. Wanting to call my mother. Not a pretty sight."

We go through a few more moves that we've repeated a hundred times before, and then class ends.

"Hey, Alita, why don't you follow me over to my place? I want to fix us some grilled chicken tacos. The meat has been marinating in the refrigerator since last night."

"Sounds like a plan. I'm right behind you, girl."

I hop in and start my car, and she follows me to the

apartment. We get out of our vehicles and quietly enter the front door.

I'm so busy chatting with Alita that at first I don't notice him. He's standing in the dining room. All the lights are on in the living area. Marlene is sitting at the table, her flabby arm raised up. Jeff is examining her bare arm.

"That's tight," he says as he raises her arm and smiles.

"Hey," I say, "what's going on in here?" I haven't seen or talked to Jeff since that day in Waffle House. Jeff whips his head around and jumps back from Marlene. He looks surprised, which is insulting. He ought to figure that I'd eventually run into him again one day.

"Hey, Sis." Marlene beams and stands up. "What's up, Alita?"

"That's what we're trying to find out," I say.

"Oh, we're just getting ready to do something really cool. At first I was skeptical"—Marlene laughs—"but Jeff has a way of convincing me to do things I may not want to do at first." She clears her throat. They lock eyes and smile, as if sharing a private joke.

"What's so funny?" Alita smiles, although I know it's her fake but genuine-looking grin. "We want to laugh, too."

Jeff opens his mouth to answer, but Marlene butts in. "It's private."

I shrug like it's no biggie. "Cool. We're just about to make ourselves something to eat. Ya'll hungry?"

Marlene looks at me oddly, like she's surprised I am not ranting and raving.

"Hey, Alita, clear the table. Make room for four," I tell her. She responds by removing old newspapers that are neatly piled in a stack on the dining room table.

Jeff, looking startled, says, "Let me help you with that, Alita."

I head for the kitchen and get busy. I remove the chicken meat from the fridge. I whip out my George Foreman Grill and get the flour tortillas, veggies, lettuce, and picante sauce. Soon the kitchen is filled with delicious aroma.

"Damn, Rachel. I haven't eaten those in a long time."

I simply smile at Jeff's comment and continue cooking. Alita sets the table. Marlene just sits and mopes. Jeff comes and stands next to me.

"Need any help?"

"Nope. I'm good."

"You sure? I'm a man who doesn't mind cooking."

"Well, I'm making this food for everyone's enjoyment, just something I feel like doing . . . and"—I smile wickedly— "you caught me at a good time."

"Um, yeah, I guess I'm lucky."

"You know what? You really are lucky."

Alita locks eyes with me.

Jeff says, "What do you mean by that?"

"Oh nothing. Just talking. Don't pay me any attention."

Jeff moves in closer. His elbow touches my rib.

"Oops, sorry. Accident."

"Jeff, I know our kitchen is tiny, but you really need to move over . . . a couple feet actually. I don't need anyone up under me while I'm trying to cook."

"Ha, you hear her say 'trying' to cook." Marlene laughs and hops up. She grabs Jeff closely by the arm. "C'mon, we don't have to stay for this. We have business to take care of."

"No, Marlene. We have time. I'm starving."

"I'll feed you, babe." She laughs again and looks at me, then tugs at Jeff's arm even tighter and tilts her head so she's looking up at him. He removes his arm from her grip and yells, "Watch that meat, it's burning."

"Oh, someone get me another spatula, hurry."

Jeff jumps back and opens a utensil drawer, hands me a spatula.

"Ouch," I say.

"What's wrong? Grease hit you?"

I nod and grimace.

"Go sit down. I got this," Jeff commands. He takes over and finishes grilling the chicken slices. I take a seat and let Alita hold an ice cube to my stinging arm, which was splattered with oil.

Marlene just sits back, shakes her head, probably thinking this was all planned.

Jeff turns off the grill and starts filling the tortillas with meat, veggies, and sauce. He serves Marlene first, then me, Alita, and himself.

Alita does a good job making my arm feel better. I revel in the fact that my thoughts are clear, my emotions appear under control.

"I can't believe we're all here, eating, acting civilized," I say to no one in particular. We're all seated at the dining room table. Jeff and Marlene are next to each other, Jeff directly across from me. He bites into his food and glances at me every few seconds. I feel weak under his constant gaze, but I keep trying to stuff my mouth with food as a distraction.

"You like?" Jeff asks Marlene but peers steadily at me.

"Yeah, it's yummy."

Jeff's cell starts to ring. He glances at the number and hops up so fast that he knocks his chair over. He answers the phone, "Hello," really loud and leaves the apartment to go talk.

"Must be important," Marlene says, as though she needs to speak up on his behalf.

"Must be," Alita says.

"Why are you doing this?" Marlene hisses. She hasn't eaten at all and has spent the last few minutes shoving her food around her plate with a fork. "What are you trying to do? Make him see what he's missing? Because he's not missing you anymore. He told me—."

"Marlene. Enough. Really. I could not care less about that man."

"For real? I'm going to tell him you said that—."

"That's not necessary. But if you feel that it is, go on and tell him. But more importantly, believe me, I don't care what you do. You can have him. So to answer your question, that's what I'm trying to do. It's called not giving a damn." I abruptly rise from the table, not hungry anymore. I nod, look at her. "Yep. I'm going to rise above this."

She sits there looking stunned.

"Invite me to the wedding," I tell her, and feel a sudden urge to go outside. My head is spinning, making me feel like I want to faint. I need to inhale some fresh air. A little bit of smoke is still lingering in the kitchen. So I say, "BRB," real loud and slip outside the front door onto our balcony. Jeff is pacing back and forth, one hand shoved in his pocket, totally involved in his conversation. But when he looks up and notices me, he ends his call and practically runs to me.

"How's your arm? You okay, Rach?"

"You haven't called me that in months . . . sounds strange now."

"Hey, I really am sorry about everything. I know you must be hurt."

"Not hurt. Fine actually," and I mean it. "Never been better."

"You can't be serious. You were just pissed at everything not too long ago."

"Things change. Things change fast sometimes," I explain to him. I can see in his eyes that he's confused, maybe even hurt. Perhaps the hurt that I once felt has been transferred to him. Affecting his mind, shattering his emotions. The funny thing is I really don't care what he says. If he can lie and say he's accidentally carrying my ring on him, the most important piece of jewelry he's ever bought in his life, then I am pretty much done with the guy. No one would believe what he told Marlene about the ring. It's not something trivial, like absent-mindedly stashing a dollar bill in his pocket.

"I don't know if things change that fast."

"Well, Jeff, I can't speak for everyone else, but sometimes a little light goes off in a person's head. They get an epiphany, things become clear, and they get what they need to move forward with life."

"Oh, so you're saying you're over me? You don't love me anymore . . . don't want me . . . just like that?"

"Excuse me, Jeff, but I think your future wife is trying to get your attention. You hear her calling you? Better go see what she wants now or else she may not give you any pussy tonight."

"That's so disgusting. I am not even trying to go there—."

"Jeff, she's already told me, okay? I smelled what you used to give me on her body weeks ago. You can lie to Marlene, but I'm not her. I'm not," I say a little more loudly than I wish. I do not want Marlene to think we are fighting over her. I'm too exhausted to go round for round with this girl. I just hope she knows what she's doing. Because now I've figured out a lot of things that I want to do.

I head back inside, ignoring Marlene's hostile stare as I pass through the front door to return to the kitchen. It's a mess. Messiness makes me feel antsy. And I use my new surge of energy to make the kitchen look more presentable, wiping off counters, putting away leftovers, and sweeping the floor.

Jeff comes in the apartment soon afterward. Marlene returns a few seconds behind him.

"Need some help?" Jeff offers.

"She's fine, Jeff, are you ready to go now?"

"Um, sure, Marlene. But don't forget, before we go, you should clean up, if you know what I mean."

"Okay." She giggles and sneaks a look at me. "I am going to hop in the shower real quick. Count to three hundred and I'll be ready. Wait until you hear the shower come on, okay?"

"Fine," Jeff says. She races from the kitchen.

"Hmm," Alita suddenly says, "I gotta get something out of my car. Be right back." She nods at me.

And Jeff and I are alone in the front area of the apartment, a place where we used to share so much happiness. I remember how he chased me around the place one time, trying to spray me with a water gun that my little cousin forgot and left over here. I screamed and dashed for the bathroom, walk-in closet, anywhere, so I could escape him. But he caught up with me, sprayed me playfully, then threw me on the carpet. He got on top of me and started kissing me with such passion that our clothes soon were peeled from our bodies. We did some foreplay, then made love on the living room floor. I got aroused wondering if Marlene was about to walk through the door. Jeff kissed and licked me all over, but he moaned like I was doing him. That day I thought how lucky I was to have him. And right then it didn't matter that, two days prior, I was angry at him for not getting back to me when I called and left a detailed voice mail. I tore into him about being inconsiderate of me when we had dinner plans. How I'd waited and waited on him to pick me up, until I realized he'd left me in the lurch. I told myself there's no way in hell I could marry a man who took me for granted. But I heard his sweet voice hours later, and he stopped by my place after midnight, unannounced, looking sheepish, apologizing and smelling good.

"Where were you?" I grilled him.

"I had to work, baby; these people had me waiting so long to show them the house that I fell asleep in the car. Then, when I woke up, I had to let them in the house, and they took their time inspecting every inch of the place."

"Okay, but why didn't you call when you woke up?"

"I couldn't get a signal, baby, you know how undependable these cell phones are. You pay up the ass every month and can't even use the phone half the time." The subject went from where he was to how he hated Sprint because "they are so freaking unreliable." And I thought about how freaking unreliable Jeff could be. And I let it go. I didn't yet terminate his contract. Because as he bitched about Sprint, he caressed my arms. My legs. And I got lost. Deep in love. Again. And the cycle repeated itself.

Although I genuinely loved him, I didn't always love what came with being with him. And now that I have to witness my sister getting caught up, I almost can't believe it. It's like my relationship is being rewound, replayed for me all over again. I don't like how it appears he's moving too fast with her, so fast that she's blinded by his apparent charms.

"Rach—."

"Don't." I feel him standing behind me. His warm breath flows against my neck. I wish he'd just stop it.

"But I wanna talk to you."

"Talk to Marlene."

"I want to talk to you."

I sigh. Tremble.

"Just hear me out," he pleads.

"Okay," I say, my back stiff with tension.

"Every time I'm with her," he whispers, "I think of you. It's like, when I am with her I'm finishing up what you and I started."

"Jeff, no. Don't do that. It's not fair to you, to her. Me."

"Listen. I know it sounds strange, but I need to do this."

I turn around. "You are going to hurt her, you know that, don't you?"

He looks exasperated. I can see his love for me all in his eyes. It makes me want to protect Marlene. But she's too far gone for me to do anything meaningful. She'll misinterpret my every action. So, as much as I hate what's happening, my hands are tied as tight as a drum.

I think of something quick.

"Um, Jeff, I know you are really bothered by the breakup. I totally understand. This has been difficult for both of us."

"Yes, it has. You don't know what kind of effect you had on me."

"And it kills me to see you with her. Truly."

He stares down at me with puppy-dog eyes.

"Come closer," I say to him. He takes one step toward me. "Closer."

Another step.

Praying my plan will work, I wrap my arms tight around his neck. I stare up at him; his cheek is so close it nearly brushes against mine.

"Is it okay if I do this?"

He nods.

"I miss you, honey. Miss your lips, your touch."

The front door opens, but I continue talking softly to Jeff.

"Let's make up, start over from scratch."

"What are you talking about?"

"Hug me," I say.

He hesitates, then wraps his arms around my waist. I squeeze him tight, closing my eyes, and pull his body against mine. He has on a long-sleeved cotton shirt and a pair of blue jeans. I moan like I'm having an orgasm. I rub my fingers across his shoulders, arms, press myself deeper against him. Our pelvises touch. I can feel his erection growing between us.

"Rachel?" Alita says. I ignore her, look at Jeff. His eyes are shut tight, mouth open. I'm taking him there.

I slide my arms down his back, grab his ass and squeeze. He moans, "Oh, God."

I take a deep breath, and rub his butt, then place both my hands on his jeans pockets. I feel around until I touch a small, hard object. I reach inside his pocket and pull out my ring.

"Jeff." I hear Marlene's shrill voice coming from the hallway.

Alita locks eyes with me. I nod. She rushes in Marlene's direction. I hear a door slam shut.

"Honey," I whisper. "Do you really want to be with her, or do you want to marry me?"

"Rachel, I want to marry you!"

I push him off me and back away. He looks hurt, confused.

I am so angry I can't speak. His actions tell me he is definitely not serious about Marlene. But I don't want him thinking he wants me, either.

"What are you doing?" he asks. "You're playing some kind of game, huh, Rachel?"

"No, you're the one playing games. Stay the fuck away from my sister."

"Y—you're crazy, Rachel. Give me back my ring."

I feel like running outside and throwing it in the bushes, but when I hear Marlene arguing with Alita, frustration makes me say fuck it. She's in too deep. I can do everything I can on her behalf, but if she's not willing to listen she'll have to learn the hard way. I hand the ring back over to Jeff.

Minutes later she emerges from her bedroom, Alita running behind her. I motion with my eyes to forget it, damage has been done.

Even though I was nervous about it, my plan was for Jeff to at least show me he's true to my sister, by not falling for my little seductress act. If he would have rejected me, I could have told her he might be serious after all. But now I know the truth about his intentions. I watch Jeff conjure up a fake smile. Observe him wrap his lanky arm around Marlene's wide shoulders. He waves bye to Alita but ignores me. And he and my sister walk out the front door.

As soon as they leave the apartment, Alita asks, "Now are you ready to sign up for some online dating?"

10

MARLENE

I'm Definitely Not Rachel

I can't believe I'm doing this. This is the thought that repeatedly enters into my brain. It's midafternoon on Saturday, several hours after we left Rachel and Alita at the apartment. I am lying down on a massage bed. All I can see are white lights. Silas, a skinny body artist with long stringy brown hair that covers one eye, has rubbed alcohol on the upper part of my right breast. My cheeks are burning red and hot. Humiliation. But also some fear. Why does the needle sound so terrifying? It's buzzing really loudly and reminds me of Blinky's electric razor. Silas carefully dips the needle in black ink and places one drop on his own skin to test it.

"Are you sure you're okay with this?" Jeff asks, smiling down at me. His eyes display both concern and excitement.

"I'm good. Let's do this. It's the Jeffrey Williams way."

We laugh.

Silas leans over me and secures a thin sheet of carbon paper above my nipple. He carefully traces a picture of a heart on top of my breast. My new heart will be about the size of two fifty-cent pieces. I also instruct Silas to put interlocking letters, "M&J," on top of the heart, but the letters should be in red ink. Using the needle, Silas hums along to an old Springsteen song blaring from a transistor radio. He rocks his head to the beat and follows the lines of the tracing, then picks up the needle. Ready or not, here I come. The needle sounds loud as hell, and when the tip finally meets my skin, it feels like a big staple is scraping across my breast.

"Ouch," I say and try to remain still.

"Sorry," Silas remarks and continues bobbing his head to the music.

Besides me and Silas, the only other person in the room is Jeff. Last night, when Jeff first brought up the body art idea, he told me when it's your first time, it's normal to bring lots of supporters: family, friends, people who can provide comfort while you go through the tattoo experience. But I couldn't think of one person who I thought would be happy for me, including Loretta. When I called her this morning and excitedly told her my plans, first thing she said to me was "You sound like a damn fool. I didn't raise you to be no fool."

"Huh," I said, instantly annoyed. "What?"

"A real woman loves her man and is down for him, but a tat? Isn't that for, like, men who are hanging around a prison yard lifting weights and plotting their escape?"

I laughed at her naiveté. "No, Mama, that's a stupid B movie stereotype. Everybody gets tats these days. A lot of celebrities and basketball players have them."

"Marlene, you are hardly a celebrity. And I have never seen you running up and down a court bouncing a ball—"

"Even Blinky has one."

"Girl, Blinky got that ugly-ass thing when he got out of the service years ago. He ain't trying to make no statement or nothing, but I guess you are."

"Well, Mama, I do love Jeff and he loves—."

"What you say? You say he loves you? Ha ha ha," she cackled. "Ooo, my precious dumb daughter, you have a lot to learn."

"Mama," I whined. "I thought you were for us, on my side. I don't like hearing you talk like this. I am not dumb."

"Well, a few punches upside my head are causing me to think a little more straight these days. That's about the only good thing I'm getting out of what happened."

Blinky doesn't know it, but Loretta has recently been thinking about kicking him out. Except she got fired from her job last week for being extra pushy with her advice to a client, so now she must rely on him more to pay the rent, buy groceries, and fill up her tank with gas so she can drive around in her big ole four-door Chrysler. I made the mistake of telling Loretta that Blinky might sock her again since her joblessness has him stressing about money and bills.

"Shut the hell up," she said, cutting me off and proceeding to curse me out until I hung up on her. I haven't mentioned her jobless situation since.

And those incidents is probably the main reason why I didn't invite Loretta to be with me while I get my first tat. She'll automatically say it's a "damn good waste of money" or something to that effect. And personally I don't care to hear her or anyone else's negativity. I consider myself grown, so I think by now I should know what I'm doing.

"That's going to be awesome when it's done," Jeff says, a glint of happiness spilling from his eyes.

"I know it is, babe. We gotta go celebrate, too. My treat."

"No, no, no, *my* treat. You paid for our dinner last time, so I insist."

"Okay, cool. I won't argue with you," I say and laugh, but stiffen up a bit, being overly paranoid that something might go wrong with the tat.

Another hour passes and then we're done. Silas quickly cleans off the tat with some rubbing alcohol, then applies

A&D ointment, a scar-healing cream that feels slightly cold on my skin.

I sit up. But before I can even get off the table, Silas says, "Do you mind if I take a photo for my portfolio?"

"Suit yourself," I tell him and pose for a picture.

Jeff reaches in his wallet and hands Silas two twenties. We admire the fancywork for a minute, then head out to the parking lot. We drove over here in Ella. I can tell that Jeff's in a good mood, because whenever he feels good, he likes to whip around in his favorite car. Plus it's super sunny in Houston this afternoon, perfect for riding in a convertible. The sun blazes so brightly, I take it as an omen that my future is so bright, nothing but good can happen from now on.

When we stop at the side of the car, Jeff grabs my hand in his and kisses me fully on the lips. I'm surprised by his sudden display of affection, but I close my eyes and kiss him back. Anything he gives me, I want to return it to him 100 percent.

"You're the best, Marlene. I love that about you. You're down for whatever. No arguing, no drama." He looks amazed. "Do you realize since we've been hanging out we've never even had a half of an argument? Unreal," he mutters, shaking his head. Then he grimaces as if he's sick or has gas or something.

"What's wrong?"

"Nothing. Don't worry about it."

"Well, if there's anything I can do to help, let me know. I got everything in my pocketbook. Tums, migraine medicine, vitamins, cold and flu pills."

"No, no thank you. The thing I got can't be cured by anything that's in your purse."

"Oh," I say flatly.

"Let's ride."

When he opens the car door, he instructs me, "Don't put your purse on the floor like you did last time. Some of your stuff fell out . . ."

"Oh, okay."

"No, it's just that I had to spend time wiping up lotion off my carpet. It'll never be the same again, you know what I'm saying?"

"Ahh, yeah. I know what you're saying," I say sweetly. "I'm sorry about that."

"No, no, it's cool." By now he's hopped in on the driver's side, and he waits a few seconds before starting the car, then drives off. I notice that about him. It seems like he says a quick prayer every time we get in the car. Like he wants the Lord to protect us or something. I think it's a good idea for him to pray even for a few seconds, because I need all the prayer I can get.

"So we gonna hang out? You gonna hang out with me? You wanna do that, Beautiful Girl?"

Blushing, I say, "Uh, you know I wanna be with you. I don't care what we do."

"You sure?" He winks.

"I'm sure."

"Good, because I am hungry again and want to grab a bite to eat. Then I need to make a run on the south side. Gotta pick up some rent from a tenant who's late."

"Oh, yeah? Who is that?"

"Some lady who's been with me for about eight months. She had been doing pretty well, you know what I'm saying, but I guess she's been having some issues lately. Hey, I don't care about all your personal problems. I need to get my money."

"Wow, I'm so proud of you, Jeff. You are so business-minded. A lot of the guys I've known have been very irresponsible. They either live with their mom who pays for everything, or they have roommates who fight over the bills. It was a mess. I would tell some of them, 'If you can't take care of yourself, how on earth can you take care of me?' "

"Yeah, well, that's the difference between a boy and a man. A real man handles his business. And I, young lady, am a real man. I guess you know that already, huh?" He gives me a wicked grin, and I blush some more, looking like a big fool.

"Oh, you must be talking about—."

"Popping that cherry, and believe me your cherry is sweet, hot, and juicyyy."

"Jeff," I squeal. "Hush."

"Oh, what? Are you ashamed of making love to your man or something? Hey, if you got it good like that you need to tell somebody. Make it known that you got a good man."

"Jeff." I laugh. "My mama told me to never tell another woman all the details of all the good things your good man does . . . so I won't be spreading the good word anytime soon."

"Hmm, interesting," he says, and his face grows serious. He doesn't say anything else to me until we get to the restaurant. We stop by Murphy's Deli and order some French onion soup, turkey pitas, and drinks to go. I'm glad Jeff wanted to get some food, since I didn't feel like eating any of Rachel's.

"I hate to eat and drive," he explains once we're back in the car, "but I need to meet this lady."

"Oh," I say and get a bright idea. I grab the Murphy Deli's bag that's sitting on a blanket on the back seat and remove one of the pitas.

"What are you doing?" he barks while driving.

"I'm taking care of you."

I carefully peel back some of the paper that's wrapped around the pita and order Jeff, "Open your mouth."

"What?" he screeches. "Don't do that!"

"Huh?"

"Put that shit, I mean, set that food back in the bag. We'll eat when we get to the house."

"But I thought—."

"Look, I'm hungry but not *that* hungry," he remarks, looking worried. "And if you are, you'll just have to exercise some patience. We'll be there in twenty. If you want to sip on that bottled water, that's okay. Just make sure to use that straw."

"Oh—" I give him a blank stare.

"Did you hear what I said? Just be a sweetie and put the food back in the bag. Hurry, before tomatoes and lettuce fall out and make a mess."

"Yeah, right. It's cool."

Inside I'm rolling my eyes, but on the outside I'll be sure to let him see me doing what he wants.

Just as he predicted, we arrive at one of his rental properties twenty minutes later. This property is located near Hobby Airport. It's a one-story duplex that is in bad need of paint. The grass looks like it hasn't been mowed in weeks.

When we pull up in the narrow driveway, a brown-skinned lady with a short Afro is standing behind an old black Nissan Sentra that's parked in front of us. We step out of the car. I see at least three other little heads through the back of the Sentra.

"Damn, Jeff, it took you long enough."

"Hey, Lola, I don't wanna hear all that. If you made me wait for my rent, then you can wait, too."

"Shit, I got better things to do and—."

"I don't wanna hear it. Where's the rent? It's five dollars extra a day every day that you're late, so you owe me seven hundred thirty-five."

She frowns and rolls her eyes. Reaches in her tiny purse and pulls out a crumpled check.

"What the fuck is this? I told you cash only, or a money order. I don't want your bouncy checks, Lola."

"I didn't have time to go to the bank or nothing, so take it or leave it."

Jeff's veins pop through his forehead looking like snakes crawling under his skin. He quietly swears under his breath.

"Don't tell me you wasted my time and gas making me fly over here and almost getting into an accident to get my money, and your money is acting funny. I don't do personal checks, Lola, you know this."

"Damn, Jeff, I got bills to pay, you not the only one with your hand stuck out. My baby daddy skipped out on child support, and I had to scrape up money the best way I can. My sister loaned me some money, but she gave me a check . . . that's why I'm giving you a check."

"Which sister?"

"Bunny."

"Sweaty Drawers?" He grins.

Lola holds her hand over her mouth and giggles. "Ooo, you know you wrong about that. She lost ten pounds recently, so she ain't as big as she used to be." Lola eyes me curiously. "She about the size of this chick," she says and nods at me.

"Anyway," Jeff says loudly. "Bunny is cool, but Lo, you know how I do. I wish you would've taken time to draw the money out the bank."

"I know, baby, I know, but I'll do that next time, I swear to God."

She smiles encouragingly at Jeff, and his scowl gradually turns into a toothy grin.

"All right," he says and snatches the check from her. "How're the kids?"

"Bad as hell. I'm about to take 'em to their Nanny, and then I gots to go to my second job. Damn shame, if their daddy would pay the child support like he's supposed to I wouldn't have to take a second job working at the damn Taco Bell."

"I bet you look real fine in that uniform, Lo."

"Whatever, Jeff. I'll be talking to you. Give me a call sometime. You know how to reach me." She gives me a piercing, nasty look and twists her butt around, switching all the way to her car.

Jeff and I stand there looking at each other. "See what I go through?"

"Whoa. That's all I have to say."

"But see, I don't do banks, and now I got this check. Can we do a third-party thing with you? I'll give you one percent."

"Huh?" I ask.

Lola loudly blows her horn, rolls down her window. "Get the fuck out the way. You heard me say I'm running late to work."

"That bitch is tripping," Jeff mutters. "Get in the car," he says to me.

We return to Jeff's ride and hop in, and he backs out the driveway and speeds down the street.

"Jeff," I say, but he just stares into space while driving. His quietness allows me to reflect on the not-so-wonderful parts of Jeffrey Williams. He seemed unnecessarily rude to his tenant. Sure, she owes him money, but acting like a butt-hole won't make her give him his money any faster. Maybe he's stressed. Or maybe he's just not as good of a man as I thought.

"So you gonna hook me up on this check?"

"Did you hear me saying 'huh' just a minute ago?"

"What? No, babe, sorry. I have a lot of stuff on my mind. What were you saying?"

"Um, never mind. It wasn't important."

"Anything that you wanna talk about I may want to talk about, too," he says and starts laughing at his own joke.

"No, it's fine. I'm probably overreacting. Loretta says a real woman never goes to extremes and overreacts in situations that don't lend themselves to high emotions."

"Your mama said that?"

"Why you ask? Are you shocked?"

"She doesn't seem like the type . . . Well, who am I to judge. Women don't always easily fit in the categories that I think they fit in. Take yourself, for example."

"Yeah? What about me?"

"On the outside you look like a woman who will put up a fight for what she believes in. Yet you're one of the sweetest young ladies I've ever met. And I've met a lot of them . . . being in this type of business, of course."

"Oh, so are you saying I'm soft?"

"You don't *look* soft . . . but I know you're the other kind of soft . . . warm . . . cozy . . . affectionate. All good things, babe."

I blush, nod. *Keep going*, I think inside.

"And when I'm doing my thing on the real estate tip, filling out paperwork, paying utility bills, checking and responding to a hundred e-mails, you're the very next thing on my mind. I wonder what you're doing throughout the day. Wonder when I can see that beautiful smile again. Then I get an unexpected call, and I hate that I have to dial you up and let you know I've had a change of plans."

"Yeah, I've noticed you did that a couple of times last week—"

"But it doesn't happen on purpose. You know how it is; sometimes you just can't plan how everything happens. Things come along that kick you in the face, and you either deal with the pain or pretend like it's not hurting." He sighs and looks like he's in pain. I hate seeing him look this way. He works hard and deserves to enjoy the fruits of his labor.

"Anything I can do to help?"

"Nope," he says.

"All right."

"Wait, yep. Do the check for me. Please."

"Jeff, I'd better not do that."

"Why not?"

"You can cash the check at a twenty-four-hour check-cashing place."

"I know that. They charge two percent."

"Oh, so you're trying to cheat me?" I laugh.

"No, no, never that. Just thought I'd ask, though. Never mind. Don't want you doing anything that makes you feel uncomfy."

"Jeff," I say quietly.

"Yeah."

"Is it okay if I eat now?"

"Huh, no. Sorry. I got distracted by Lo and forgot all about the food. Tell you what, if you promise to be real careful, go ahead and take a bite out of that pita. Or if you're very hungry, let me hurry up and drop you back off at your spot. I got some things to do myself."

"What? I thought we were gonna hang out."

"I thought we were, too, but Baby Doll, I gotta be about my business. Gotta take care of some things that just came up."

"Oh, Jeff. I'm sorry. I was looking forward—."

"We'll do something tomorrow. Promise. And I don't make promises too often."

"Then why did I take a shower? What was that about?"

"I know you want it, girl, but sometimes a man has to do things that shoves sex to the bottom of the to-do list. Real talk."

I want to say something nasty, but since he's noticed we haven't had our first fight I will shut up and wait until we really have something substantial to argue about.

"Tell you what. Take me to my mama's. I want to go see about her and my father."

"No problem."

We head over to Blinky's. I see Aunt Perry's car parked outside their house. I grab my food and wave bye to Jeff. He blows the horn and answers his cell before speeding off down the street.

I ring the doorbell. Perry opens the door. "Hey, knuckle-head girl. What you doing over here?"

"Oh, I got dropped off. I'm going to need a ride home later. How long will you be over here?"

"Not long. I came to see my big brother." She finally opens the door and whispers in my ear as I slide past her try-ing to get in the house. "Your daddy asked me for some money. I told him he's got two working daughters. Humph, he said he didn't want to bother ya'll."

"Hmm, that's fine with me," I tell her. "Daddy," I scream and walk directly to the den. He's sitting in the La-Z-Boy. "Turn on some lights in here," I snap. When I cut on the lamp, I see a thick bandage on the corner of his forehead.

"Oh, how'd that happen?"

"What? Got stung by a wasp."

"Does the wasp wear head scarves and bracelets?"

"Hush, Pretty Girl."

Aunt Perry prances into the den and plops on the sofa. "Have a seat, girl, nobody's going to bite you."

She looks me up and down, then moves closer when she notices the upper side of my breast.

She partially pulls down the front of my shirt. "What in the hell?"

"Hey," I say angrily. "Don't be touching me like that."

"Well, well, well. You went and got you something that really expresses how you feel about that little boy. I was going to ask, but this here tells me more than what your mouth would've said. Humph, Blinky, you see your daughter got a tat? On her tit?"

"Auntie, please." I stand up, feeling humiliated.

"Sit back down, girl. I'm just messing with you."

I reluctantly sit down and wonder why I asked Jeff to take me over here.

"Your sister see it yet?" Perry asks.

I shake my head.

"Have you thought about how it's going to affect her?"

"Perry, she won't care. She's over Jeff."

"Since when?"

"Today!"

"Please."

"Look, I don't have time to worry about people judging me about my decisions. I know what I'm doing."

"But 'M and J'?" She shakes her head. "Did he get a tat with *your* initials?"

"No, this was just for me, Perry. Dang, can we change the subject? Where's my mama?"

"She's trying to get another job," Blinky says. "So she says."

Aunt Perry starts cackling. "You all are a mess. You better hope she's not trying to find another place to stay."

"Aw, I'm not worried about her leaving me. She's threatened to do that so many times ... Ha, I dare her to leave. We'll make up in no time flat. Loretta loves me. "

"She's probably only staying with you to save face, Blinky." When my Aunt Perry gets on a roll, it's hard to stop her.

"If she leaves you, Brooke will never let her hear the end of it. I'm sure glad that lady went on with her life." She stares at me. "And your sister is going to go on with hers."

"Keep me out of this conversation, will you?" I say. "Loretta is not me. I'm not her. And I'm definitely not Rachel."

"We know you not, Pretty Girl," says Blinky. "And we love you just the way you are."

"I know you do, Daddy. But sometimes I'm not sure about Aunt Perry."

"Girl, stop tripping. I love you, too. That's why I stay on you. If I didn't care about you, I'd let you do whatever you want. Don't you know I used to change your dirty diapers when you were a baby? Holding my nose and trying to wipe up your shit?"

"Auntie, please!" I say and stand up.

"No, listen. We're grown. We can talk. As long as I have breath in my body I'll be trying to guide you right. Trying to keep you from making mistakes that can ruin your life. That's what family does. Now come here and give me a hug, and I'm going to give you a ride home whether you like it or not."

11

RACHEL

Make Myself Happy

I'm in my bedroom seated in front of my desk. I watch Alita, who's standing next to me, point and click. She's on the Internet and just logged in to SoulSingles.com, a singles dating community.

"Girl, just read some of the other women's profiles so you can get idea of how to set up yours."

"Wow, I can't believe there are so many people on this site."

"Yep, and some folks like to make the rounds and register on all the dating sites. Match, eHarmony, BlackSingles, and there are some Christian sites, too."

"Humph, I'll remember that one for my sis," I tell her.

"Aw, that's cold. Anyway, Rachel, congrats on even taking the first step and signing up. Oh, excuse me for calling you Rachel. I meant to say HoneyBrownTX."

"Ha ha ha, funny funny funny."

"No, for real girl, that's a nice name. But you should keep going."

"Shoot, they want to know so much info. I'm not sure if I'm ready for this."

"I'm telling you, once you get started and begin to receive flirts and e-mails, you'll be addicted. Your ego will blow up as big as one of Pam Anderson's breasts. It'll be fun, but you still have to watch out for the crazies."

"What? I thought you said there weren't any crazies on here."

"Oh, I didn't say that. I said crazy men are everywhere."

"Ain't that the truth," I murmur. "Anyway, help me, girl. What should I say?"

"Do the easy stuff first. You're a nonsmoker, you don't really drink that much. You want kids, right?"

"Mmm hmm. Do I give my real weight?"

"Yes. Once you put your photo up there, people are going to see how you look, anyway. You're not big or anything, but believe me, brothas looking for love like the thick sistas, too, and the white ones, the Hispanics, older women, you name it."

"Hmmm," I tell her and begin to fill out the personal info for my dating profile.

"Ugh, I sound so lame."

Alita chuckles. "You *are* lame. Just kidding. No, you gotta spruce it up a bit. That's why you need to get in touch with my cousin London. She could even write some of this stuff for you. Girl, she goes out on two dates a week, sometimes three."

"I'm not surprised. That chick is a bona fide knockout."

"Well, she's just having a little fun. She knows she's not halfway serious about some of these guys, but it lets her filter out what type of companion she doesn't want."

"I see." I point and click, browsing the site looking at different men's profiles. "Why don't some guys have their photos? That's weird."

"I dunno. They may not have had their photos approved yet. Or they're ugly. Or maybe married."

"Ha ha, that would be terrible to see your husband's picture up on one of these sites."

"Girl, if a wife sees her hubby's profile on SoulSingles, then she's no better than he is. Am I right, or am I on crack?"

"You are definitely not on crack . . . this time, Alita."

"Aw, hush your mouth. Or I'm going to hook you up with Magilla Gorilla."

"I don't think so. I am hoping to meet someone who is honest, a good communicator, and handsome, of course. I think he should be an old-fashioned gentleman. Oh jeez, I don't know. That sounds lame, too. I'm starting to get frustrated."

"Calm down. We have plenty of time. What's today? Saturday? We should have everything posted in the next couple days. That'll give you time to get some hits and set up some dates for next weekend."

I start grinning. "Oh, yeah, right, sure. And in two more weeks I expect to be engaged to a wealthy man. And I guess I'll be married and on a honeymoon in eight weeks."

"And divorced one month after that. Hollywood-style stuff, huh, Rach—oops, HoneyBrownTX."

"No Hollywood stuff for me," I state firmly. "I'm looking for the real deal. If I am sincere in my quest for love, there's no reason to connect with a man who's not as genuine as I am."

I do a couple of searches for single men between the ages of twenty-four and thirty-four and click on a member profile. The guy's screen name is WriteBro4U.

"Oh," I tell Alita, "maybe he's an author, or a poet. That would be different."

I glance at his personal info.

Height: 5'8"

Weight: 115 lbs.

"Oh, hell no. If I put on heels, I'd have to look down on top of his head."

Alita giggles. "Try to be open. London dates guys who are taller and shorter than her. The short guys are funnier—"

"That's because they gotta be—"

"And the tall guys feel they don't have to do much to impress a woman because they're relying on their height or good looks."

"Okay, something to consider."

I click on a section called Opinions.

"Let's see what WriteBro4U is about," I murmur. "Oh, God, look at his first answer. They want his opinion on abortions. He put 'Sometimes.'"

"Dang, okay, we know what he's been up to, huh?"

"Yeah. I've got to get out of this brotha's page. He's not for me."

"Don't give up so fast. You may find you have so many other traits in common with this man."

"That's all right. We'll never know, because I wouldn't give him the time of day."

"Suit yourself, lady. You have too many rules or something. It may take you a while to find someone you like."

"Oh, yeah right, two whole weeks instead of three long days."

"Smarty," she says and pretends to karate chop me.

"Aww," I playfully scream. "No, stop, stay back," I say, mimicking what we say in self-defense class. "Hey, I'm really happy we're taking the class. I may need it once I start going on some dates."

"Let's hope you won't have to go Mike Tyson on anybody, but you never know." She jumps up. "Hey, I gotta go to the bathroom, sweetie."

"Take your time, Hardly Berry. I'm going to continue searching around for my future baby daddy."

I flick through several profiles and wrinkle my nose in frustration. I had no idea finding a new guy would be so difficult. My thoughts settle on Jeff, and I wonder if he's the one that got away. But I convince myself that if he really were that good, and truly belonged to me, he wouldn't be trying to date my sister regardless of his asinine reason for being with her.

I entertain some thoughts for several minutes and begin typing in a section called In My Own Words:

*Hey, what's up, world? My name is—oops, you almost got me. For this site, I want to be known as Honey-BrownTX. Why? Well, I am a proud Texas girl, born and raised in Houston. Texas is my roots and there's no better place in the world than my home state. Secondly, my skin is as brown as the sweetness of a honeycomb, but my outward appearance is not important. The things inside of me are what matter the most. This is my first time seeking a mate on a dating site. I am not here to play games. In fact, I've signed up not just to meet my dream guy, but I'm here to discover things, important things, about myself as a woman, and hopefully about you, too. I've experienced several relationships in the past; some made me extremely happy, others made me question my judgment. Which brings me to my personal philosophy: **Make yourself happy as long as you aren't making someone else unhappy along the way.** I came across these words on the Internet one day, and they perfectly describe where I am right now. I want love. I want happiness. But if my being happy means that I gotta hurt someone else, I'll delay my happiness. The type of fulfillment I'm looking for must be pure, honest, and suitable. Feel free to hit me up if you feel what I'm saying.*

My fingers stop clicking the keyboard. My shirt is now clinging to me. I feel a pool of wetness forming in my armpit. Writing that material has taken a lot out of me. I unloaded my heart, emotions, everything I have, into what I want to say. Emptying my soul feels unusually good, and my spirit feels lighter.

Alita returns to my room, glancing over my shoulder.

"Hmm, girlfriend, you've put the wow factor in your profile."

"Amazing, huh?"

"Sure is. Now fill out some more stuff, then we'll submit your profile, okay?"

"All right, I'll answer a few more questions."

I click on Opinions and type the first things that pop in my mind:

OPINIONS

ABORTION:	Nope, hopefully never.
ANIMAL RIGHTS:	If the animal is a rat, no. But for King Kong? Hell, yeah.
BILL CLINTON:	Unforgettable Prez.
CAPITAL PUNISHMENT:	Only in extreme cases (e.g., Jeffrey Dahmer).
DEMOCRATS:	No more Bushit.
MARTIN LUTHER KING JR.:	Still a major influence on the world.
MICHAEL JACKSON:	He should have his own reality show.
RELIGION:	Not sure where it fits in my life, although I do believe in God.
REPUBLICANS:	Not everyone can be on welfare.
REV. JESSE JACKSON:	Keep one eye open around him.
SCHOOL PRAYER:	It definitely can't hurt. Amen.

"All right. I'm tired, girl," I say and push my swivel chair back from my desk.

"I think you have enough to get started. One last thing, though—you need to post a photo."

"Hmm, I hate taking pictures. Not very photogenic."

"Just submit your best photo."

"My favorite slash best photo is one where Jeff and I are standing cheek to cheek. I love that picture, but no way it's going on SoulSingles."

"Then take a new picture."

"Shoot, look at my hair. I've got a couple of pimples on my face. Yuck. No one's going to be attracted to me."

"Girl, if these ugly-ass men have enough nerve to put their pictures up there—"

"You calling me ugly, Alita?"

"No, fool. You're cute as a button. You just don't realize it." Alita places her hands on her hips, then smiles. "Hey, let's play a little game. But we gotta hook up with London and see if she'll be in on it. Knowing my cousin, she'll say yes."

Alita gets her cousin on the phone, and they chitchat for a few. "London is in the area, actually at First Colony Mall. I told her we'll meet her there."

"What's she doing at the mall?"

"Some guy gave her a JCPenney gift card. So she's checking out jewelry. They're having a diamond and gold sale. Seventy percent off."

"Hmm, must be nice. Let's go," I say, excited.

We get in my car and it takes ten minutes to get to the mall, park, and reach the jewelry department. The well-lit displays make the diamond rings, earrings, and necklaces look so alluring. We spot London immediately. She favors the singer Leona Lewis. Tall and shapely with those long Shirley Temple curls cascading down her back. She's rocking some

7 for All Mankind wide-leg jeans, red pumps, and a black Ed Hardy T-shirt with the ugly skull graphic on the front.

Every guy that passes by does a double take. It must be the fact that her big round booty looks great in her tight jeans.

"Hey hey, now," Alita yells. "What's up, Cousin?"

"Oh, hey, cuz. Hi, Rachel. I'm almost finished."

"Find anything?" Alita asks.

"Yeah, I want some more gold hoop earrings. These are perfect," she says and asks the dark-haired female salesclerk to ring up her purchase. I notice that even the salesclerk is blushing and can't take her eyes off London.

London beams and barely notices all the attention that people are giving her. Scattered customers standing idly nearby. Several older men who obviously were walking hand in hand with their senior wives.

"Hey, London, we don't want to keep you long. I just wanted to say hello, and I gotta ask you for a huge favor. It has to do with my friend," she says and nods at me. We've just left the jewelry department and are now walking through the busy, noisy mall.

Teen girls are hanging out, clutching tiny purses to their sides. Thirty-something moms are pushing their toddlers in strollers. Dozens of men are walking around in packs, ogling women, loudly laughing and flirting.

"No problem," London says. "What do you need me to do?"

"Well," Alita says, smiling. "We've signed Rachel up on SoulSingles."

"Oh, cool. That site is a trip. But I've met a couple decent guys on there, and we still hook up from time to time."

"Good for you, London," I tell her. "That's all I want. Maybe meet some guys who'll turn out to be good friends, potential companions. I'm not exactly looking for a husband or anything."

"You can find anything and everything on the site," London replies.

"Anyway," Alita says. "We've done everything except Rachel's picture. I really want a photo that stands out. Do you have any old ones we can use?"

"Are you joking? I don't think that's a good idea."

"C'mon, please. We'll post it up there for just a couple of days. Until we take a nice picture of Rachel, Photoshop it—"

"Hey," I say, pretending to be annoyed.

Alita giggles. "No, seriously. I don't want to deceive any guy, but it'll be fun to see who contacts Rachel if we post your sexy photo up on the site."

"Ya'll are being naughty." London smirks. "But hey, what the heck? It's not like guys don't post fake profiles, fake photos. Equal opportunity, right, ladies?"

I smile but feel a little uncomfortable. What if they lust over London's gorgeous pictures, ask me out on a date, see me in person, and then get pissed off because I look nothing like my photo?

"Ladies, I dunno. I told them I'm not playing games. So maybe we should just take a thousand photos of me, and hope one turns out good."

"We'll do both," Alita says. "Now, London, promise me you'll e-mail like five photos. They can be old, I don't care. I just feel mischievous."

"You're feeling naughty on my account. What if I miss out on a good man behind you wanting to play?"

"Rachel, c'mon. Just one day. Post London's pic for one freaking day. Jeez, live a little."

I roll my eyes and fume inside. Alita continues to nag me, tugs my elbow, and laughs uproariously, sounding so loud it's like she's trying to embarrass me in front of everyone at the mall. I finally say, "Okay, okay, okay. One day only. I hope I don't regret this."

Alita, London, and I hang out at the mall for another half-hour, window shopping, oohing and ahhing over cute shoes, and spraying ourselves with sweet-smelling perfume at Sephora. We group hug and wave bye to London. On the way back to my apartment, Alita says says she's gotta meet Hen for dinner and a movie. She tells me she'll e-mail me late tonight and makes me promise to load one of London's pictures.

I'm perched on the couch in the living room that night when I hear a clamor outside my apartment. I stand in front of the window and pull back the shade. Marlene and Aunt Perry are standing next to Perry's cute little Mazda yapping away.

Intrigued, I step outside on the balcony. Perry points at me. Marlene turns around and stares at me, then looks back at my aunt.

"Go ahead," I hear Perry say. "Ask her."

Even more curious, I run down the stairs and walk up to them. "Ask me what?"

"Your knucklehead sister wants to know if you'd like to go to service with her tomorrow. It's Women's Day, and you're supposed to bring all the women you can. I told Marlene I'll go, but only if you go, too."

"Say what?" I screech. "You're pulling me into something . . ."

"It's not just something," Marlene says, and finally looks at me. "It's church."

"Jeez, I dunno. I may be busy," I reply.

"Busy doing what?" Perry asks. "Scratching your ass? Sleeping till noon, then going out to eat at Denny's?"

"Perry," I begin.

"Perry nothing. As your favorite and most lovable aunt, I insist that you go."

"What? When's the last time *you* went to church?"

"It was when Brian McKnight came to sing."

"Brian McKnight was at ST?" I question Marlene. It's a shame I missed that event. Brian McKnight is for older folks, but I still like a couple of his songs.

"Yeah, girl. He performed at a Christmas concert. I'm telling you, we have a lot of exciting things going on there. You'd like it. For real."

"What time shall I pick y'all up?" Aunt Perry asks.

"We all can't fit in your car," I blurt.

"That's a lame excuse. We'll take two cars if we have to. But, yeah, I think we should go. Shoot, I may even bend Loretta's arm and get her to go. Brooke, too."

"Yeah, right," I heartily chuckle. "No way on earth that's gonna happen."

"Anyway, be ready by eleven."

She whips around real fast, like it's a done deal, hops in her itty-bitty car, and a minute later speeds away, leaving Marlene and me standing there looking and feeling awkward.

"What's that all about?" I ask Marlene. We begin walking up the stairs until we're back inside the apartment. I guess we both feel too hyper to have a seat; both of us remain standing and resume our conversation.

"Aunt Perry is on a little roll, I guess. She . . . sees things in the family that bother her . . . She's trying to take the lead . . . make some things happen."

"What brought it on, though?"

Marlene hesitates and clears her throat. "I guess now is as good a time as any." She faces me with a scared look and yanks on her shirt so that her upper chest is exposed. "I got this tat today. Perry pitched a fit. She said I need counseling, not body art." She laughs, then stops abruptly. "True be told, I need both of 'em."

"Oh my God, you *do* need counseling!" I say in shock, tears swimming in my eyes. "Girl, that tat was a foolish decision. You haven't known the guy that long. You don't seem to be using your brain at all." I throw up my hands, walk in a circle, come back. "If being with a man makes you lose sight of who you truly are, maybe you don't need him."

"I didn't ask for, neither do I want, to hear your advice, Rachel. That's all I've been getting from people lately. Folks all up in my business, trying to run my life. I'm grown and I can do what I want to do. Have you ever thought about that?"

I want to say more but don't.

Marlene continues. "I find it so hypocritical that my mama does whatever she wants and no one says much. Brooke walks around not caring about anyone's feelings because she's angry about old junk. And Perry, really, she has some nerve preaching to me. Her two precious kids. I mean, where is their father? She's forty-something years old and acts like she's lost her mind with her midlife crisis behavior."

"And your point is?"

"All of us Draper women—"

"*Merrell.*"

"All of us women tend to do what we feel is right, until we find out we're wrong. If I'm making a mistake, let me make it. You get it? You can't live for me any more than I can live for you, Sis."

She grimaces and her eyes glaze over, making her seem lost in thought. "God knows when you were barely a teen and got interested in guys, I tried so very hard to keep you focused on class, homework, chores. I tried to tell you right from wrong, tried to be the example, but sometimes you wouldn't listen, remember?"

I nod, feeling frustrated.

"And when your mom would blame me for the things you did, I would feel frustrated. And who can forget the trouble that we got into because you hung out with your little friends and shoplifted little apple pies and bags of potato chips from the corner store? Loretta called your mom and told her that the store manager threatened to call the police on you. And when Brooke told her that I was in the store, too, while ya'll did your little dirt, she had my mama put me on the phone."

Marlene pauses with this incredulous look on her face. "I tried to explain to her that I had to go to the bathroom and didn't witness what happened. Yet Loretta screamed at me so loud I–I thought the woman *hated* me. She cursed me at the top of her lungs. I was only thirteen. I didn't understand. Her harsh words hurt me back then. The memory hurts me even now. Brooke said I ought to be more responsible when it came to you. I should have taken you into the bathroom with me. That month when she was gone made me feel like I was forced to do the things that she wasn't able to do. Making sure you stayed out of trouble."

"I sort of remember that. She made ya'll put me on punishment. I thought it was unfair since she wasn't even around back then."

"And when I tried my best to watch you, but you still did what you wanted, I threw up my hands, had to let you go, not mother you so much. I couldn't wait until your mom was able to resume her role, and be your mom like she was supposed to be."

"That was temporary."

"Yes, you're right. She got herself together and came and got you. Raised you, all that, but for a while there, I felt like . . ." Marlene gasps, breaks down, falls to her knees.

"Are you okay?" I ask, still looking at my sister.

"I guess what I'm trying to say is that . . . I just wish people would try to understand. Life is hard for all of us, even for me, Sis. I swear to God, I'm not trying to hurt anybody. No, I'm not. I'm not. I'm not," she sobs, her shoulders bobbing up and down as she breaks down. I guess she's referring to why she feels she must do what she's doing with Jeff. Dating him, the tat, everything.

"Okay, stop crying, please. I hate when you do that," I say and rub her arms.

"I'm just doing what comes natural. Looking for love. It just happens to be with someone who . . . It's not intentional . . ."

"But Marlene . . . a tattoo?" I shake my head, amazed. "I remember Jeff asked me to do that for him, but I said no. We'd only known each other three months." I stare at her. "See what I'm saying? You have no filters anymore . . . You're just down for whatever, and that's what scares me about you. And him," I scoff. "Don't even get me started on him. He doesn't know what the hell he's doing."

"Maybe he's still hurting, Rachel." She's stopped crying. Her voice is calm, sure. "You hurt the man big-time. He might be seeking to heal his wounds. I may be the source of his healing. You never know."

"But—"

"And if I am the source, don't you want the best for Jeff? Let him be healed . . . even if it's through me?"

I stare at her incredulously. I swear she thinks she's the mother of Jesus, or maybe his aunt. Like she's doing something noble and significant. This can't be right. Feels too wrong.

Suddenly, my sister gives me a sad look, then wobbles away to her room.

Exhausted, I go to my own room, shut the door, and collapse on my bed. But I remember that I need to check my e-mail. I drag myself to my desk, click on new mail, and open an attachment from Alita.

London is wearing a deep-orange bikini. She's grinning, looking confident, beautiful, and alluring.

What kind of attention will I get with that picture? I feel a little guilty for wanting to do this. It seems wrong, naughty, but what's the worst that can happen?

I download her picture to my hard drive. Log in to Soul-Singles and add the photo. I go back to bed fantasizing about the changes that can potentially renew my life. I cannot wait.

MARLENE

Not Too Proud to Cry for Help

My favorite accessories are stylish hats that I can pull over my forehead, so that my hair can be neatly tucked underneath. I also adore big black sunglasses, which are back in style. When I clothe myself with both of these fashion necessities, I feel so powerful. Protected. In control.

That's how I choose to dress this Sunday morning. Women's Day. I'm a woman, and today is my day. Forget Rachel. Forget Perry. Even Loretta. I need to hear words that soothe my soul and piece together my spirit. All this yada, yada, yada stuff is getting old. No matter what my female relatives say to me today, if it's funky sounding, I am going to tell them to talk to the hand.

I complete my look by whisking my favorite double-breasted skirt suit from my closet. It's purple and has a fake fur collar that looks good on me. I shower and dress, then head for the kitchen. My sister has already started the coffee and is making some grits. I can hear the grease popping from the bacon that's in the oven.

"You look cute, Marlene."

"So do you."

She smirks, knowing I'm kidding, because she still has on a striped bathrobe. "You are still coming with us, right?"

"Yeah, I'll come. But I tell you, I'm not enthused. I'm doing this as a favor to Aunt Perry."

"Oh, boy, then God's really gonna bless you," I respond with glee. "Wait and see."

"Can't wait."

It feels good that my sister and I are communicating better, rather than constantly arguing. That's how we are sometimes. We can be yelling, screaming, and threatening each other one day, and borrowing each other's jewelry or purses the next and talking as if nothing bad ever happened.

"You're welcome to breakfast. There's enough for everybody. Aunt Perry and Kiki should be here any minute."

A knock at the door signals their arrival. I rush to open the door, scoop my cousin Kiki in my arms, and press my lips against her little cheek. "Uh yuck. Don't kiss me, 'Lene." She's always had a hard time saying my name.

"You look adorable," I tell her. I smudge lip balm off her face with the tips of my fingers.

"Hey, Auntie Perry." I whirl around and proceed to drop some bread slices into the toaster.

"What up, what up?" Aunt Perry says. She looks fabulous. Her tailored black suit perfectly fits her tiny body. "Let's get our church on," she announces, then looks about her surroundings, giving us proud stares. "Wow, this is feeling kinda nice. I am so excited to be with y'all, you just don't know. Usually on Sunday morning, I'm l-a-y-i-n-g with some m-a-n," she whispers and nods conspiratorially at Kiki, who's staring at her mom with a blank look. "But for once I'm starting my week off right. Praising the Lord, getting into the word, and spending time with my family."

"Amen, Auntie," I say. I start humming a song by CeCe Winans and finish overseeing the toast, spreading strawberry jam on everybody's slices. Soon we all sit at the dining room table together with our plates full and eat breakfast.

"What you got up today after church, Niece?" says Aunt Perry to Rachel.

"Nothing much . . . I'm waiting to see what jumps off," she replies.

"And you?" Perry asks, nodding at me.

"Um, gotta take care of some business . . . with you-know-who."

"Jeff? You can say his name. Like I told you last time, I don't care what y'all do," Rachel says.

"Whoa, are you fu—oops—are you effing kidding me?" Aunt Perry asks Rachel.

"Nope, not kidding. I'm moving on. Not that it's easy, but it's the better thing, the right thing to do."

"Hmm, this I gotta see. It's not easy getting over a relationship."

"No, it's not, but we all gotta do it at some point." Rachel smiles. I'm not sure if she's trying to be funny or what, so I take the high road and keep my mouth shut.

"It would have been nice if Loretta could have come. But she wanted to be up under Blinky today."

"I'll bet she does," Rachel says, smirking.

"Rachel, that's not nice. Get your mind out of the gutter. She's probably trying to repair their relationship, spend quality time with her man."

"Being up under a man is quality time, all right," Rachel says, laughing out loud.

Irritated, I say, "Rachel, please stop it. I'm not in the mood for this . . . not right before church."

"Aww, leave your sister alone, Marlene. I can tell she's just nervous about showing up at Solomon's Temple. She doesn't mean to be rude."

I slam the table with my free hand. Everyone jumps, shaken. "That's it. Why does everyone stand up for her all the time? Like I'm always in the wrong?"

"Calm down," says Kiki.

"You be quiet, little girl; no one was talking to you," I tell my cousin.

"Okay, hold up," Perry interrupts. "Leave my daughter out of this. Even she can see that things are getting out of hand. Don't tell me a four-year-old has more sense than you."

"More sense than both of us," I say, agreeing and feeling ashamed. "And that's not cool. I–I'm sorry. I've been tripping, and Perry, you're right. I'm making a big deal out of nothing. And I definitely don't want to step up in church with a bad attitude. I'm not trying to be 'that' girl."

"That's much better, Marlene,"

"Much better, 'Lene," says Kiki.

We finish eating breakfast and are forced to listen to Kiki recite numbers one through one hundred. I eat till my plate is spotless.

"Hey, according to my Timex, it's getting late," Auntie Perry says, rising up and removing her plate and utensils from the table. "So do what y'all have to do and meet me in my car, pronto."

Rachel rushes to get dressed. Moments later we all pile in Aunt Perry's Mazda and speed off toward Solomon's Temple. We make a little lighthearted small talk all the way to church. When we arrive, I anxiously rush inside the immense sanctuary that's pulsating with spirited energy. Foot stomps. Hand claps. Shouts and yelps. It feels like heaven to be among almost a thousand well-dressed African Americans who love to sing and lift up their hands to the ceiling during a two-hour church service. An usher leads us to our seats, the middle of a very long pew. And once I sit, but before I can get truly relaxed, the congregation is asked to stand up. We're instructed to hug the person standing next to us.

"Come here and give me a hug, niece." I turn to my right and wrap my arms tightly around Aunt Perry, who squeezes me so tight I gasp. "Thanks for inviting me," she murmurs, her mouth touching my hair. When we stop embracing, I detect sincerity in her eyes. I turn to my left side. Rachel avoids eye contact with me. She looks awkward, like she's self-conscious that she doesn't fit in.

"Hey, Little Bit, I'm so glad you're here."

"Um, yeah," she says. I take the initiative and reach over to pull her neck into my chest. Just like I'd do when she was a little girl. She's not a little girl anymore, yet I sense her vulnerability, a combination of strength and weakness that is apparent when a woman has important issues on her mind.

The worship leader says, "Grab the person's hand next to you and let's pray." I entwine my fingers though Rachel's and close my eyes. This moment helps me recall the countless times I was charged by my parents to take care of Rachel: look both ways before we'd cross the street, keep her close to me when we'd go grocery shopping with Loretta.

Rachel isn't like Kiki anymore; she doesn't count on me to be the leader who tells her what to do, what to say, how to dress, I think to myself. What is my role now that we're older, now that we both are adult enough to follow our own decisions, and make our own mistakes? Do I still have to be the example, even though it's a role I don't want at times?

After reciting a soul-stirring prayer that makes me feel lighthearted and hopeful, we settle back in our seats and continue enjoying the program. The latest announcements are being loudly broadcast on two huge TV monitors, as if we're at a concert in the Toyota Center. Then we let loose by clapping our hands and singing along with the one hundred–

member women's choir. I feel good. More relaxed. God knows I need a break from the drama I've endured the past few weeks.

A woman named Sister Palmer gives a minisermon in honor of Women's Day. She wears a floor-length white robe and paces across the stage, pointing her finger and raising her voice, like she's a prophetess straight from the Bible.

Finally, the man of the hour takes the stage. Observes the crowd. Big Bible always glued to his hand, Pastor Solomon is outfitted in a black clergy robe lined with gold brocade. He looks spiritual yet hip, like he's comfortably connected to his flock.

Pastor says, "Some of y'all think you can slide into heaven based on good works you did twenty years ago. But your current deeds aren't as exemplary as they were in the past. What if you get to the gates of heaven and God says, 'What have you done for me lately?'

"Would you say, 'Hey Lord, I didn't know you were into Janet Jackson'?"

"And the Lord would answer, 'Is Janet Jackson into me?' "

Aunt Perry says, "Hey now," and high fives me.

Pastor Solomon continues his forty-minute sermon, telling stories and jokes, reading scripture, and making me think about things that help me clear my cluttered mind. He says, "Marinate on this a minute: *If it's in God's hands, it's in good hands.*" He asks us to repeat his thought of the week throughout the rest of his message.

"Don't be afraid; do not be afraid, don't be afraid, to pray, good people. Yeah, you heard right, y'all need to pray. Oh, oh, oh, I know ya'll sophisticated, educated, you watch TV One, and drive Hummers up and down West Bellfort Street, but you can never get so high in life that you think you've got it so good that you don't need to pray. You say, 'They took prayer out of schools,' yeah, but as long as you still have a mouth, you can pray. As long as you still have a mind, you can pray. As long as you still have breath . . . even bad breath," he jokes, and waits for us to collectively reply, "You can pray."

"There ya go." He laughs and scans the congregation, looking over the heads of the people. "I do believe that some of y'all ladies are awake this morning. That's a good thing," he continues. "Don't be so controlling over certain areas of your life: your money, your mansion, and your man. Whether you know it or not, everything you possess came from God's hand. Not from Chevron, not Houston Independent School District, not Continental Airlines, and not even from your sugar daddy. So if you can give back to God what he's freely given to you, you know you're on the right track. If it's in God's hands . . ." He goes on for several more minutes saying that God will bless us with the things we desire, but we must be careful that those things don't become an obsession, or it can lead to us worshipping things made by men. "American Idolatry," he jokes. "Paula and Simon ain't seen nothing yet."

The service concludes with a call for salvation; an invitation is also extended to those who have special prayer requests. I sit attentively up in my seat; this is the most intriguing part of church. Observing people who, from the outside appearance, look as though they have life neatly wrapped around their finger. But when life begins to get overwhelming, they're not too proud to cry for help. It's amazing to see people walk to the front looking one way, and returning to their pew looking another.

Aunt Perry glances at me, her face looking pale and dull, which is a stark contrast to her normal fiery appearance. I whisper, "You all right? Wanna go up there? I'll go with you if you want."

"Naw, I'm cool."

Kiki says, "I wanna go."

"Shut up, fool."

"Aunt Perry," I gasp. "Don't call her that. You ought to be ashamed of yourself. She's just a baby."

"Why she wanna go? Kiki doesn't know what she's doing."

"Yes, I do, Mommy."

"Oh, yeah, why you going up there? You're four years old, you don't have any problems."

"I'm going to pray for you, Mommy," Kiki says, with wide-eyed innocence. "And for Cousin Rachel, and 'Lene, and Uncle Blinky."

"Let's go, baby," Aunt Perry says and grabs Kiki's skinny hand. I smile with pride and watch Perry scoot past the other folks seated on our pew until she reaches the aisle. But instead of heading for the altar, she yanks Kiki and steers her in the opposite direction, as if she's leaving. I am stunned, embarrassed. Rachel and I lock eyes, exchange shrugs.

When church finally wraps up and we're dismissed, we depart the sanctuary and impatiently press through the throng of folks who are socializing, buying DVDs of the sermon, and standing in line to obtain tickets to an upcoming women's conference. We finally spot Aunt Perry in the front lobby looking standoffish and bored.

"Hey, Aunt Perry," I say and give her a solid hug. "I'm glad you came, I mean that. I hope you enjoyed yourself."

"It was cool," she says and looks at my sister. "Did you have a good time, Rachel? You think you want to come back next Sunday?"

"Um, I know I won't be coming back next Sunday."

"You didn't have a good time?" I interject, shocked and a little hurt by her words.

"I did what I agreed to do. Nothing more, nothing less."

"Dang, Rachel, that sounds horrible," I tell her. "I'm going to pray for you."

"Pray for yourself, Marlene," she says.

"Oh, you two, c'mon. Can't my two nieces at least wait until they're in the parking lot before they start cutting up?"

"We're not cutting up," Rachel speaks up.

"Rachel, if you think I can't detect this chilly attitude coming from you, that's been inside of you since we stepped foot in the place, you need to know you're not talking to a fool," Aunt Perry says. "If you really didn't want to go, you should have said no."

"No, it's not that—"

"Never mind. Let it go. My good mood is quickly turning funky," Perry says and tries to regroup. "Well, I can't talk for you, but at least I got something good out of the message."

"I'm not saying I didn't get anything. It was fine," Rachel says. "It's just that I could have watched this type of thing on TV."

I roll my eyes, grit my teeth. "What did you get out of the message, Aunt Perry?"

"I–I may not have had the guts to walk to the front for prayer," she starts, "but it turned out okay. I had to beg the ushers to let me go 'cause they're real strict about leaving during prayer, but they saw Kiki and allowed us to leave. And when we went to the ladies' room—" she stops and sniffs. "We go in there and do our thing. This wrinkled-up old lady who doesn't even know me, took one look at us and asked real nicely, 'May I pray with you?' I couldn't say anything but 'Yeah, lady.' And she did. And . . . it felt nice. So I learned, God can find you even when you may think you're slick, when you are trying your best to hide from Him . . . even behind a stall."

"That's crazy, but beautiful, Aunt Perry," I say and smile.

"No, seriously," Perry continues, "I really got into some parts of the service; others I'm not too sure about. But overall, it was off the chain."

Rachel steps up to us. "What she said," she murmurs and points at Perry.

We all laugh and know that's about as much as Rachel's going to allow. She may not be speaking what I sense is on the inside, but it's cool. I may not know exactly how she feels, but someone more important than me knows and that's what counts. I feel hopeful, relieved. We leave church, and my aunt drives us back to our apartment. We thank her for the ride and jump out of the car ready to go inside. But Aunt Perry rolls down her window, chatting. Kiki is in the backseat behind her mom. She rolls down her window, too, and stares intently at us.

"My two nieces looked so beautiful, like Serena and Venus, or Beyoncé and Solange. You made me so proud today. And you, Rachel, you shock me sometimes. I want to take a picture of you, show Blinky how much his daughters have grown and matured."

"Uh, I'd love to, but I really have to be going." I glance at my watch.

"Why? What are you in a hurry for?" Aunt Perry asks.

"What am I in a hurry for? Um, I have a lunch engagement. Or is it brunch? I just know I'm going out to eat with someone around two o'clock."

"Oh, Jeff must be coming any minute, huh?" Aunt Perry replies.

I don't say anything.

"It'll only take a second, dang knucklehead girl." With the car still running she grabs her camera phone and hops out the car.

"Go ahead, stand together. Smile for the camera."

"Aunt Perry, this is silly. We're too old for this," Rachel complains.

"You're never too old to document special family moments. So get to grinning because by the time I count to three, whatever comes out in the picture is what Blinky is gonna see."

"I hate you," Rachel pouts.

"And I love you," Aunt Perry says. "One, two . . ."

I grab Rachel by the waist and grin.

"Three," Kiki says from inside the car, "Yayyy," she yells and claps her hands.

The flash goes off. Rachel disengages herself, turns around, and climbs up the flight of stairs to our unit.

"Anyway, thanks for everything. You'll have to join us again one day," I tell my aunt.

"All right, sweetie. Bye. And thanks. Thanks so much. I mean that." Aunt Perry smiles back and returns to her car.

When I get in the apartment, Rachel is in the kitchen with the refrigerator door open. But the fridge is practically empty. We haven't done any major grocery shopping for the week, and the last bit of food we had was eaten during breakfast.

"Oh, well," she says. "I'll just make a peanut butter and jelly sandwich."

"Um, that sounds good."

"No, it doesn't." She turns around and looks at me like I'm crazy.

I don't say anything.

"At least you have a date. Or someone you can share a meal with. Must be nice." Rachel abruptly shuts up, like she's thinking. "Oh, snap, I gotta go check my Yahoo mail." She kicks off her shoes and leaves them in the center of the floor as she races through the living room. After a while I hear these yelps and cackling noises. Curious, I venture down the hall, twist open the doorknob, and enter her room. I can see her sitting at her tiny desk settled in front of the computer, smiling big-time, and peering closely at the monitor.

"Oh, hell no," I hear her say. "He is much too light, much too short, much too everything."

"Girl, what are you in here doing?"

"Um, nothing," she quickly says and laughs, then grows serious. "Well, to be honest, I'm doing something I never, ever thought I'd do before."

"Which is?"

"Cyber love, baby."

"Oh, for real? Dang, Rachel, that's not even your style."

"I know ... But sometimes you gotta do things differently if you want a different outcome. Anyway, I got tons of hits. Hmm, wonder why," she says and giggles to herself. "Girl, this stuff is a trip. Oh my God, look at this dude's profile. Four feet five and two hundred fifty pounds? Plus no picture? You've gotta be kidding me."

She keeps clicking her mouse, making negative sounds, and shaking her head.

"Dang, no one stands out so far. I may have to change up some of my search criteria, 'cause these so-called matches suck. Oh, look at this. This guy looks promising."

I roll my eyes and smile, leave the room so I can freshen up for my outing with Jeff. My hair looks a mess and needs a little bit of touching up. I head to the bathroom and plug in my curling iron.

When I last talked to Jeff, he said he wants to see me today, that we can go grab a bite to eat this afternoon, and then he suggested taking a nice leisurely ride until we reach downtown. He's been talking nonstop about going to Discovery Green, a place he described as the perfect outdoor spot for walking, people watching, and laughing at little kids who are having a ball playing in the water fountain. I told him it sounded great and suggested that he hit me up when he was ready. He said he'd be ready by two.

Holding the curling iron steadily in my hand, I carefully clip some strands of hair and begin winding the wand. After I'm satisfied with my hairstyle, I grease my dry scalp, and swipe some Lookin' Good for Jesus lip balm across my lips. I wait ten minutes, go look out the window, and check my cell phone's voice mail. No new messages. No new anything.

Bored and agitated, I return to Rachel's room to see what she's up to. She's still leaning toward her monitor, sending e-mails. She's laughing and seems thoroughly engaged. That irritates me.

"What's so funny?"

"Huh?" she asks, sounding distracted. "Oh, this one here is a trip. He sent me a flirt, then immediately e-mailed me, gave me his Yahoo address, his IM info, phone number, the works. Jeez, dude is moving a little too fast for me."

"So, what did you sign up—"

"Oops, hold on. Two guys are trying to IM me at the same time. They see I'm online. Oh, shit, I'm in trouble now."

"Hey, Rachel—"

"Shhh, be quiet Marlene. I'm trying . . . okay, he's in Jamaica, New York. Duh, can't he read and understand English? I said in my profile that I'd rather date guys who live no more than five hundred miles away. Oh, he can read, he just can't count, huh?" She starts cracking up. I want to crack her in her mouth. Since when is something on a computer more important than what I've got to say? Hmm, some nerve. I don't care. I got better things to do . . . if only my "better" would hurry his butt up and come on. Maybe I'll call him. No, nope, no. I don't want it to seem like I'm desperate, checking up on him. I gotta act as if I haven't noticed he's not here. I gotta do something to keep busy, or else I'll go lose my cool. Rachel interrupts my train of thought.

"Oh, Marlene, okay, you gotta check out this guy. He's—"

"I don't want to hear it, Rachel."

"But hold on. His screen name is OldSkool214, but he says to call him Smoky. He claims he's really feeling me, my profile, and just wants to get to know me better. He says he loves my photo, but would love to see who the real me is, behind the gorgeous face and body. And the best thing is he's local."

I frown. "He sounds like a nut bag."

"Girl, stop. I am a little curious."

"Curiosity killed the—"

"Jeez, now two other guys are trying to IM me. I haven't even replied to the first two yet. Goodness. Who has time for this?"

"Why'd you get on the site if you're not going to do what you're expected to do, Rachel? Huh?"

Rachel finally stops clicking her mouse and turns to stare at me with a puzzled expression etched on her face. "Why are you still here?" she asks and casually glances at the wall clock. "I thought you would have skedaddled with what's-his-face."

"Apparently, what's-his-face is running somewhat late."

"And you hate waiting on folks." She cackles. "Jeff had better have a damn good excuse for making a sista wait on his ass."

She makes a "that's a shame" noise in her throat. I settle on her bed, then lie back on the comforter, and let my eyes wander to the ceiling. I am starting to feel like the people I see at church. Well-packaged on the outside, but the outside veils what's on the inside. When it comes to Jeff's and my relationship, I have my pride, but what am I getting in exchange for it? When you lose pride, you start doing things you never imagined you'd do.

"I think I am having second thoughts about all this."

"Wh–what?" Rachel screeches.

"I mean, he's a good man and all, but sometimes he can be . . ."

"What? Go ahead. Say it." She turns off her monitor and fully swivels her chair and gives me her complete attention.

"He's not always respectful and considerate. Maybe it's just me. Maybe he's just being a man. You know they're thinkers more than feelers. So I can accept that—"

"But?"

"But as women, why do we always have to be understanding when it comes to guys' flaws? It's like they're born to be a certain way. Insensitive at times. Self-centered. Rude. And we are forced to accept men just the way they are."

"Preach, girl."

"No, really. How many guys start off great? They act sweet and have great attention to detail . . . They're always on time. They pay for dates—"

"Jeff doesn't pay for dates anymore?"

I stare at her, think. "He still does from time to time."

"But."

"He's asked to borrow money. And he has me doing strange monetary transactions."

"Nooo. Dang, girl, asking to borrow money is asking a bit much. Jeff's not rich, but he has enough. What's he need your money for?"

"I was hoping . . . you'd be able to tell me," I say with a twinge of sadness. "You know him way better than I do."

"Jeez, girl. I dunno. I am trying to forget him, trying to move on, and now you are asking me to psychoanalyze his actions? Give you advice about my ex? That takes a lot of nerve, Marlene."

"I was only asking—"

"You may be asking the wrong person."

"Okay, then forget it, Rachel. Just forget I brought it up. But according to what you've recently told me, you are over him. You couldn't care less what he's doing. So if that's true, what's the harm in talking to me?"

"As much as I hate hearing myself admit this, I'm Jeff's ex, dummy—"

"I am not dumb; don't ever call me that again."

"Dummy."

I sit up and pounce at her like a tigress. I ball my fingers into a solid fist and swing at her head like it's a volley ball. But Rachel is quick; she jumps from the chair, dodging and ducking me in one swift move. She stands back a few inches away with her feet spaced apart, hands drawn to her side.

I catch my breath, laugh at how goofy she looks. "Oh, so you think you're one of Charlie's Angels now, huh? Which one?"

"Fuck you, Marlene."

"Rachel, stop the profanity. Jeez, do you have any respect for the church?"

"Oh, like you do. That's what I hate about you, girl. You're a hypocrite who can't see her own self. Look in the mirror, Marlene. Open up your eyes, look in a fucking mirror, and see yourself for who you really are, not who you tell yourself you are, but who you really are."

I want to swing at her again, but I lack the energy, focus. My mind is too split to do any harm to her. Plus she's not the true reason for my attitude. It's way past two-thirty, almost three. Jeff could have called to explain his whereabouts. Is that too much to ask? What's so hard about showing consideration to the one you claim you like? If this is how he treats people he likes, how does he treat those he doesn't like? Or maybe I'm overreacting. Guys are set up so different from women that he probably doesn't realize his tardiness irks me. He says he cares about me, so no way he'd be doing this stuff on purpose. And that's fine. But why is he becoming slack lately? Women always want to know why. But how many times are we given a suitable answer? I wish I knew.

RACHEL

Bastard of the Year

My *mama once said* that if you want revenge on someone who's done you wrong, don't do anything. She said the wrongs that people commit will always catch up to them, and the only thing I'm required to do is sit back and witness the big payback. So when I see Marlene look so despondent about Jeff's recent behavior, the first thing I do is think about my mother's advice. Could this be what she's referring to? If it is, there really is a God. I never imagined that she, the one who seems so crazy and boldly in love with Jeff, would start to have doubts about the guy.

So while she's here trying to get me to answer her silly little questions, I feel torn. One part of me wants to jump up and down, pump my fists in the air, and scream "hallelujah." I want to laugh loud and hard like I'm in the comedy club. Giggle right in her face and tell the girl, "You're getting just what your ass deserves." The other part of me, the wiser part, says not to do anything too over the top. Shut my mouth, hush up with the I-told-you-so stuff, and simply wait it out. Let Marlene talk. My job is to listen and gain as much information as possible.

But because I am the way that I am, my solution is to settle for a combination of both.

We're still in my bedroom. I've just called her a hypocrite. But she doesn't seem fazed or bothered by my words. I wonder if she's losing the will to fight.

"Marlene, are you okay? You have this strange look on your face."

"I'm not surprised. I think it's only because I am so hungry. I didn't eat much breakfast, trying to save my appetite for this afternoon." She takes her hand, makes wide circles on her belly as she strokes its roundness.

"Forgive me for asking, Marlene, but what's stopping you from picking up a phone and calling the guy?"

"Oh, Rachel. I hate when I am waiting, and I give in and call. I just don't like doing it."

"Ha, better you than me."

"Why are you saying that?"

"Fuck Jeff. I mean, really . . . it's just making me mad hearing you talk this way. It's not like it's a once-in-a-lifetime event that's going on this afternoon, and like if you aren't able to go, then you're really missing out on something big."

"Like Discovery Green."

"Oh, well, yeah, but still. That's not about anything, either." Actually, that hurts. I remember asking Jeff to take me there, too, but something would always come up, so we never got to go.

"So what would you do if you were in my shoes?"

I smile and think about her question. If she only knew that if I were in her shoes, so many things would be different. If things had turned out the way they should have, and we were able to resolve any premarital concerns, Jeff and I would probably be headed down the aisle by now. She'd be my maid of honor. I'd be on the road to perhaps the best times of my life. Getting married, doing the honeymoon, setting up the Mr. and Mrs. Jeffrey Williams household.

None of these very real alternatives would be occurring now. We wouldn't be having this conversation, and I definitely would have no reason to be signing up with some freaking online dating site. So her question is both pointless . . . and cruel.

"Marlene, I think you should either shit or get off the pot."

"Eww."

"Stop it, girl, get real for once in your life. You get annoyed at me for cussing, yet the guy you're attracted to also cusses sometimes. Or had you overlooked that part of him? He's no better than me."

"Okay, Rachel, you are right. But I guess it's a little different because he's a guy, the man I'm attracted to, and you're—"

"Just your sister? So that automatically gives you the right to be stricter with me than with the guy you're sleeping with?"

"Please. I get it, okay? I'll try to be easier on you . . . Rachel." She starts vigorously massaging her forehead, and I can sense her weariness. I actually feel sorry for Marlene. But before I give in to the temptation of going to pat her on the back, I remember the awful things she's said to me lately. How she didn't care about my feelings when I pleaded with her to leave Jeff alone. Her only priority was Marlene Draper. And I decide then to not let my heart grow soft. Let her suffer a little longer. By ignoring my wishes, she's invited herself to fully experience any misery that comes with dating your sister's ex.

"Okay, let me just think a bit," Marlene speaks up. "It's been an hour now. No Jeff, no calls. I wonder if something bad has happened. He deals with some shady characters sometimes. His tenants can be hostile. And I know that he's angry at a couple of tenants who haven't paid rent. He wants to evict them. Maybe that's what he's doing right now. Trying to make that paper . . . for me."

I sit back and listen to Marlene come up with all kinds of excuses, feeble attempts to cover her man's misconduct. Yep, she really does love him. Maybe it's my cue to step out of the way. A woman in love is like a blind person walking down the middle of the street. Everyone in the blind person's path will have to move out of his way.

Alita, London, and I are laughing our asses off. It's midweek, a few days after I agreed to meet OldSkool214, aka Smoky. He and I swapped dozens of e-mails on Sunday, then chatted on the phone yesterday. And now my girls and I are extra hyped because I told Smoky I'd be happy to meet him in a public place for a cup of coffee. So we agreed upon a Starbucks that's on Westheimer and Fondren.

The girls are sitting in my car while I sit outdoors at a green metal round table. And when Smoky arrives, I immediately know it's him. Very few black folks come to this spot. And if they do it's usually going to be early in the morning, on their way to work. But it's almost eight at night. And this black guy pulls up in a chocolate-colored Jaguar. Old but classy. Dude takes his time getting out of the car. I can see him looking at himself in his rearview. Eventually, when he emerges, he walks so slow it looks like he's floating on air. He's wearing a black T-shirt with white letters that say, "It's Hard Out Here for a Republican." And his blue jeans are crisply ironed.

I see his eyes moving around, like he's looking for the girl he saw in the profile. I wave at him. He sees me, hesitates, waves back.

"Smoky?"

He looks around and behind him even though we're the only two people in the café area.

"Hello, Smoky." I rise up and smile.

"Do I know you?"

"We met online."

He looks confused. "Okay?"

It's hard not to laugh. "How has your day gone so far?"

He stares at me. I point at the seat next to me. He pulls out the chair, still peering at me, and slowly sits down.

"My day has gone all right."

The moment is awkward. I feel like getting up and leaving.

But he takes one last look at me and slumps in his seat, pulls out a pack of cigarettes. Holds them toward me. I shake my head. He shrugs and lights up one.

"I didn't know that you smoked. Your profile said you're a nonsmoker."

"Things change."

I stiffen. Wait for him to talk.

"What did you say your name was again?"

"I've never given my name, but my screen name is HoneyBrownTX."

"Oh, all right," he says, but there's no flicker of recognition on his face. He starts inhaling from his cigarette.

"How long have you been on the dating site?" I ask.

"Two years, five months."

I gasp. "Why so long? Doesn't that cost a lot of money?"

"It takes that long to find who you're feeling, and who's feeling you, you know what I'm saying?"

"I can imagine."

Soon the smoke from his smoking habit nearly causes me to choke. The air is thick with the stifling smell of marijuana. I stare at him in disbelief, but he keeps taking a drag on his "cigarette."

For the next several minutes, I try to ignore the smoke, and I ask him frivolous questions. He politely answers. Even though he's calm, pleasant, and seems nonthreatening, I can never truly relax. Something about him bothers me.

I cough and clear my throat, glance at my watch. "Well, it's almost that time."

"Oh, yeah, you got to go to your second job, right? You watch some kids who live in River Oaks?"

With a frozen smile plastered on my face, I nod emphatically. "You remembered. You have an excellent memory, Smoky."

I hop up so fast my purse falls to the ground. My leather checkbook falls out, and my driver's license photo is showing through the clear plastic sleeve.

Smoky says, "Let me get that." He reaches for my checkbook, glances at the photo, stares at me briefly, then hands it over.

"Well, anyway, like you said, I gotta be going so I can babysit all those kids. Nice meeting you. Good-bye."

I don't wait for him to say anything. I just start walking east down Westheimer, never looking back. My cell rings. It's him. I ignore the call. The cell rings again.

"Hey, Alita. Y'all see me. Come get me. When it comes to this Internet dating stuff, it's time for me to go back to the drawing board."

Alita's car pulls up next to me minutes later, and I climb in the backseat.

"You sure know how to pick 'em—"

"Don't start, Alita."

London says, "Now we know why he wants you to call him 'Smoky.' "

"Yeah," I say, blushing, "I should have read between the lines. Anyway, he's definitely coming off my favorites. And I'm blocking him from e-mailing me."

"You do what you need to do, girl," Alita says.

I sigh, feeling disappointed. "I know I just got on the site, but if this is how it's going to be, I'm not sure I'll ever connect with the right kind of man."

"Stop stressing," London says. "You're there to have fun, but sure, you want to make that love connection, too. You're bound to go through some undesirables first before you meet the cream-of-the-crop type guys."

"Hmm, I hope you're right."

"Change your search criteria, girl. Don't settle. Be specific." Alita lectures me like she is the online dating pro or something.

"But won't that limit my opportunities?"

"Only one way to find out," Alita says.

They drop me off at home. Once I get inside and settled in my bedroom, I immediately log on to the Internet. I delete five messages that Smoky has sent me in the past half hour. The fact that he didn't even comment on my appearance and how I look nothing like my profile photo really shows me he isn't serious at all. He'll date anything, anybody, no standards. Well, I don't wanna be that girl. I am not interested in meeting someone as long as he's a member of the opposite sex and that's it. No way.

I remember the day I met Jeff. I remember feeling and looking fantastic. I just got my hair done and had a fresh cut and perm. I sported a pair of my favorite jeans and a Tennessee Titans jersey signed by Vince Young. You could walk into any room in that two-story house and you'd find a stunning looking woman. Half the women were college educated or professionals in their field. I recognized this other distinctive woman because she's always appearing in *Houston Style Magazine* touting her successful Cajun restaurant. So even though competition was fierce, that day I just wanted to relax and enjoy myself. I was comfortably seated in the great room on this huge couch that could fit twenty people. The ceilings were fifteen feet high, there was a sixty-five-inch flat-screen television, a wet bar, and plenty of buffalo wings and sauce, chips and dip, cold bottles of beer, and other goodies.

One guy saw me, sat next to me, immediately introduced himself. I felt flattered that he'd single me out. But when a taller, more well-endowed woman entered the room, talking loud and smiling, the guy who made me feel good made me feel bad when he got up and struck up a conversation with the Next Woman. I tried not to let his rejection bother me, but when the couple started dancing and there wasn't any music playing, I had enough. I quietly excused myself and sought a spot that was less busy. I noticed a room down the hallway with some French doors and decided to go in there. Soothing music played on a radio. I sat on the sofa, soon fell asleep. I woke up when I heard someone talking to me.

"Hey, there, you look so adorable I didn't want to wake you. But they're about to serve dessert . . ."

I opened my eyes and blinked. "Who are you?"

"Jeff. Jeffrey Williams." He extended his hand. And when I extended mine he shook it but held my fingers tight in his grasp while he continued introducing himself. I felt so at ease with him. I sat up. Listened. Asked questions. Laughed at his jokes. He asked if I minded if he sat. I didn't. And we talked for an hour, not thinking about dessert or who was winning the football game.

I felt an odd sense of pleasure by the way Jeff's eyes penetrated mine. His lips were thick and curled when he smiled. He made me feel warm, gooey, and sexy. I flirted with him, too, knowing full well that it might be the first and last conversation I ever had with this man. But it didn't matter. I went for it, not making a fool of myself or seeming desperate for attention. I felt fully comfortable being who I was, Rachel Merrell. Not a beauty queen, no college degree, not the owner of a successful business. Just an ordinary girl, with an ordinary life, who wanted to experience good things with genuine people.

By the time the evening ended, Jeff had asked for my phone number, and I was happy that he knew my birthday, favorite color, all-time-favorite movies, restaurants, and a lot about my background. I felt safe with him, an extraordinary thing to realize when you've just met someone. And even though, ultimately, our ending turned out worse than our beginning, I want another chance at love. I don't care how many failed relationships I experience, I hold on to the hope that there's someone special out there designed just for me. A man who treats me with kindness and respect. Someone who makes me laugh, listens to my troubles, and shares my enthusiasm for life and love. I've learned so much in the past month or so. I'm ready for the promise of true love again.

I log back on to the SoulSingles site and start clicking on the criteria, making sure that it will help me to find the exact type of guy I want.

I set up new parameters and do another search. It's amazing how dozens of profiles pop up. Yayyy me. But as I click through them one by one, discouragement fills my heart. Men who can't spell ("She must have a *since* of humor"). Shallow guys ("Big booty/dime pieces only"). Or, worst of all, men who refuse to fill out the entire profile. Those guys aren't serious. They can be compared to people looking for a job but instead of fully completing the application, they simply write: see résumé. Not impressive.

But one profile catches my eye. First, it has a photo of a giant teddy bear sitting behind the wheel of a Cadillac convertible. That makes me smile. *It seems he's got a sense of humor.* Second, I love that he considers himself a workaholic, doesn't visit bars, has no kids, and says he's super confident. His screen name is COCKY247.

I decide to send him a flirt. Tell him I saw his profile. Let him know I think we might get along and should chat sometime. I push back from my desk and decide to chill out in the living room. I am in the mood to watch a good romantic comedy. Marlene is looking stiff and sitting at the dining room table, tapping her hand against her purse. Her eyes look vacant while she stares into space.

"Hey," I say. "What's up?"

"Not a whole lot."

"I hope you aren't still waiting on him."

"What? Oh, well, he apologized for the other day." Marlene was so upset at Jeff for not showing up or calling Sunday afternoon. I had to talk her out of calling him and leaving a nasty voice mail. I told her to just leave it alone. And she did.

"Oh, yeah, when?"

"Monday. He explained that he's been sick and was under some medication that makes him drowsy. He was knocked out all afternoon and didn't wake up till two in the morning."

"Hmm, I remember how when Jeff would get sick he would really be down for the count."

"That's kind of how he explained it to me. So I accepted his apology. He said he'll make it up to me. In a special way."

"I see," I tell her. "What's he gonna do?"

"Wouldn't say. Like it's a big surprise."

"Figures." I stop and think aloud. "I cannot believe I'm having a conversation with you about my ex and I'm not freaking out like normal."

"Me, either." She looks almost apologetic. "Maybe Jeff and I being together is fate. That the reason you're not so hung up over us anymore is because you two were never meant to be."

Even though I feel I'm getting over him, her words sting. "Um, I'm not sure about all that. I know he loved me. I loved him. Our partnership was real, even if it didn't work out."

"Yeah, but—"

"Anyway, if you don't mind, I want to pop in a DVD."

"You're not bothering me, Rachel."

Right then, I hear a loud knock on our front door. It's twilight by now. I go to the door and look through the peephole. But it's too dark to see clearly what's happening outside. So I unlock the door and open it. A flicker of light captures my attention. I step out on the balcony. The cool air feels good against my skin. Jeff is standing near the railing, a huge smile on his face. It's obvious he's made a table setting for two on our balcony. I notice some empty Olive Garden bags neatly folded on one of the wrought iron chairs. There's spaghetti and meatballs, Greek salad, a basket of bread sticks, and a bottle of wine with two wineglasses.

"Wh–what's this for?"

"Where's that cute older sister of yours?" he asks, his voice filled with excitement.

I flinch but point toward the door. "In there."

"Go get her."

I stare at him, irritated by his pushiness.

"Pretty please, with sugar on top?"

"Okay," I cheerfully tell him, but inside I am furious.

I bounce back inside the apartment. "Hey, Marlene,

there's someone outside waiting for you. And it looks like you won't need your purse or your money . . . this time."

"Why you—"

"Just go," I tell her with more annoyance in my voice than I want her to hear.

She gives me a puzzled look but does what I tell her. I watch her go outside on the balcony. She squeals in delight. And there's no doubt in my mind that she's grabbed him and kissed him. I return to my room, no longer caring to watch a stupid and pointless DVD.

I pick up my cell phone and call my mama. "Hey, can I ask you a question?" I say when she answers the phone.

"Sure, Little Bit."

"How long does it take to get over a man who you loved?"

"Some men, it won't take long at all. It's either because they treated you so bad toward the end that you know ain't no way you could possibly put up with a man like that. Or it may take you a lifetime to get over him. Your love for that man runs so deep that you love him even if you can't be with him anymore. You never stop thinking of him. Even if you go on to be with other people, he's always in your heart."

"I see." I sigh. "I don't know how to feel sometimes, Mama." I bite my bottom lip. "And I may act strong, act like I don't care, but . . ."

"I know, baby girl. I know. It hurts so much when it's right there in your face. Some people have no class. Your sister, I swear to God."

"I'm trying to be a good girl. I don't want to lay hands on my sister anymore. I am sick of cursing her out. I am trying to do right, Mama. But what has it gotten me? I'm still all alone." I gasp and catch my breath, trying to hold back a sob. "I'm all alone searching for a movie to look at to fill up my time, and she . . . he brought food over for them to eat . . . on a balcony. Mama? Do you know how that makes me . . . ?"

"It's like the fucking movie is playing out in front of you, instead of on the TV. Damn shame. That Jeff is the bastard of the year, yes he is. I don't like to say stuff like this around you, because I know you're still stupidly sweet on him. But . . ."

"Mama, it's as if I never truly knew him. He's not acting like the man I used to know. I don't like the man he's become, but I miss the man he used to be. The one I fell in love with. It sounds weird, but that's the only way I can explain it."

"Well, if it helps any, think less of who he used to be, but focus more on who Jeff is right now, this very second. How is the man acting now? Is he respectful? Grounded? Loving? Loyal? What he's doing now is way more important than how great he was when you first met. But, the funny thing is, the man he seemed to be in the beginning really wasn't him." Mama sounds stunned, like she's discovering horrible truths about Jeff herself.

"Hmm, it's awful, unreal." I nod and wipe some hot tears that slide down my cheeks. I don't want to cry. But I don't know how else to deal with the hurt that lives inside of me. Hurt I've never fully processed. "Mama, I guess I know what you mean. It's like Jeff is showing his true nature." I sniff and wipe my nose. "And if that's how he really is, could I have truly been in love, or was I just deceiving myself?"

"Ha," Mama yelps like she's reflecting on ancient memories. "God knows I swore up and down I loved this man or that one. At the time he's all I could think about, couldn't imagine living a day without hearing his voice. But then, when the relationship is over, I look at his picture and don't feel a thing. The sun doesn't rise and fall on the guy anymore. And I question why all the love I used to have went away. Where is the love that I swore would last forever?"

"That's how I feel, Mama. And that's why I wonder if my relationship is all I imagined it to be. It's what I've thought about when it came to me and Jeff. I still don't know the truth."

"Time will tell, Little Bit. Time always tells."

Mama and I talk a few more minutes. I promise to drive out and check on her this week. "Yes," she says. "Do that. I need you. Been wanting to see you in person." It would do me good to help her with housecleaning and other chores that have been neglected.

Right now I could use something to drink. My throat feels dry, like I've been sleeping with my mouth open all night. Plus my tongue feels thick and gummy, probably because of my crying spell. When I enter the kitchen, the lights are off in the living room. The DVD player is running. I can see the movie *Love Jones* flashing across the big-screen TV. Marlene's huge butt is sitting directly on Jeff's lap, her huge arm snugly wrapped around his neck. They look happy and relaxed on a corner of the couch. I notice sounds of lips smacking against each other every couple of seconds as they watch the movie. Bile rises to the top of my throat. I hold it in. I rush to the refrigerator and pour a glass of cold lemonade and return to my room as soon as I can.

"I gotta do something, gotta get out of here," I say aloud. I arch my neck and chug down the whole glass of lemonade in a few gulps. It tastes sweet, cold, and good.

Something tells me to go check my SoulSingles account.

"Hey now," I say to myself. COCKY247 has sent me a flirt and two e-mails. I see that he sent these to me as soon as I sent him a flirt a while ago. I like his responsiveness. His flirt is pretty standard. His e-mail isn't.

Hello HoneyBrownTX. Your screen name is pretty. Let me cut to the chase. I've been on this site for three months. Sure, I've met a couple of women here and there. Things didn't work out. No hard feelings. But there's something about your photo. I love the fire in your eyes. And your smile makes me want to get to know you for myself, so I can make you smile. I am an honest, hardworking black man who loves life and enjoys experiencing good things (when I get the time). I am not in a serious relationship. No baby mama drama. No priors. Sound good so far? Enough about me. I want to hear more from you. Oh, I've attached my photo so you can decide if you want to meet me in person or not. Please be kind. It's not my best photo (plus I look way more handsome in person). You can call me Denzel. Cocky247 is just an attention-getter (smile).

I decide to review his profile again. We have so much in common. He likes going out for long rides in the country and wants to travel to Europe. He loves music, the same artists as me (T.I., The.Dream, Ciara, and Rihanna). And he loves the NBA (favorite team: the Spurs).

"This is sounding kinda good here." I pick up my cell and speed dial Alita.

"What's up, Hardly Berry? Is London with you? I want her to do something for me."

"Yep, she's here. I'll put you on speaker."

"Yo, Mama, what's going on?" London says.

"Girl, I am sitting here at my computer, and there's this guy . . . I am really feeling the things he's telling me. His words are like poetry. I want you to go meet him for me."

"No problem. When?"

"Don't know. I haven't written him back yet. When's a good time for you?"

"Friday night is cool. Um, let's say dinner around seven?"

"Okay, but hold up, I gotta check his schedule." I laugh and feel excited yet mischievous.

"I want to do this," I continue saying, "but what if he's my dream man? If he knows I posted a fake photo, he may not want to have anything to do with me. I am scared of messing up my chances."

"So what are you thinking of doing?" Alita asks. "Do you want to come clean now? Or come clean during y'alls fuck session?" She bursts out laughing.

"Oh, you've got jokes, huh?" I say, irritated. "Please, Alita, it's not funny. I'm having a serious anxiety attack. I can feel my shoulders tensing up." I take a deep breath. "But I want to do this. And I pray that he's a hundred times better than weed-smoking Smoky."

"So true," London says. "Anyway, so what's this guy look like so I'll know who to look for at our date?"

"Oh, snap," I yelp. "He sent me an attachment, but I was so busy reading his profile that I forgot to take a look. Let me open it now."

I click on the photo and wait for the picture to upload.

I gape. Stand to my feet. Hold my fingers to my neck. Gasp.

"Damn, girl," Alita says. "Is he *that* fine? You sound like you're about to faint."

"I am," I manage to tell her. "The photo on this guy's profile . . . is Jeff."

I sit down, nervously run my fingers through my hair. "What's he doing on this man's . . . Maybe he's doing a friend a favor and letting him use his photo, like us?" It's more like a question than a statement. Because my mind is zooming in so many different directions, none of what I'm thinking makes sense.

"Mother . . ." Alita says. "Are you serious? Jeff is on the down-low on a dating site?"

London starts giggling in the background. "Ooo wee, we're going to have some fun, ya'll. Set up the date, Rachel. Set it up. He doesn't know me. I'll fix his ass."

"Wait, ladies," I tell her and start whispering. "Check this out. Oh my God. Jeff is a few feet away in my living room, probably licking Marlene's toes. Yuck! I hate to think where his mouth has been last." I stand up, pace the room. "What should I do? Tell me," I plead.

"I think you should answer him like everything is normal," Alita tells me. "Set up the fucking date. And I don't care how hard it is for you, do not talk to Jeff and let him know you're aware of the shit he's trying to pull."

— 14 —

MARLENE

There's Something You Need to Know About Jeff

"*You feel so good* I wanna bite you," Jeff tells me. His middle finger is moving back and forth in my vagina. And it's very juicy down there, so wet I can hear swishing sounds.

"Oh, Jeff, stop it."

"No, I can't stop, Beautiful Girl." He thrusts his finger deeper inside me. It hurts, but I like this type of pain. My eyes roll in the back of my head. "Let's go," I moan. "Right now."

He twists and turns his finger and develops a back and forth rhythm. My hips rock with him trying to match his pace. He slowly removes his finger from inside me and stands up. He reaches toward me and hoists me up in his arms. I feel like a kid being carried by her father.

"Oh my God," I say laughing but trying not to be too loud. "You're shocking me, Jeff. That's what I like about you, love about you." I rest my head against his warm neck and enjoy the feel of his skin against mine.

"You love me?"

I nod, then move my face toward his lips and kiss his mouth and his chin.

"That tickles," he complains, "but keep going."

I laugh and kiss him again. It feels so good to be with Jeff right now. He's been pulling out all the stops tonight. I love how romantic he is. He surprised me with dinner on the balcony from my favorite restaurant. He made me open my mouth and fed me delicious spaghetti. I shivered when he slowly inserted that fork in my mouth. I could taste his tongue and his body right then and there. He didn't even let me pick up my own bread sticks, said that he wanted to take care of everything. He poured me a tall glass of wine. And he entwined his hand around mine and we toasted.

"To us," he proclaimed.

"To us," I repeated and took a sip of the best wine I've ever tasted.

We relaxed on the balcony, him looking me deep in my eyes in a way he's never looked at me before. And it's easy to predict that this man will be in my bed tonight. But it's getting late. I have to get up early to go to work. Jeff's been so busy lately, working hard. But we need this. I deserve this.

Jeff drops me on the bed and cracks up when the mattress bounces and the bed squeaks. "It's like sailing in a boat on the ocean," he says, winking. "Hey, don't go anywhere."

He stares at me and walks backward until he reaches my bedroom door. He secures the lock without taking his eyes off me. It's like he's in a zone. A love zone.

"May I undress you?" he asks.

I nod and wait for him to come to me.

He removes his leather jacket. I can hear his e-mail buzzer going off on his cell. He picks up his device, pushes a button, and the buzzing sound ceases. I want to melt even more. When a man is with a woman and he turns off his cell phone, you know he wants her undivided attention. And right now he's letting me know that nothing is more important than the time we're about to spend together.

"You're so sexy," he tells me. "I'll bet you haven't heard that too often, have you?"

"I dunno." I shrug, not trying to remember what other men have said to me in the past. Who cares? All I care about is spending time with Jeffrey Williams. He possesses a magnetism that's difficult to ignore. Even when I've gotten upset with him for being inconsiderate, and I tell myself I won't brush aside his mess anymore, those feelings disappear each time he calls. He starts off calling me sweet names that make my ears tingle. Then he apologizes: "I'm sorry, baby." He promises he'll do better. Then he talks about the future and what he wants us to do together. Instead of screaming because I'm mad, I want to scream with happiness.

And having him here right now, in my bed, is part of my secret fantasy.

"Hey, Beautiful Girl, how'd you get so beautiful?"

"I dunno. From my parents?"

"Shhh, be quiet. I need to concentrate."

Jeff removes a long-sleeved shirt and drops it to the floor. I sit back in bed against several pillows. Oh my God, oh my goodness. I can't wait to hold him in my arms.

He smiles, nods. Bends down and unties his shoelaces and kicks off his shoes.

"You see this?" he asks, looking down at himself. The front of his pants looks like an ear of corn is stuffed inside.

"That you? Or a sock?"

"All me, baby. And you got me in this position."

"Uh oh, are you upset about it?" I tease.

"Very. You're going to have to be punished. But trust me, it's going to hurt me more than it's going to hurt you."

"Okay, Daddy." I gasp and scoot back in the bed.

I love how he's making me wait. The longer I wait the hotter it feels between my legs. I am so focused on Jeff that I barely remember my sister is right across the hallway. Part of me hopes that she's fallen asleep and stays asleep. Another part of me wonders if she can hear us.

Jeff unzips his blue jeans. He has on a tight pair of briefs. I clamp my legs together because my legs are trembling.

"You like that?" he asks. "You want this?"

He slides in bed and reaches for my nipples, caressing them through my bra. I close my eyes and move my mouth until it finds his. He opens his mouth and inserts his tongue deep. I love how Jeff cradles me in his arms while kissing me. It feels like he loves me. I moan and squirm. His tongue is so long I feel like choking. And his lips are so thick. I place my mouth over his bottom lip and suck on it. His hands move down my thighs, stroking me with fervor. We kiss and explore each other's mouths. I come up for air.

"You about ready to turn off that light?" I ask.

"Let's do it with the lights on. It makes things more intense."

"Maybe for you."

"Why are you looking like that? You don't want me to see your body?"

"I just feel more comfortable in the dark."

"But I want to see and feel what I'm getting, you got it?"

I smile but wonder why he insists on having his way so much. He stares down at me and breaks into a grin, like he's admiring me. I unsnap my bra.

"Hey, that tat looks good, Beautiful Girl. I love that you had so much faith in me, and in us. Your tat proves it. M and J. Marlene and Jeff. That means a lot to me. Sometimes I don't realize how good I have it."

"Why do you say that?"

"Because, woman. I hustle so much that it takes a lot for me to slow down and think about my life. To really count up my blessings and know good things are happening. I like that you're down for me, Marlene. You don't bitch and moan and kick me to the curb when I screw up."

"Oh, you're talking about how you've slipped lately?"

"But, see, you understand how it is for a man. We are under a lot of pressure. I have all these mortgages to pay. Folks are acting funny with their money. The economy is starting to suck. And people don't always want to do right. But when I know my girl is holding it down for me, that makes me feel like I can relax a little. You get what I'm saying?" His eyes look sincere, and I am glad that I haven't gone off on him like I've been tempted to do when he's gotten me upset.

"Jeff, all I ask is that you be respectful. Tell me what's going on so I won't have to wonder and worry."

"You never have to worry. The answer will always be the same." He looks down at me and kisses my nipple. "I'm working."

He kisses my stomach. "I'm running after tenants."

He kisses me on the lips and the kiss lasts longer than normal. "And I'm thinking about the next time I can be with you."

"It all sounds good, but my mama told me to always watch what a man says. She says you know he's real if his actions line up with his words."

"Your mother is always saying a lot, but what does she have to show for all her words? You told me what happened to her. How she let your dad pop her upside her head."

"Hey, now wait a minute—"

"Hold on, you look so cute when you're mad. I'm just telling the truth. Most women who nag out men are women who don't have a man, or they're having big-time problems with their man. A woman in a truly fulfilled relationship is not going to constantly give all these warnings about men."

"Yeah, but—"

"But nothing. Be quiet, or else I'm going to put something on you." He pulls off his underwear and reaches for his pants pocket. Retrieves a condom packet and places it on the bed next to us.

"I love you, but I'm not ready to have a baby with you or anybody else."

I sit up. "What do you mean with anybody else? Who else is there?"

He pushes me back down on the bed and gets on top of me. He starts kissing me on my neck and running his hands through my hair. I try to move my legs so he falls off, but he stays on me, locking me down with his arms and legs.

"Don't get away from me. I've been waiting all day for this. I've missed you, Marlene. Got it? Now lay back and relax so your man can get you off."

Oh, wow, sounds intriguing. I forget about what I'm mad at, and I lay back in anticipation. He moves his head down until his face is between my legs.

"Are you sure you don't want to turn off the lights?"

"Shhh." He sticks out his tongue and starts licking and kissing my vagina.

"Oh my goodness," I gasp.

"You taste deliciously sweet. Like a lollipop." He continues going down on me. I grab a pillow and place it on top of my face. I pump my hips, twisting and turning, trying to lock in that good feeling so it can last as long as possible. He's only the second man ever to go down on me. And Jeff is so good at this I gotta think twice. My mama said if you can find a man who has a Ph.D. in eating twat, then make sure that man is at the top of your list. And you'd better not ever tell another woman how good he is at eating you out. It'll be like a neighborhood dog letting the other dogs know where he can get free food. Every other dog would be trying to hang out at that spot, too. So I forget about any issue I've wanted to discuss with Jeff. I enjoy having him between my legs, making me moan, shake, and tremble with indescribable pleasure.

"Oh, Jesus," I start screaming, my lips pressed into the pillow that covers my face.

"Are you coming, Marlene?"

"Yes, Jeff, yes."

"I can't hear you. Marlene, pull that pillow off your face and let me know who's making you come."

I snatch the pillow off my face and tilt my head. "Jeffrey Williams is making me come. Ahh, ahh, ahhh." I yell so loud that at first Jeff looks startled. Then his eyes enlarge. I keep screaming and jerking so much I feel him beginning to smile like he's proud of how loud he made me scream.

"Damn, I didn't know it was that good. You been holding in some stress, baby?"

"Ohhh, Jeff, mmm." My hands tremble like I'm standing outside butt naked in freezing temperature. "Hold me, please," I moan.

"Wait a sec," he says. Jeff hops up and goes to my bedroom door, opens it, peeps out, then jumps back in the bed. The door is still open. He's propped next to me, looking down at me and grinning with unbelievable joy. I guess he's proud because he made me come so violently.

"Let's keep going. You ready for round two?"

"Jeff, you gotta be kidding."

"No, Beautiful Girl. You inspire me."

"You wear me out. I'm sleepy."

"Really? Damn. Brother got skills, huh?"

"Mad skills, Jeff. I feel sticky and wet, though, like I want to take a quick shower."

"O—okay. I'll be waiting for you right here."

It takes me a few seconds to muster up enough strength to even sit up. I want to run and tell someone about how Jeff and I have fantastic sex, but who can I tell? Not a soul. This is something that I'll have to keep to myself.

"Need some help?"

I nod.

Jeff grabs me by the shoulders and pulls me into a sitting position.

"Damn girl, you're making my head swell. And I'm not talking about the head on my shoulders."

"Oh, Jeff," I say, blushing. "You're a nasty man."

"But you're nastier than me. Looks like a raw egg was just cracked and opened on your privates."

"What?"

"It's really nasty looking down there. Go get in the shower." He hops out of bed and goes straight to his PDA. He presses a button and I hear it powering up. Several rings chime out one after another.

"Damn, who's been calling, e-mailing?" He frowns. "Must be tenants."

He stands up and absentmindedly slides on his underwear while reading a message at the same time.

"Hey, why are you getting dressed?" I pout. He ignores me. "After I shower, don't you want to cuddle and go another round like you said?"

He sits back on the other side of the bed. Reads his PDA. Starts smiling and talking to himself. Frustrated, I roll out of the bed and walk to him. Put my hands on my hips and clear my throat. He acts like I'm not even there. His eyes look glassy and bright. I reach out and snatch his phone from his hand.

He has seventeen Yahoo messages. I try to click on a message from a HoneyBrownTX, but Jeff rips the phone from out my hand.

"What the hell is your problem? Never mess with a black man's phone. That's like messing with my money. With my car."

"With your woman?" I ask with attitude. "Who is Honey-Brown whatever her name is?"

"Stay out of my phone, Marlene. You're going too far."

"What did you call me?"

"What? I said Marlene. It's not like I called you a bitch. Or a nosy-ass bitch."

"Jeffrey Williams, what is your problem?"

"No, no, no. Don't put this on me. We just had a great time in bed. You were screaming my name. And now you gotta mess up the moment because you're insecure? This is wack." He is screaming louder than I was when I was having an orgasm. He must be out of his mind. All this drama over some cell phone junk?

My mama always told me if a man acts real defensive and hovers over his cell phone constantly, he's got something to hide. Because if everything was legit, there'd be no reason to guard your phone like it's a winning lottery ticket. I don't like how he's behaving at all. Come to think of it, whenever we're together, he always has one hand on that freaking phone. And when we've been out at a restaurant, he'll excuse himself several times. His phone will be glued to his hand. No man has to pee that many times in that short a period. I asked him if he has a weak bladder one time. He looked at me like I was crazy. Asked me what I'm asking him personal questions like that for. And I was too shocked to even reply. So I never asked about his stupid bladder again.

"Jeffrey, please lower your voice—"

"No, Marlene. The problem is not my voice. You gotta respect the boundaries, man. Respect other people's property. It's the golden rule."

"The golden rule is do unto others as you would have them do unto you," I spit back.

"Bingo, Marlene. If you don't want me snooping into your shit, then don't peep into mine. Everyone knows that."

"My mama said—."

"Fuck your mama. She just needs to get dicked down anyway. That's her problem. I've met women like her before. Old, horny, and mad as fuck. Mad cause the dick isn't rock hard as it used to be."

"Shut up talking about my mother like that. You don't know her like that."

"Marlene, you don't know who I know or what I know. I know that much."

"And stop calling me Marlene. I'm Beautiful Girl." I'm in his face rotating my neck and wagging my finger. I've never seen him look so mad before. He's breathing hard, and his mouth is all pointed like he's a nasty-looking rat.

My head is spinning. I sit down. "You hear what I said. If your golden rule is not touching your property, then you should know my property is my family. My mama. Keep her name out of your mouth."

"Fine. Done deal. I don't like hearing what she has to say, anyway. Loser."

I lose it. Hop up so fast that I twist my ankle and crumple to the floor. "Oww. See what you've done, Jeff."

"I haven't done anything." He looks down at me, like he's safe and I'm vulnerable. And I know then that even the best sex in the world can't get rid of deep problems a couple may experience. Orgasms won't stop arguments. I think my orgasm caused an argument. And now my ankle is starting to ache with a nagging pain.

"Jeff, it hurts. I'm talking really hurts." I look up at him. The anger in his eyes lessens. He reaches out his free hand to me and pulls me up off the floor. I limp over to the bed.

"Lie down," he commands.

I lie back. He arranges the pillows so that I feel more comfortable. He examines my ankle, briefly rubs his fingers across the swelling. He reaches down, glances at me, then kisses my toes.

"That feel better . . . Beautiful Girl?"

I nod, thankful that he's not acting like a butthole. I'm still naked. And I hate the creamy wet feeling that is in between my legs and spread out like little dots on my thighs.

"I really need to take a shower."

"All right, go ahead."

"Do you want to take one with me?"

"What?"

"Jeff, we've never showered together. It'll be fun."

"I dunno. I gotta roll out," he says.

"You always rolling out, running here and there. Slow down, Jeff. Those houses aren't going anywhere. I wanted to spend more time with you."

"I dunno—"

"Plus you stink too. You smell like penis and p—"

"Okay, okay." He says yes, but he looks mad. I don't care. We ought to do what I want to do for a change. Why I always gotta do things the Jeffrey Williams way, anyway? Sure, I know I said I'd do it. But my feelings are different now from when we first met. It's obvious he likes me as much as I like him. That I don't doubt. But he could stand to be more giving, less self-centered. Especially since he gets whatever he asks of me. Time, sex, money, treats, love, and attention. Surely I deserve the same things.

He helps me get out of bed.

"Get my robe, please. It's in the closet." He places his PDA on the bed for a second, but then picks it back up. He goes to my closet and finds my sky blue silk robe. He helps me put my arms through the sleeves, and he even puts down his PDA for a minute so he can secure the belt around my waist. He looks lovingly down at me and kisses my lips.

"That feel better, Beautiful Girl?"

"Much better, boyfriend."

He stiffens then offers a dazed smile. "C'mon," he says, patting me on the butt. "Let's go get washed up. But after that, I'm serious, I got to go. Something's come up, and you know me. I'm always about my business."

"Hmm."

"Please, don't be like that. I thought you said that's one of the qualities you love about me. Has that changed? Do you still love me, Beautiful Girl?"

Oh, God, why is he doing this to me? I tilt back my head, stare up into his beautiful eyes, and nod. He smiles and plants small kisses on my cheeks and forehead. I giggle and move back. "Stop it. I can smell myself. Let's go. Now."

We slowly walk through the living area to the bathroom. I grab a fresh bar of Ivory soap and a bottle of shower gel.

Jeff pulls off his underwear. "You don't have anything more masculine smelling than that?"

"If I did you'd be pissed. So my answer is no. Deal with it. Nothing wrong with a man smelling like candy apple." I laugh.

"Yeah, you think that's funny, but I'm the one who has to deal with weird looks once I step outside your door."

"Ha, it's better than smelling like penis and p—"

"Hush," he says, laughing. "I get your point."

We step in the shower, and when I turn the knob the water is instantly steaming hot. Jeff stands in front of me and lets the water splash all over his face, arms, and chest. I squirt shower gel on his back and rub it into his skin until it's lathered and soapy.

"You're going to turn gay," I sing. He laughs but lets me clean him thoroughly. Even though the shower is loud, I can hear beeping and buzzing sounds. Jeff turns around to face me and gives me an innocent look.

"Jeff, did you actually bring your cell phone in the bathroom?"

"Yeah, I don't want to miss an important call."

"Who or what could be more important than me, huh? Tell me that."

When he doesn't reply and just has this incredibly stupid look on his face, I roll my eyes and carefully step out of the shower. Water is dripping from my body to the floor, but I don't care. His buzzing PDA is on the counter. I see he's gotten eight more messages since I last looked.

"Hey, what are you doing?"

I don't say anything and press a button to try to read an e-mail, but it says "locked."

Soon I feel him right behind me. "What the fuck you doing, Marlene?" He grabs his phone from my hand.

"I see you have a password on your phone, so why you gotta snatch it from me? You think I may figure out your code?"

"You never know."

"You're going to get electrocuted."

"And you're going to get hurt."

"What did you say?"

"Huh, girl, quit playing. Let's finish taking the shower. I gotta wash your back."

"No, finish what you were saying. What do you mean I'm going to get hurt, Jeff?"

"You are going to get electrocuted, too, that's what I meant."

"Lame."

"Okay, please get back in the shower. I'm putting my cell phone down, see me?" He places it on the counter and steps back in the shower.

"Come on, Beautiful Girl," he sings.

I try to let the cell phone issue go and get back in the shower. He lathers the soap, and I have fun letting him squeeze my breasts and rub the wash cloth between my legs. We end up French kissing so long that the water turns luke-warm. As soon as we're done showering, drying off, and getting dressed, he tells me he'll call later, that he has to go. I am disappointed but ask him to drive safe.

As soon as Jeff leaves, and I shut the door behind him, Rachel quickly emerges from her bedroom.

"I heard y'all in there getting freaky," she says, cutting to the chase.

"Okay, what about it?"

"Marlene, there's something you need to know about Jeff."

15

RACHEL

Sampling the Same Goods

I am standing in front of Marlene acting as serious as I've ever been. But she looks distracted. She winces when she attempts to walk to the couch.

"Why are you walking like that?"

"My ankle hurts. It'll be okay. I just need to sit down."

I wait until she's seated, then I sit next to her. "Like I was saying before, you need to slow your roll with this man."

"Rachel, can you do me a huge favor, please?"

Before I can answer, I hear loud, consistent knocks on the front door. "Damn, who the hell is it?" I rush and fling open the door.

Alita and London storm in. Alita takes one look at Marlene. "Hey, Marlene, how are you doing?"

"Not too good. Can y'all make yourselves useful? Please go to the pharmacy and pick up something for swelling. I'm sure my injury will be fine in a day or so, but it really hurts right now."

Alita sits down and gingerly brushes her finger across Marlene's skin, carefully inspecting it. "Oh, wow, yeah, Rachel. Let's go to CVS, get her something. Plus, I want to ask you something. Get your purse. Hell, forget the purse. I'll pay for the medicine."

"Aren't you an angel?" I say.

"Bump that, you're paying me back soon as we get back."

"I knew it was too good to be true."

"A lot of things are too good to be true," she replies, but that's another story. "Okay, Marlene. We're going to the store and we'll hook you up."

"Thanks," Marlene says. We follow behind London, who holds open the door for us. Alita grabs my hand and forces me out of the house. I feel so naked. No purse. No cell phone.

"Jesus, why are you rushing me? I was trying to warn Marlene—"

"No, fool. That's the last thing you should do. I told you on the phone to keep this on the DL. You gotta make sure Jeff takes the bait before you go squealing on a brotha. You need some proof. She's not going to take you at your word."

"But the picture—"

"No, girl, forget all that." We jump in Alita's ride, and she's driving and talking like a chatterbox. "Do what I tell you. Chill with the warnings. Get him to talk to London on the phone. Let her get some info from him. We need more info. Got it?"

"I guess."

"We need to see how many lies the bastard has been telling. Ohhh, I am so pissed I could go off on somebody."

"As long as it's not me. Damn, Alita. Okay, I'll go along with your little plan."

We arrive at CVS. Alita plants a twenty-dollar bill in my hand. I start walking up and down the aisles searching the shelves for some healing ointment.

"Has Jeff answered your e-mails yet?" London asks, swinging her fists and boxing the air. "Girl, I want to get it popping."

"You two are funny. But no, he's been too busy sexing up my sister."

"Eww, that's plain ole nasty," Alita says. "He must really think he has a lot of game. I can't believe your rejection of Jeff has turned him into such a—"

"Don't say it," I say, cutting her off. "What really trips me out is how I indicated what characteristics I want in a man on the dating site. And my ideal man turns out to be my ex. What the hell is wrong with me?"

Alita starts cracking up and holding her belly.

"Hardly Berry, you're one to laugh. Don't forget it took the real Halle Berry to go through a ton of bad relationships before she hooked up with her dream guy."

"A white man at that," London says.

"No, a Canadian," Alita corrects her. "A much younger, much richer, savvier dream man. I'm glad for her."

"But you feel sorry for me, huh?" I read the labels and details of several ointments and end up picking a fast-healing cream that costs about fifteen bucks. "Got it. I'm ready."

We walk to the cashier line of the pharmacy area. We're the only customers. I spot one pharmacist in the back doing whatever pharmacists do. And this other female Asian pharmacist is too busy filling a prescription to acknowledge me.

I clear my throat. The Asian lady looks up but keeps working.

"Let's give her a couple minutes."

We begin casually browsing the counter, which has a small display of tabloids. *Star* magazine, *National Enquirer*. I thumb through a story about Jennifer Aniston's latest breakup but get bored after two paragraphs. I couldn't care less about Jen's problems. All I want to do is purchase the medicine and go home.

To fill time, Alita strikes up a conversation about how she beat Big Hen at some video game. I halfway listen to my friend rambling; the other half of me can't stop gawking at a tall, middle-aged white man with dark brown hair who swiftly walks over and stands in front of the counter right next to us. He's dressed in a classic black dress suit, crisp white shirt, and plain red tie. Within seconds the Asian lady stops what she's doing and approaches the cash register. "How are you today, sir? May I help you?" she says, her eyes making direct contact with the man.

"Hold on," I mutter softly, not believing my eyes. "Can you believe what she just did?" I ask Alita, talking a little louder.

"Yep, I can, we're used to it. Obama or no Obama, some things won't ever change." Alita shakes her head back and forth like she wants to explode with frustration. I want to blow up, too. But this is a battle that I don't want to engage in just now. Too many other issues deserve my attention.

We quietly wait until the Asian lady provides the white man quick, efficient, and super-friendly customer service. As soon as he happily leaves with his CVS bag in his hand, the lady acts like she doesn't even want to say hello to us. She continues scribbling notes on a notepad, making me feel invisible and unwanted.

"I can't believe this shit," I say to Alita. "I feel like asking for the manager. Get her rude ass written up."

"She's not worth it," London says. "Just pay for your stuff and go. Or you can go to the front cash register and pay."

"No, those lines are always way too long, but I guess I can do that next time."

The girls and I tap our feet, loudly sighing and glancing at our watches. Finally the Asian lady asks, "May I help you with something?"

"Are your eyes working okay, lady?" I ask, not able to

hide my annoyance. London lightly shoves me in the ribs. The lady frowns as if I have vomited on her fingers, but she goes ahead and rings up my order. When she hands me my change, she places the change on top of the receipt on top of my hand, as if she doesn't want her skin to touch mine.

I storm away from the counter. "I swear I'm never coming to this store again. That lady is a minority like me. Who is she trying to fool? I don't care if she gives herself an American name—"

"Rachel, chill. Who cares about her? It's over and done. You need to focus on what you're going to do about your scandalous ex. That's the real world."

"Yeah, you're right," I say to Alita, trying to calm down. We drive back to my apartment and drop off the ointment to Marlene. She's propped up on the couch, resting on some throw pillows. The TV is so loud I'm surprised she hasn't gone deaf. She's watching *The Break-Up* starring Jennifer Aniston, of all people.

"I hope you feel better," I tell her, then skip out of the door so the rest of us can congregate on the balcony.

"Hmm," Alita says, looking around at the burned-out candles. "So this is where your scandalous ex romanced your sister with the dinner, the wine. He's a two-timing Casanova. So I'm not impressed."

"Well, I was very envious," I confess to Alita and London. "I don't like that he's doing things with her that he didn't do with me. I feel like he knows how to push my buttons. Like he's doing this shit on purpose. I don't appreciate it. I'm trying to be a saint—"

"You are no saint."

"Shut up, Alita. I said I'm *trying* to be one. But it's not working. I want to pay him back for every hurtful thing he's doing."

"His day is coming," Alita assures me. "Don't worry."

I feel my cell phone vibrating in my pocket and casually pick it up and glance at the screen. "Oh, snap, COCKY247 has written us back, London." I laugh. "He says to name the time and the place. He'll open up his packed schedule to meet us. He gives a phone number, but I don't recognize it. Hmm, that's odd."

"It's not his landline?" Alita asks.

"Nope. It's a one-eight-hundred number."

"Call it now. Do it."

"Wait, wait." I giggle. "I want to read the other e-mails first." I scroll through Jeff's messages. "He says he's a native Houstonian. His Ph.D. was given to him by the streets. He's had his heart broken before, but he's willing to give love a try till he gets it right. Oh, no, he didn't."

"You see what he's trying to do, don't you?"

"What is he doing, Alita?"

"This man is trying to prove that he's vulnerable, human. He's showing that he's a strong man, and if he gets hurt, he's emotionally strong enough to bounce back."

"I swear, Alita, you ought to be on the XM Cosmo station. You're full of relationship analyses."

"I missed my calling working at Wal-Mart, huh? Girl, you won't believe the things customers tell me. Women trying to explain to me why they're buying a box of thirty-six condoms. How they got an STD from the last man they slept with. They've been forced to take control of their sexual life before they end up losing their life."

"That's deep. Women have to do what they have to do in this day and age."

"Sure enough. I remember this one customer. This lady had all kinds of sex stuff in her shopping cart. So I'm trying to be funny, right. Telling her she must be getting ready for a sensuous weekend. That lady tells me, and she couldn't be any older than thirty-five, she says she's buying this stuff for her seventeen-year-old daughter, who she caught fucking in her bed while she should've been at school. And the man her daughter was fucking was someone the mom used to date."

"Oh shoot, so he was a thirty-something guy messing with a seventeen-year-old girl?"

"No, fool. This guy was twenty. The woman is a big-time cougar who got a rude awakening. She said the men she's attracted to end up trying to be with her *and* her teenager."

"That's awful. It must've felt weird for her to buy condoms for her daughter and her ex. Better her than me, though."

Alita shoots me an odd look. A weird feeling passes through me, giving me a reality check. Who the hell am I to scrutinize her customer's sex life? I'm no better than her or anyone else. And Marlene, poor thing, she's unknowingly getting caught in the drama. Surely there have to be enough men to go around so that women won't have to all be sampling the same goods.

"Anyway, my point is, I hear and see a lot of things out there," Alita says. "I am in a secure relationship, but I get scared sometimes, too. What if an Adonis steps in my line one day, gives me his phone number, and propositions me? It hasn't happened yet, but what if it does?"

I tell her, "The fact that you're worried about it happening says everything, Alita. Shit, and if that's the case we're all in trouble. We're all getting screwed without the Vaseline."

"No, I disagree," London says. "We are adult enough to know what we're getting ourselves into. No more excuses. Jeff knows what he's doing. Marlene knew what she was doing when she made the decision to step out with your ex.

And we know what we're doing posting fake photos online. We do what we choose to do, and it's up to us to face the consequences of our actions."

I can't argue with London. Because as bad and guilty as I feel, I still want to pay Jeff back for what he's doing. When Jeff and Marlene were getting busy tossing each other's salad tonight, I went back to the SoulSingles website. Jeff has so many favorites I couldn't count them all. Women from California to Maryland, Texas to Illinois. And the profile said he's been on the site even when he knew me. That's foul. I never totally felt that he was stepping out on me, but now it's obvious certain things weren't right with him. I truly wish that the good and honorable parts of him could have been evident 100 percent of the time, instead of 50 percent.

"Well, in light of what London says, I am willing to face whatever is in store for me by pretending that I'm her."

We stop chatting and enjoy the evening's cool breeze as we stand by my front door. I guiltily glance toward the living room window. Through the curtains I can see shadows of my sister, hugging a pillow, looking dreamily at the television. I feel sad when I realize her fantasy is about to come to an end.

"Are we ready to make the call?" London pulls out a cheat sheet that I typed up for her. She is familiar with all my favorites that I listed on the dating site. And I told her it's okay with me if she wants to fabricate any other information once she finally talks to Jeff. I really don't care anymore.

"Well, even though I doubt Marlene can hear us out here, let's walk down these stairs just in case," I say.

Once we're on the first level, I recite the 1–800 number and give London the okay sign.

"Put him on speaker," Alita says.

"Good idea." London presses a button and we hear a line ringing. It rings four times, then a voice comes on. "You've reached J.A.W. Enterprises. Leave your name and number to get a call-back."

The voice mail indicator beeps so fast that London looks startled, but she quickly recovers. "Hello, this is Honey-BrownTX. We met on SoulSingles. I'm giving you a call to see what you're up to. Call me back. I'm sure you see my number on caller ID. Lock me in so you'll know how to reach me. I look forward to hearing from you. Stay sweet."

She disconnects the line.

"Hmm, that must be a business cell. I don't think he had that when we were together."

"You learn something new every day," Alita says.

"London, did you make sure your voice mail has a generic greeting on it in case Jeff tries to call you back?" I ask.

"Absolutely. I never record my own voice on cell phone greetings," London replies. "Well, I guess we should be heading out. It's getting very late, and it's about time Alita took me home. We'll be in touch, Rachel. Stay on your grind."

"Sure enough. Thanks for everything, both of you. I owe you big-time."

I wave bye and go back in the apartment. Marlene is snoring with her mouth wide open. The closing credits are going off from *The Break-Up* movie. It's after midnight. I stare at my sister through the darkness. There's a look of contentment on her face. Who am I to interrupt her moments of happiness? God knows they don't come often or easily, not for any of us. Yet I think she deserves to know the truth.

I tap her on the shoulder.

"Sis, get up. You need to get in your own bed."

"Leave me alone."

"Wake up, Marlene."

"Nooo, I don't know what he's doing."

"Huh? You're talking in your sleep?"

"I found that money so it's mine."

I giggle and lean close to her ear, so close I can hear her breathing. "Your man is a two-timer, did you know that?"

She tries to shift and turn to the other side, but winces. "Ouch."

"Hmm, your little ankle must be hurting. Maybe it's best you sleep on the couch. Doesn't look like you'll be going to work in the morning."

She snorts loudly, sounding like a hog. Unable to resist myself, I press my mouth close to her ear, "Jeffrey Williams is cheating on you."

Marlene's eyes pop open. She sits up and squints at me. "Did you say something?"

"I said you should go get in your own bed. That's what I said."

"What time is it?"

"Almost twelve-thirty."

"Oh, shoot. Hand me my cell." Her phone is sitting nearby on the coffee table. I pick it up, and she snatches the phone from my hand.

She opens the phone. "Dang, I can't believe this. He told me . . ." She looks up at me and attempts to hide her true feelings.

"Did you enjoy the dinner that Jeff brought over to you tonight?"

"What? Oh, yeah. It was cool. He totally surprised me."

"I'll bet he did."

"He's doing a lot better."

"Oh, yeah," I say and sit on the edge of the couch so that I'm facing her. "What's he doing better? Care to be specific?"

"Um, just in general. Nothing specific. I like how things are progressing."

"That's good. I'm glad for you."

"Are you really?" she says, looking doubtful.

"Yeah, if this is the man you think you wanna be with, and there's no one out there better than Jeff, then you get what you deserve."

"What?"

"I mean, you two are meant for each other. It's fate."

"Oh, all right. Thanks." She doesn't sound too convincing.

"Anyway, just thought I'd see if you were going to get in your bed. I'm about to get in mine. See ya later, Marlene." I go on to bed and fall asleep fairly quickly. When I wake up in the morning, Marlene is still spread out on the couch snoring loud. It's like she's superglued to the fabric. I wonder if she even got up to use the restroom.

It's eight o'clock, so I figure Marlene must have called in sick. I check my e-mail. COCKY247 has written twice. And London has texted me. She wants me to call when I get a chance. But I see my mama called me at six this morning, which is unusual for her. She knows I don't get up until after seven. I pick up my phone and redial her.

"Hey, Little Bit. I've been wanting to talk to you for the longest."

"Well, I just woke up, but—"

"No, I mean for a long time. Longer than just the past twelve hours. You hear what I'm saying?"

"I–I guess so. What's up?"

"There's something I want to show you . . . tell you. Stop over here before you go to work. But come now if you can."

"Now?"

"Yeah, may as well get it over with."

"Is this something that can be done over the phone, Mama?"

"Never."

Confused, I tell her I'll be right over. I take my shower and skip breakfast. On the way over to my mama's, Alita calls.

"You getting ready for work?" she asks.

"No, where are you, Alita?"

"I'm on my break. Let me call London and click her in on the conversation. She and I talked a bit last night, and you need to hear this."

"Oh, great," I say and instantly feel uncomfortable. My shoulders feel hard as concrete. This isn't good. Why does everything have to happen all at the same time?

Alita comes back on the line.

"Okay, London, real quick. Tell her."

"Hey, Rachel, good morning. Girl, your ex is a piece of work. He actually called me at, like, almost one-thirty in the morning, talking about how he's been working like a slave with no benefits all day, which to me doesn't make a bit of sense. But he was turning on the charm big-time. He told me how much he loves the way my voice sounds, like a sweet little kitten. He said I look so good in my picture that he could practically feel the softness of my skin. And he told me my photo looks better than Kim Kardashian, but he prefers to see me in person."

"Oh, did he now?"

"He kept asking me my real name, but I wouldn't tell him. Oh, and we talked quite a while, and eventually the conversation turned to sex. And he says he loves to spend time with a cuddy buddy, and he's long overdue for some sex. I wanted to laugh. So typical. Your boy ended the conversation by telling me he's a millionaire in the making, and he wants a woman by his side who complements his lifestyle."

"Oh, brother. So what did you say to him?"

"I was mostly listening. Trying to read between the lines. I asked him about getting his heart broke. He said that women always mess up when they have a good man; he said a woman will go up a hill and down a road trying to find a way to screw up her relationship, because she doesn't always feel confident enough to be with a king. Told me everybody can't be a Beyoncé and Jay-Z."

"He's comparing himself to Jay-Z? And he thinks he's a king now?" I ask. "King of Bullshit, that's what he is."

"So," London continues, chuckling, "he kept saying he wants to see me tonight. That's kind of fast. I told him I'll have to get back with him on that. Oh, and he sent me another photo. Shirtless, girl. He's packing. I was shocked." We laugh and I grow even more uncomfortable. It's like I'm sharing my secrets, things that ought to be private.

"Let me know how to proceed as far as this date thing is concerned. I got something for his ass," London says, laughing hysterically. I give a weak laugh and get off the phone. It's time to see what my mama wants.

I go in through the side door and find her in the kitchen gulping from a shot glass.

"Mama, isn't it a little too early in the morning to be doing all that?" I grab the glass from her and take a sniff. "Whiskey?" I say and crinkle my nose. "You must really be on something. This is not like you."

"Well, I, you know—"

"God, you're acting weird. Just tell me. Is it about Blinky?"

"No, no."

"Loretta?"

"Naw, not Loretta."

"Marlene?"

"Nooo, not her, either."

"Mama, just spit it out."

"I can't spit it out, that's why I had to write it out. Go on ahead. Read this."

She holds out a handwritten letter. I recognize her tiny lettering. My heart beats wildly inside of me. "You read. I'm going in the kitchen. I'll be back later."

"No, Mama, don't leave me now. You're scaring me, and I want you to be here with me."

She gives me a stony look, but her feet remain planted on the kitchen tile. I take a deep breath and start reading.

My Dearest Little Bit,

You got no idea how hard it is for me to right this. I thought about it mini times, but never had the guts to tell you. But I no your in pain. And your pain is spreadin to other people. As a real woman, I gotta do what I gotta do. First, I love you with all my heart. I wood never try to hurt you on purpus. But you should no that . . .

Oh, God, I think inside. What on earth could my mama want to tell me?

A long time ago, when you first met jeff, he tried to go with me.

My hands are shaking so much, and I'm holding Mama's letter so tight that the flimsy piece of paper is getting wrinkled. Where did Jeff try to go with my mom?

He looked at me, told me that you musta got your prettyness from me. He called me Ma. Asked if it was okay to call me that. I said sure. Then he moved closer and closer to me. He touched my face.

What?

He leaned down and smiled at me. I didn't like kissing him at all, I swair Rachel. I spat right after it was over. Spat his poison all on my kitchen floor. I told him to get out. No, I said to get the fuck out. He looked scared. He asked, What's wrong Ma? I said, Ma? You must mean Ma-nipyoulation. Don't be calling me Ma. He made me promise not to tell you. And I said ok. But jeff is not pryority. You are. I am sorry to tell you. But he's a bad man. I am glad you didn't marry jeff.

I've read the last word and I'm standing in the middle of my mother's living room with my mouth so wide open an entire fist could fit in it. I press my knuckles against my mouth, shove my fist in my mouth. And I scream.

"Afhgh, sheiooo, weiwot." None of the words I'm trying to say make sense. But the words streaking across my mind do.

What kind of mess is this?

My Jeff?

And my mama?

Had a thing?

Right under my nose.

My vision is so blurry that the words from my mama's letter disappear before my eyes. But the memory of her confession remains glued in my soul.

I stand there screaming with my fist in my mouth I don't know how long. After a while, I feel my mama standing behind me. Feel her little skinny hands clutch me from behind. She pulls me into her body. Like she's trying to protect me.

I swing around, take my fist out my mouth, and push her so hard she flies back a few steps.

"Don't touch me," I scream at the top of my lungs. "You're an awful person. You're not even a person. You're an awful *thing*. You are a million times worse than Loretta."

Mama's eyes grow so huge I can see fear wrapped tightly around them. I'm glad she's scared. No other way she ought to feel right now except scared.

"Don't you ever talk to me again in your life! We're through!"

And I walk out.

16

MARLENE

Chain of Fools

I've managed to drop down to the carpet and crawl from the living room to my bedroom. I felt guilty for calling in sick, but I need to rest and stay off this ankle. Only thing is it's hard trying to do things around the house by myself. Rachel's gone to work. I can't get Jeff on his cell. I wish I could take back the ten times I've called him. But technology proves a woman's desperation. The missed calls will show up on his phone. He may begin to despise me if he thinks I need him too much.

As much as I don't want to do this, I'm going to have to swallow my pride and take a chance. I am lying in my bed with the covers off so my ankle can get some air. My tiny portable TV that doesn't get the clearest picture is on, but I don't care about any television show that's on right now. My stomach is growling, and my underarms are wet with perspiration. So many needs, so few answers.

I pick up my cell phone. Dial a number.

"I can't believe you're calling me. What's the occasion?"

"Mama, how you been doing? You okay?"

"Marlene, you know me. I'll always be all right."

"How's the job search coming along?"

"I've got a few interviews lined up. As a matter of fact, I have one this afternoon. I need to stop by the store and get some panty hose, though. All my other pairs are either dirty or ripped. But I know this job is mine."

"What is it?"

"It's another counseling position. Mentoring young women who have gotten themselves knocked up and feel like their life is over. I can tell them how I went on and got my education, made something of myself regardless of being a single parent."

"Hmm, that sounds right up your alley." I think for a second. "You know that's what I like about you. You're willing to share your troubles with other women and let them know there's a way out of any challenging situation."

"Got to stay positive, no matter what you're up against."

"Well, I need your help." I explain to Loretta how I'm stuck in bed. I'm hungry. And being rubbed down with a washcloth, warm water, and soap would make my day. "And I would love to have something to read. *Us Weekly, People, National Enquirer.*"

"Humph, I'm shocked you haven't just whipped out your Bible. From what I understand, that's the book that can always be found right next to your bedside. Is that still true?"

"No, ma'am," I say in a quiet voice.

"Oh, so where is it then?"

"Under my bed."

"Hmm, that can only mean one thing. Something else much more valuable to you has taken the place of your beloved Bible. Tell me the truth, Marlene. Is it a man? You've been having sex? And you're too ashamed to sleep with some guy and have the Bible right next to you on your bedside, staring you in the face at the same—"

"Mama, please stop, please. Your mind is always running a hundred miles an hour when it needs to slow down like it's in a school zone. Slow down, listen, learn. 'Cause you may be my parent, but you don't know everything, you know."

I hear her heartily laugh, like there's hardly anything I say can say to truly move her.

"I know enough. Tell you what. I'm sorry for saying what I said. I want you to relax. No need to be stressing you out."

"Yeah, well, I have noticed a couple gray hairs on my head. And it shocked me to death."

"You've been dealing with some stuff, huh?"

"My ankle hurts so much it's throbbing."

"Where's your man at? He sets his own hours, right? Don't tell me he's *that* busy."

"No, I just saw him yesterday."

"Oh, ya'll had some wild sex and you injured yourself? I've heard of some freaky shit with the blindfolds and the chains and whips, but damn—"

"You don't know what you're talking about."

"And apparently you know everything I don't know. And I want to hear more. So stay put. Help is on the way."

She abruptly hangs up on me. I roll my eyes and lie back on my pillows, thoughtfully gazing up at the ceiling.

Am I being punished? My behavior hasn't been the most positive lately. Maybe I'm reaping what I've sown. Rachel would always say that to me. That she hoped I got what I deserve. I bite my bottom lip and my throat thickens with soreness. *I just feel awful. And it's no fun when you feel your worst, and no one is around to help you.*

And why would they? I ask myself. *Who wants to be around a know-it-all, stubborn, conceited female who acts like she has a direct line to God, when in actuality I think God is caller IDing me? When's the last time he's answered my prayers? I believe in God, and I know I'm his child, but it's no secret I'm not his best child.*

I fall asleep with tears streaming down my cheeks, snot stuck in my nose, making it hard for me to breathe. Last thought I have is *If I'm lucky, maybe I'll choke on my own spit . . . and die.*

When I wake up, the first face I see is Rachel's. She's silent. Staring down at me. Looking at me like she doesn't know who I am.

"What are you doing here?" I mumble. "Why aren't you at work?" It's almost eleven, and I know she's a stickler for trying to get to work a little bit early.

"Bastards. All of 'em. Fucking bastards. Can't trust nobody. No one. Soon as you turn your back, somebody's plunging a sharp knife in you and twisting it around so you can bleed some more. I can't believe her. I can't. Bitch."

I wince and try my best to sit up, so I can have a clear view of my sister and make sure I can hear everything she's saying.

"What happened? Something happened at work? You got into it with your boss?" I know that once before, Rachel and her boss, Twila, got into a shouting match. Twila wrote up Rachel and docked her two days' pay. Since then Rachel said she's been on her best behavior, but maybe Twila's getting on her last nerve again.

"Nothing happened at work." She laughs, then quickly hushes. "I did call in, though. I can't work under these conditions. No way." Rachel is walking back and forth, raising her hands, laughing, then looking pissed, like her cheeks are about to burst.

"Don't pay those people any mind. I hope the folks at my job aren't talking about me behind my back for calling in sick, too."

"Well, Marlene, I hadn't planned on calling in. I was on my way to work, but I got a little phone call. Loretta told me to stop whatever I was doing and go straight home. I told her I wasn't in the mood; it just wasn't a good time for her foolishness, but she started crying."

"My mama? Crying?"

"Girl, yes! It sounded . . . yuck, it was so awful, like a hound dog wailing in the wee hours of the morning. She sounded like I've never heard her sound before."

"She sounded . . . "

"Human."

I nod, halfway understanding. "Why'd she ask you to come home?"

"She said I need to step it up, come see about you. I told her, well shit, I need someone to come see about *me*. Why I always gotta be the hero? Or is it the shero?"

"Oh, really? You're here . . . Rachel. Because my mama asked you to come . . . see about me?"

She nods emphatically like she's is in a daze and can't believe it herself.

"At first I said no. But a few minutes later I was like 'Why the hell not?' It's probably all my fault that you're in this mess, anyway. Let me try to undo what I've done. It's all fucked . . . fuck, fuck, fuck. I hate . . . " Rachel's eyes immediately well up. It almost looks like she's wearing bifocals. Soon her tears spill over, and she quickly wipes them away. I don't know what to say. I would hug her, but I'm stuck and can't get up.

"Are you all right, Sis?"

"No. Yes. Look, I know you don't understand. But I just gotta face some things, unbelievably tough things, then I'll be all right." Satisfied with her answer, I watch her leave the room and hear her clattering around the kitchen for several minutes. When she returns, her cheeks appear rosier, eyes more alert and focused.

"Hey, Marlene. I–I warmed you up a pot of chicken noodle soup. Not that you're sneezing and wheezing and blowing your nose . . . but chicken noodle soup . . . seemed like the right thing to do."

I slowly nod at my sister, thoughtfully considering her gesture. In one way I wish she'd just leave my room. I will handle this on my own. But seeing her act vulnerable and confused is so rare; it's like I can't peel my eyes off her.

"I want you to eat some soup, but first . . . you need to know two things. I just don't know which to tell you first." Her loud laughter sounds choppy, ugly.

"Rachel, what on earth is going on?"

"Jeff is a cheater, a liar. He's not a good man, Marlene."

"What? I know he's no Will Smith, no Denzel—"

"He's more like a man you've known for years, but then he does something wrong and gets arrested. The incident is splashed across the TV, the papers. Other people who know him come out the woodwork and say things you've never heard before, describe him in such foreign terms that you're convinced he can't be the same person. That's Jeff!"

She comes and sits next to me on the bed. "The man you think you love—"

"What? I *do* care for him." I bite my bottom lip. "I love him, Sis."

"No, you just think you do."

"I *know* I do."

She gives me a sad, sympathetic look. "Why?"

"I–I miss him when we're not together."

"Get a dog, then," she sputters.

"He makes me laugh."

"Go to the comedy club."

"And"—I think twice before answering—"I like the orgasms he gives me."

"Eww," she says, standing up. "Get a fucking vibrator. You can always buy something that will lick your vagina real good if you're not too ashamed to use it. You don't need him to make you feel good."

"I know, but I still want him."

"Listen up. The guy who you miss, laugh at, and have sex with is doing the same shit with other women."

"I don't know why you're saying that, Rachel. Jeez."

"Jeez, nothing. Look, dummy, I'm trying to help you."

I spring up out of the bed and hobble up to Rachel, standing right under her nose. I grab her by her shoulders and shake her so hard that her eyes enlarge as round as quarters.

"I am not dumb, not stupid, none of that, do you hear me? You have no reason to call me that. Wait, yes, you do. You're the ultimate hater."

"Let go of me," she screams. She balls up some paper that's been in her hands and runs out of the room. I hear the front door slam. But I can tell she hasn't locked it.

Wow, she must really be pissed. Too bad. So am I. I manage to walk over to the front door and secure the lock. Smoke rises from the big pot of soup that boils on the stove top. Feeling guilty, I go and turn off the burner.

I've gotta change into a different shirt, at the least, I think to myself and hobble across the living room, aiming for the closet. But when I'm halfway to my room, my uninjured foot kicks a crumpled-up piece of paper.

This is what Rachel had in her hand all that time she was in here. I lean over and pick up the balled-up paper, then stand to read it.

Brooke. I can tell her writing anywhere. Plus, poor thing, she never was the best speller. But it's not the misspelled words; it's the words she's saying that make me slowly lower myself to my bed in a sitting position.

"Oh, no," I say to myself.

"Rachel!" I scream, even though I know she can't hear me.

Fifteen minutes later, I'm in my car speeding down Highway 6. I speed dial Rachel ten times before she answers.

"What?"

"Sis, I'm so sorry. I am so upset; I don't know what to think."

"Oh, you've finally accepted how du—"

"Hear me out. Please. I read . . . Brooke's letter. And I'm scared."

"Nothing to be scared of," Rachel murmurs.

"Brooke is something else."

"Both of them are something else. They were both wrong: he for doing what he did, and she for allowing him to kiss her, and for not immediately telling me. I'm so angry with them, I don't know what to do."

"I know you're mad. I am, too. I'm more shocked than anything. But it's not all about you. This is about us, Sis. We're in this together."

"Damn, Marlene. Can you believe this?" I hear her sob.

"Hey, where are you?"

"Alita's. Big Hen is taking a vacation day. Golfing. I called Alita and she told me it was okay to come by her job and get the town house key. So I'll be chilling over here."

"That's good. But what about Jeff? Are you going to talk to him about what happened with him and Brooke? Because if you don't, I will—"

"No, Marlene. Don't say anything to him. You need to stop being concerned about what he's done in the past, and think more about what he's doing now."

"You're scaring me. What's he doing?"

"I've been trying to tell you that he's a cheater, girl. He dates other women, Marlene."

"No." I don't want to hear it. It hurts to listen. "Are you positive?"

"Look, remember last night? You and Jeff were in the bed having a good ole time? Well, he had just texted this girl telling her about himself and trying to hook up."

"How do you know all this?"

She explains about the dating site. That Jeff has a profile and secretly dates other women.

"Oh, no. I just can't believe it."

"Believe it."

Even if a woman has a gut feeling about her man and the things he may be doing behind her back, she always hopes for the best, that she's imagining things and that he really can be trusted.

"Marlene, I've set up a fake date with Jeff. He's taken the bait and has agreed to meet London at a restaurant. I think you should go there, too."

"Catch him in the act?"

"Exactly."

"Oh, you don't know how bad I want to call this man. If it's all true, he owes me some answers."

"No, that's where you're wrong. You may want answers, but I doubt you'll get them. This type of guy feels entitled. He wants to have his cake—"

"His icing, his candles, and the presents that come with the damn cake."

"There ya go, Marlene. You're finally getting it."

"Truth be told, I'm devastated. Rachel, I truly fell in love with Jeff."

"Well, I did, too, Marlene."

I feel foolish. I can feel my cheeks and whole face burning and growing warmer with shame. I want to shake this bad feeling. Do something to counter how I feel.

"We're going to pay this bastard back, too. The hell with forgiveness, giving him another chance," Rachel says. "No, no, *hell* no. I don't ever want him to do another woman like he's done me."

"Like he's done *me*."

"Stop repeating what I say, Marlene."

"Under the circumstances, I can't help it, Rachel."

"Shame, shame, shame."

Rachel starts humming this familiar-sounding melody. I can tell she's coming out of her anger. From anger to strength. "Hey, Marlene, remember that old-school song that Blinky likes to play all the time?"

"You mean besides James Brown?"

"Right. Aretha Franklin. 'Chain, chain, chain,' " Rachel starts singing. " 'Chain of fools.' "

"Girl, how do you remember the words to that old song?"

"Blinky plays it so much I can't help but memorize them." She sings, " 'Five long years I thought you were my man. But I found out I'm just a link in your chain.' "

I'm still driving around. Headed toward Jeff's house. I have never gone to his place unannounced. But he's been avoiding my calls. And sometimes circumstances drive a woman to do things she's never done before, things she doesn't necessarily want to do. Tire Slashing 101. Introduction to Spray Painting. She does something headline-like, trying to make him feel bad and regret what he's done. Later on, the defense attorney calls it "temporary insanity."

But as long as her man keeps screwing up, it'll never be temporary, and she will always be insane.

"Marlene, I've been talking, and you're not saying anything. What are you doing? Where are you?"

I've just pulled up in front of Jeff's house. His precious Ella is sitting in the driveway, looking arrogant with that stupid car cover spread over it. I think about how he won't let me eat in his car. He's also put a big towel in there, insisting I sit on it and not on his custom-made leather seats. He wears special gloves that he uses to open the doors. And all this time I thought he was being a perfect gentleman, opening my door. Ha!

"Earth to Marlene, earth to Marlene."

That punk. I can't believe he favors an ugly, overpriced piece of metal over me. The longer I gape at his dumb car, the angrier I become. I unlock my door and press my weight on the steering wheel to give myself enough strength to get out of the car. I stand there, in the driveway, staring at Ella as if she's the other woman. I take a wobbly step toward the car.

"Marlene." I hear Rachel singing my name from inside my cell phone, which is now safely tucked in my jacket pocket.

I take another step. The sun is shining brightly. And something captures my attention out of the corner of my eye. Lying in plain view on the grass is a pair of lopping shears. The handles are at least two feet long. And check out at that beautiful steel blade. How would Jeff feel if he came home and saw big gashes all over his precious Ella?

I reach down and grab the shears and hold the wooden handles securely in my hands. I take one more step and hear words that sound as if they're being broadcast from a loudspeaker.

"You are too close to the car. Please move away. Thank you."

"Marlene? Are you messing with Jeff's ride? Girl, get the hell away from it, you're messing up."

I reach inside my pocket and pick up my cell phone. "Rachel, I can't believe him. When did he find time to get this security device?"

"You can ask him all those questions, but it won't be today. You need to stay low, Sis. Join the crew and be in our scheme."

Like the car says, I back away, but it's only because the siren starts blaring. Neighbors are looking at me like I'm a felon.

That's it.

I give up.

RACHEL

Just Say No

I am holding my cell phone in my hand. The screen indicates I have five new messages.

"Little Bit—" I press seven and delete.

"Hey, it's me. I know you must be—" I press seven again.

"Call me. We need to—" Seven, seven, seven. Funny how the number seven is supposed to mean lucky, but when it comes to a cell phone it means get rid of, erase, strike out, eliminate. Delete my deceitful mother from my cell phone; remove her completely from my life.

I know that because of her, I have life. But when the life your mother gives you makes you want to put your hands around a throat and not stop squeezing until a face turns blue, you're no longer living. You have a heart that's beating, but there's no feeling inside of it. There's nothing.

My cell phone rings. Because caller ID doesn't say "Mama," I answer.

"Hi, Daughter Number Two."

I don't say anything.

"I've been hearing some things about you."

"And I've been hearing stuff about you, Daddy."

"Now hold on. You wrong for what you doing. Your mama is over there almost hysterical. Her blood pressure is so high no amount of medicine is going to help her. Is that what you want? You trying to kill your mama?"

"She's killed me, Daddy," I say stonily. "I have nothing to say to her. And if you don't stop lecturing me, you'll be next in line."

"If . . . you . . . don't . . . shut . . . up . . . and . . . listen . . . yougonnamakemedosomethingIregret." Blinky's voice is sharp, like a blast of wind blowing past my ears.

"Daddy—"

"Shut up. I know you're mad. I know you're hurt. But you can't make a rash decision. You gotta forgive her. Family is all you got."

"Why didn't she think of that . . . before she did what she did? If family is so important, she wouldn't have put herself in that position. I mean, why me? What have I done, Daddy? Marlene. Mama. Which family member is gonna hurt me next? I may as well not have a family."

"I know, baby girl. I know what you're saying, but you're wrong. You need your family even if things aren't going perfect."

"Alita is more of a sister to me, a mother to me, than Mama or Marlene," I tell him. "Marlene is finding out things, bad things, about Jeff. And I have tried, and I'm still trying to protect her. But what's the point? Huh?"

"Role switching."

"What?"

"People take on roles they didn't expect to be taking. Sometimes you act older than Marlene. You're the responsible, more logical one. Sometimes the mother turns into the daughter. The mama starts to act like the offspring. Our roles change as we grow up, get older."

"Oh, so you're saying that's why my mama practically hooked up with my man? Because it was her time to morph into her daughter? Switch roles? That's the stupidest thing I've ever heard," I say bitterly. "Nice try, Blinky. You know, for a sixty-year-old man, you're sounding more like an eight-year-old. No, you're about as smart as Kiki. She has more sense than all of us."

"Are you finished? You done?" he asks.

"No, I'm not. I have a good mind to just say fuck it. Move out the apartment. Go live with Alita."

"Ain't she living with her man?"

"Yeah, but she wouldn't mind."

"No woman wants to live with another woman while she's living in her own house with her man."

"I guess you'd know all about stuff like that, huh, Blinky?"

He grows quiet. And I don't care. Let him think hard about his own actions. The things I've been hearing about for so long that it's like listening to a popular bedtime story.

"Is everything I've heard about you true, Blinky? You were first dating my mama. Told her you loved her. But you started catching feelings for my mama's best friend. And you get Loretta pregnant. Is that how the story goes?"

Daddy is so quiet I'm afraid he's hung up.

"Oh, so you have nothing to say for yourself? Figures. You're no better than Jeff. As a matter of fact, you're just like him. I can't stand any of ya'll."

"If you want to hear the true story, you're going to have to listen and let me tell my story."

"I'm listening."

"Sometimes when you're young, you think you're invincible. As a man—and maybe women are like this, too—you think you can do what you want, when you want, until you learn that there's a price to pay for so-called freedom. When I was with Brooke, man oh man, she was the first thing I thought about when I woke up in the morning, the last thing on my mind when my eyes closed at night. I loved her more than life itself. She was gutsy, funny, and yes, your mama was finer than a girl in a picture show. She did what she wanted, when she wanted. I didn't like it, but I learned to deal with it. So when I started acting like her, tit for tat, well, Brooke couldn't stand it.

"One night, I came home late. I wasn't doing anything, just shooting pool all night with my man friends. But she asked me where I'd been. I didn't like her tone of voice. I told her it was none of her business. We were living with each other. And as far as Brooke was concerned, I was her common law husband. And according to her, if you live with your woman, you need to answer to that woman, or else get your ass out. But I was defiant. And I wouldn't tell her. I wasn't doing anything wrong. I resented being accused of being unfaithful. She got mad at me and hit me in my eye. She's small but it hurt. I hit her back. We got into it. I left the house. First person she called, crying and carrying on, was her best friend. She told Loretta she hated me. Loretta was like, 'You want me to check on him? He's probably at his hangout.' Brooke was like, 'I don't give a damn what you do. You can go fuck him for all I care.' And Loretta did."

I just shake my head in disbelief. My mama *never* told me that story.

"I did what a man naturally does. I was hurting. Ego bruised. My girl cursing me out, making me feel like a snake. A man has feelings. We have emotions even if y'all women accuse us of not having 'em. Shoot, we cry. I did. That night I cried in Loretta's arms. It just happened. Wasn't planned. She just felt sorry for me. She saw I was a good man. I was doing the best I could. And I did love your mama, but she didn't know how to appreciate my love. She doubted my sincerity. What else could I do, Daughter? Tell me, what else could I do?"

"You could have proved her wrong, Daddy. You could have proved you loved my mama by not sleeping with Loretta."

Blinky doesn't say anything.

"You could have said no to Loretta. Mama could have said no to Jeff. Jeff could have said the same thing to Brooke. And that's why society is fucked up today. No one can just say no."

"I–I, um—"

"I'm right and nobody can tell me I'm wrong. Daddy, I'm not perfect, but some things you just don't do. It's like everyone has an excuse. Why they drink too much. Why they get hooked on drugs. Why they sleep around with people they should leave alone. We're trying our best to get good things, but we're doing bad things trying to get the good."

"But Daughter—"

"It's just like that old lady Camilla Parker Bowles. She may have eventually snared and married Prince Charles, but she will never earn true honor the way she could have had it if their courtship had been played out the right way. With decency and integrity. Humph, she's not even called a princess, but a *duchess*, which sounds so much uglier and unattractive than a princess. Get my drift?"

"I get it, Daughter."

"Now like I said before, I'm not perfect, Daddy. I'm working on it. If Jeff and Mama did me wrong, I have a right to work through my anger."

"Yeah, you have a right to be mad. Brooke was mad at me for getting Loretta pregnant. And Loretta got mad at me when I got Brooke pregnant."

"See there. We reap what we sow, and I think Jeff should reap something really bad for all the things he's doing. His ass should be in the back of a speeding ambulance by now."

"But if you pay him back, who's going to pay *you* back?"

"Nobody. Because I haven't done anything wrong."

"Think about your words, Daughter. Think about your attitude. Because if you do things against Jeff and even your mama, believe me, somebody is going to pay you back."

"I don't know about that."

"Well, I do. I'm warning you. Leave well enough alone."

"Oh, should I throw a party then? Break out a bottle of champagne and make a toast to Mama, to Jeff, to Marlene?" I can't take it anymore. "Daddy, I can't listen to you. I gotta get out this town house. I gotta do something before I go crazy."

I show Blinky respect by thanking him for calling and saying good-bye and that I'll call him later. I have listened to my father. Now it's time to listen to myself. I'm taking on a parent role now (if I want to go by Blinky's insane theory). I'm still very upset, and I vow to do what I think is best.

I call Marlene. "Please tell me you're laying low. I'm on my way home right now. But I'm starving so I'm going to pick up Chinese."

"Okay, bring me back some kung pao shrimp—"

"And pork egg foo young," we say at the same time. I know her favorites.

"And just so you know, Marlene, I just talked to Blinky. My mama called him, probably trying to get him to side with her."

"I still can't believe what happened."

"That sounds funny coming from you."

"What did you say?"

"I'm saying that now that the shoe is on the other foot, I

think it's amazing that you're amazed what another woman will do when it comes to someone else's man. Did you hear that?"

"Look, Rachel. If I would have known Jeff was a jerk—"

"You never would have messed around with him? Oh, but if he was a good and upright man, that would make it right?"

"You don't have to yell—"

"I'm angry, you understand? I never thought in a million years we'd be going through this stuff. It's not us. So give me a minute, okay? I'm working through my anger."

"Well, as long as you still bring me my Chinese food, I don't care what you do."

"That's sad."

"And don't forget the wonton soup."

"Pitiful."

"And lots of fortune cookies."

"Bye, Marlene."

I hang up and dash over to our favorite Chinese joint, a restaurant off Bellaire Boulevard in a section known as Chinatown.

When I go in, I decide to eat my lunch there and bring Marlene's home. Make her wait. I ask for the moo goo gai pan lunch special, and place an order for Marlene. A cute Asian waitress dressed in a white blouse and black slacks is responsible for the area where I am sitting, close to the cash register. After she takes my initial order, she frequently walks past my table but refills my glass of tea only one time after I manage to flag her down. When I've finished eating, I signal to the waitress. After ten minutes she hands me Marlene's food. Then she issues me the check and folds her arms while she waits next to my table.

"How you pay?"

"With cash. Why do you ask?" I tell her, irritated, because I don't like her questioning me how I'm planning on paying. She watches me withdraw a twenty from my wallet, takes the money, then rushes away to ring up the transaction. I keep my eyes on her and notice her closely examining the currency I gave her, as if I'm trying to use counterfeit money. When she returns, she hands me a ten, two singles, and some change. Again she folds her hands and stands at my table, making me feel uncomfortable. I just sit there and play with the coins, annoyed at her behavior. She reminds me of the pharmacist I encountered at the CVS store. And the more I think about the way I was treated that night, the more agitated I get.

Finally she backs away from my table and attends to other customers who are waving at her. When I look at the front counter and plainly see that two white male customers who were served by my waitress are paying for their meal at the register, I angrily snatch my purse and storm out of the restaurant, not leaving her even a dollar tip.

Before my feet can even hit the parking lot, the waitress bolts through the restaurant door. "You cheap. You stingy. I work hard."

"You work hard at making sure my money isn't fake," I retort, "but you're a terrible waitress." I stop and stare at her. "I don't think you need to stand over black people and make sure they pay their tab." Still seething inside, I quickly get in my car and rush home.

As soon as I enter the apartment, I go collapse on Marlene's bed and stiffly lie next to her, still reeling from my unpleasant experience.

"I'm sorry, Sis," Marlene says, assuming she's the one who got me bent out of shape. "I didn't mean to stress you out. You're right. I was wrong. I just can't figure out why Jeff would be out there doing his thing. Why do that when he has me?"

"That's what we need to figure out," I tell her. "Okay, here's the deal." I begin to describe how we're all going to the restaurant to watch London and Jeff. I ask her to please act normal so Jeff won't catch on. "He's in for a rude awakening. I hate to make him an example, but as women, we must protect and assert ourselves," I say. "I'm more upset with him than with you. He was my lover; he chose to be with me. You're my family and you didn't get to cast a vote . . . as far as being my sister."

Marlene agrees with me and promises to stick to the plan.

A couple nights later I hear Marlene on speaker phone talking to Jeff.

"Can we go check out a movie tonight, sweetie?"

"Nooo, Little Mama. I gotta meet up with a tenant."

"Oh, yeah? Which one?"

"Aw, some lady."

"Does the lady have a name?"

"You're being silly."

"No, I just don't know why we can't run and take care of your business and then go to the movies. You know I've been anxious to see the new Tyler Perry."

"Tyler Perry movies bash men. You know I'm not down with that."

I roll my eyes. "Oh, Jeff, it's just entertainment," Marlene says. "Plus I need a good laugh. Thank God my ankle feels better. And I really want to get out the house."

"Stay home and watch some of those unopened DVDs y'all have laying around there. I'll take you out tomorrow."

"Hmm, okay. But can you stop over tonight when you're done with your tenant?"

"Huh? I don't know how long it's going to take. Chasing down money is stressful. I provide them with a home. All I ask is that they pay up on time. But some folks paying late, some aren't paying at all. That's messing with my pockets."

"I heard that. Anyway, can I expect you later on?"

"Argh, Marlene, please, enough with the questions. I don't know what I'll be doing later, but I promise to call you first if I can swing by. Will that do?"

She makes a face but says, "That'll work. See ya later, Jeff."

Marlene hangs up the phone and chuckles to herself. "That's one of the hardest conversations I've ever had in my life." She pauses and reflects. "In some ways I hope you're wrong. I pray that this online stuff is just Jeff's way of meeting potential tenants. I know for sure that he's been struggling lately. One couple skipped out, moving their belongings in the middle of the night with no warning and leaving the place in shambles."

"Well, in my opinion, if he wanted to attract new tenants he'd advertise in the paper like a normal businessman. Trust me, he's up to something."

"Well, let's go see what he's up to."

Marlene and I agree to ride with Alita, who decides to borrow Big Hen's pickup. London travels solo to the restaurant in her black sedan. When setting up the date, London suggested meeting at someplace simple, friendly, and inexpensive and recommended a popular Vietnamese sandwich shop located downtown that serves banh mi sandwiches and vermicelli shrimp bowls, her favorites. But Jeff insisted on going all out and suggested Benihana.

"Oh, he's trying to show off," I told London. "But do what he says."

So it's now seven o'clock. Alita, Marlene, and I are huddled at a table in the far corner of the restaurant. London made sure to request a teppanyaki table. London looks so gorgeous, she's absolutely glowing. She got blond highlights in her long and luxurious hair. She's wearing a beautiful peach-colored dress suit that perfectly complements her unblemished skin. And her makeup is impeccable yet natural looking. She sits at the head of the table with an air of confidence even though there's another family sitting across from her. I find it extraordinary that she's comfortable enough to laugh and joke with people she's only met several minutes before.

Alita and I thought it best to sit next to each other so we can enjoy a full view of Jeff's shenanigans. Poor Marlene is smiling so hard it looks like her face is about to explode. I can tell she's nervous. I sense she's still hoping against hope. Wishing that this whole thing turns out to be a huge misunderstanding.

"Okay, we may as well order something while we're here. My cousin shouldn't be the only who gets to eat good food tonight."

"Have you seen the prices on this menu?" I balk.

"Order what you like," Marlene says. "I'll pay. I don't have an appetite."

"Your not being hungry is like Jesse Jackson saying no thanks when asked to be interviewed by CNN."

"Oh, be quiet. I couldn't eat or drink anything if you paid me," Marlene says somberly. "My stomach is in so many knots, even the best-tasting food can't enter in."

"Hmm, you do feel bad. Oh, well, let's order," I say with enthusiasm and snatch up the menu, happy that Marlene is willing to pay.

London sends me a text that says, *"He's on his way. Said he had some business to handle."*

"Hmm," I say aloud. "Maybe his tenant alibi has some truth to it."

"Yeah, see," says Marlene. "I told you, cut the man some slack. He may have messed up with Brooke, but it doesn't mean he's a completely soulless person."

"Marlene, please. If you can't say anything worth listening to, just hush."

She starts to open her mouth, but I place my fingers to my lips and shake my head. From where I'm sitting, I can see Jeff being led into the restaurant in the direction of London's table.

"Look at how sharp he's dressed," Alita chirps. "If he's trying to collect cash from tenants, wouldn't he show up looking poor and needy?"

Good point. Even from here I can see that the man has a fresh haircut. He's wearing a business suit that costs at least a grand. And I know Jeff well enough to remember that he loves silk ties with unique patterns.

"Brother Boy is looking good," Alita says, eyeing him. "But he's still foul. And that's the most important issue."

We watch him confidently stride over to London. She stands up and grins. He pulls one hand from his back and presents her with a bouquet.

"Incredible," Alita says and whistles.

"Now can you believe it?" I question my sister. "Would a landlord give his potential tenant flowers?"

"Only if he's trying to sleep with her," Marlene mumbles. She sneaks a couple of peeks at them every few minutes. "This is driving me nuts. What is he saying to her?"

I text London. Wait a few minutes. She's too busy looking him in his face grinning and nodding to pay any attention to her cell phone. I want to walk over there so bad, but I know it's not the time or the place.

"What's up with your cousin?" I casually ask Alita.

"Oh, child, please. London is a professional dater. She's used to men ogling her, taking her places. Believe me, none of this stuff fazes that girl."

"I hope you're right."

"Now don't tell me you're starting to act funky."

"No, no, no," I say hurriedly. "I'm just making sure we stick to the master plan. I wish I knew what they were talking about."

"She's going to tell you everything, word for word, when it's all over."

"Do you see how he's grinning at London?" Marlene asks. Her eyes carry a type of hurt that only a brokenhearted woman knows. "I remember that's the way he looked at me the first time we went out to celebrate my promotion. It doesn't seem all that long ago." Her voice sounds heavy with sadness.

"Don't worry, Sis," I assure Marlene. "Jeffrey Williams is going to get double for our trouble."

MARLENE

You've Made Me So Happy

The next afternoon, Aunt Perry, Alita, my sister, and I decide to go shopping at the Galleria Mall. Rachel and Alita completed their self-defense class a couple hours ago. Rachel is ecstatic that she got through the dreaded final test—dreaded because although the women experience lots of repetitive training and drills, none of the class is eager to do the actual fighting that'll test their skills.

"Ya'll should have seen me," Rachel brags. "All the women were suited up from head to toe in protective plastic clothing. When it was my turn, I felt like a mummy, really stiff, and it was hard to see through that helmet they made us put on. But when I went in the fight room and I saw those big guys in their fight gear coming after me, I lost it. Everything Floyd taught me flew out the window," she says, laughing, "but I fought those guys like I was fighting for my life. Screaming, punching, kicking, hitting. I used thoughts of Jeff as my motivation and kicked one guy hard in his balls."

"There ya go," Aunt Perry says. She's walking around holding a Thirsty's cup, but she's pretending like her strawberry-banana yogurt smoothie is some Alizé. "That was your chance to take out your aggression on other men and not on Jeff. Not saying the man doesn't deserve it, but it grieves me to hear ya'll talking about what you wish you could do to the guy. Damn, I want to stomp Jeff's ass to the ground myself, but I'm no fool. And I hope you young ladies aren't, either."

"Oh, Aunt Perry," Rachel complains, but she knows better than to say anything when my aunt gives her the look.

"Aunt Perry, nothing. I want you to focus on other things besides jacking up Jeff."

"Aren't you the one who encouraged my sister to whip my butt not too long ago?" I remind her.

"Look. I'm old. You're still young. You got your whole lives ahead of you. It's one thing to have a fight with your sis. It's a whole other ball game to be laying your hands on a non–family member. He could press assault charges. There're plenty of women in prison who will tell you it wasn't worth it."

I decide to ignore my aunt. Ever since she went to church with me, she's had a changed attitude. I am glad for her, but I'm wondering when the real Perry is gonna make an appearance.

We're fighting a huge crowd of people who are streaming through the Galleria Mall like an army of ants. Kids, teens, elderly, and middle-aged moms rush from store to store checking out sales and doing some people watching. Saturday is always the busiest day at this spot. And I must admit, it feels great to be out, not tied down at home. Earlier this morning, I went to work. I felt so embarrassed for committing major errors while dealing with customers who were transacting business via the drive-through.

Aunt Perry does her best to console me. "Honey, look at it this way. We know you're not trying to mess up people's accounts on purpose. Right? Right! Not my niece. We know your head ain't on straight because you're worried about your man. What he's doing. Who he's with. A lot of women go through that. Your customers should understand."

"Yeah, but I want to gain their trust. They're not trying to be waited on by a cute but incompetent teller. People are already wary of banks as it is."

"They didn't fire you, did they? So that means you get another chance to do better next time around, sweetie," she says. "And no, I do not want to open an account with ya'll."

"Perryyyy," I complain, but my auntie is successful at getting me to smile.

"Hey," she says, motioning at Alita and Rachel. "I want to look at something in this store. Can you two meet us in front of the skating rink in a half hour?"

"Okay," Rachel says. "I'm going to see if there are any stores out here that sell personal Tasers."

Rachel and Alita huddle together and walk away, talking nonstop.

"Did she say what I just think she said?" Aunt Perry asks.

"She's very serious, Auntie. Rachel may seem like she's handling things well, but I know she's very upset with Jeff. Last night, when we got home from the restaurant, she did something I never thought she'd do."

"She ate a whole gallon of ice cream."

"No, silly, she dumped everything Jeff ever gave her in a garbage bag and took it out to the trash compactor. That was surreal. He gave her a journal one time, a nice pair of gold hoop earrings, then there was this pretty dress he bought her right before they got engaged. A gorgeous hot pink dress that had yellow elephants on it. It never fit her, but she accepted the gift because she was shocked he'd buy something like that for her. She never wore it but kept it in the back of her closet."

"Mmm, girl, I still have a napkin a guy used to write his name and my name on it. Pete and Perry. Haha," she cackles. "Those were the days. Holding on is hard. But staying attached when you need to be free is harder."

Aunt Perry thoughtfully gazes at me. "Come on. I want to show you something."

We pass alongside the skating rink, watching cute elementary school kids impatiently waiting for their turn to break loose on the ice. The air feels so chilly when we walk by that I find myself rushing through the mall.

"Slow down. You're going to miss it."

"Miss what?" I ask.

"Wow, it's still there. See that?"

I follow my aunt into EB Games. We stand behind a Hispanic kid whose hands are glued to an Xbox game console.

"See right there?" She points. "Notice how part of the top corner of this game is chipped off? Like it's broken?"

"Yeah, Auntie, I see it. So what?"

"I did that, that's what."

"Excuse me?"

"I called myself being big and bad trying to pay back this man who I felt treated me like trash. He borrowed . . . oh, my Lord, I'm ashamed to say this, but maybe it'll help. He borrowed fifteen hundred dollars from me. Begged me to get a cash advance on my credit card."

"Hmm, interesting."

"I–I knew I shouldn't have done it, but I was crazy about the guy. He knew it, too. I can't believe I barely put up a fight. God knows I really couldn't afford to give him that money."

"You gave it to him?"

"Ha, I sure did. As soon as he got that money, girl, I could barely get his ass on the phone. Overnight, he suddenly became too busy for a sista. He avoided me for two weeks,

Marlene. Told me he was 'working on it' and warned me if I didn't back off, he wasn't giving me a dime back. Well, what he have to say that for?"

"Oh, God, what did you do?"

"I knew he loved coming here to the Galleria every Saturday. He was younger than me and very much into playing video games. Shit, was that a hint and a half for my ass or what? So, when I see him up here buying a stupid video game, yet he says he can't pay me back, well, this is what's left of this console."

"Oh, Lord, Auntie Perry, you're so crazy. Whatever happened to the guy?"

"Last I heard he was serving a little time in Humble. And he's keeping busy trying not to drop the soap."

"Mmm-mmm."

"But funny thing about it, I have nothing to do with him being in jail. Sure, we got into it right here at this very store. I'm shocked the manager doesn't remember me. We tore some stuff up," she says and gently rubs the top corner of the console that looks like someone took a hammer to it.

"But no one pressed charges. Manager asked us to leave. We did. Escorted by mall security. And I got so sick of people staring at us I said never again."

"That's a funny story. But it has nothing to do with me."

"I see it in your eyes. Seriously. You're always looking out of it. I know it has everything to do with Jeff. Whatever you plan to do, let it be. I'm lucky enough to be standing here with you, my favorite niece—"

"Hold up, I'm not your favorite."

"Yes, you are. I just tell what's-her-face that 'cause she's the youngest. But when you were born, my very first niece, girl, I held you in my arms, nuzzled your little cheeks, and thanked God you had all your fingers and toes and a head full of hair."

"Oh, stop it. You make me want to cry."

"As long as you're crying for the right reasons, go ahead and cry."

"Oh, Auntie."

"I love you, Marlene, and I don't want anything bad to happen to you. I'm sick of bad things going on in our family. And we got to stop it. The grown folks need to step in and take some of the responsibility. Blinky is my brother, but he's not right in the head. We know this."

My aunt's voice sounds so funny I want to burst out laughing. But I don't. I'm enjoying this too much. It feels like home. Feels like love.

"Let's get out of here. Too many bad memories, but at the same time, I feel proud that I can walk in here and know that I'm not trying to be the woman I used to be. I can be better than what I used to be."

"You know, Auntie, you're sounding a lot like my pastor."

"Ya think? That's an honor coming from my knuckle-head niece." She hugs me close, and we leave the game store.

"No, seriously, you remind me of this woman at church. Sister Palmer. Remember her?"

"Not really," my aunt says.

"She spoke briefly on Women's Day. We only got a little taste of how she ministers. But I think we should all attend the Women's Conference, which starts next week. I could use some new inspiration. Things have been so crappy lately, I have nothing to lose."

"You could lose some weight."

"Okay, maybe, but besides that, smarty, I have nothing better to do."

"I'll have to check my schedule. Just remind me, okay, sweetie? Now, let's go this way." I say all right and walk alongside my aunt. I can't help but notice hot guys checking her out, offering her confident smiles as we pass by.

"Hey, now. See these men giving you the eye? You're not paying any attention to any of them. Why not?"

"I don't care to meet a man off the street. I actually want to join your church's Singles Ministry."

"Auntie, stop joking around."

"Do I have a smile on my face? Do you see the whites of my teeth?"

"Oh, well, alrighty then. Funny thing is, I may have to join with you. I still care about Jeff. What? I know it's crazy, but it's hard to go from liking a man one day to outright hating him the next; I don't care what he does."

"Pitiful."

"Real."

"Okay, fine. You still got the hots for the man. But it doesn't mean you can't be setting up the next guy."

"Auntie," I say and blush.

"Men do it all the time. They'll have their main girl and are always looking to upgrade. They take being alone much worse than women do. Hell, I've been single for a couple years now. I am about ready to cash in some coochie coupons."

"Oh, it's been a while, huh?"

"Girl, now I'm starting to blush. It's a rare day in hell when I can openly talk about sex with my niece. But like I said before. We grown. We need to talk about this stuff."

I nod at her, but the Sunglass Hut draws my attention over to its counter. I adore cool sunglasses. "Oh my God, these are so tight. Look at these." I point to some gray oversized shades with rounded edges. The word *Gabbana* is engraved in all caps on the sides.

"Here, try them on," suggests a cute, perfectly tanned salesman with black, wavy, movie-star hair.

"Oh my God. These look so good."

"Yeah, you look so awesome in them," the guy says, egging me on.

"How much?" I ask.

"Only three hundred."

"That's about two hundred more than what I'd care to pay," I pout. Shoot, if Jeff had paid me back some of the money he owes me, paying cash for these beautiful shades would be no problem. I love the glasses, but it'll be kind of a tight squeeze, especially since I voluntarily splurged on our dinner last night at Benihana.

"So may I ring them up for you, Miss Lady? These glasses were made for you."

"Yeah, but they might be mistaking me for Queen Latifah or someone else important . . . and rich," I joke. I shake my head at the guy, who quietly moves on to the next potential buyer.

"Shame, shame, shame." Right then that Aretha Franklin "Chain of Fools" song goes through my head. Humiliated, I think about how I've been acting so foolish when it comes to Jeff. I don't understand why he begs me for money. Like a dummy, a couple of times I've told him okay, with a big, crazy-looking smile on my silly-looking face. Just thinking about it makes me mad and regretful, especially considering how Jeff dined with London last night, bought her beautiful flowers, and talked with her so long I got sick of sitting in that restaurant being tortured.

I deserve better than that.

"Hey, Marlene. Can you wait for me by the skating rink? I need to take care of something."

"Fine with me," I tell her. I gaze over at the dozens of children who are breezing by, the sounds of their skates slicing across the ice as they spin, turn, and dip. Some skaters glide effortlessly, looking like birds soaring peacefully through the sky; others try to stay balanced and hold on to the wall, or they cling to other skaters so they don't fall down and embarrass themselves.

I admire the ones who skate with precision. Even though they're moving backward, they appear so calm, confident, in control. I want to be like that, I think to myself. Not like the ones who grip the wall, afraid to let go, too petrified to take the fall.

Humble yourselves before the Lord, and he will lift you up.

Is that you, Lord? And are you talking to me? I feel silly talking to God inside my head while hanging out at one of the most popular malls in America. But didn't Pastor Solomon say we can pray about anything, anytime? As long as we have a mind, we can pray. And if we can talk to God anytime and anyplace, isn't it fair to think He can talk to us anywhere, too? That even the Houston Galleria can't force him out?

Fortunately for me, my Aunt Perry saunters up to me with a huge grin that shows all her sparkling white teeth.

"Happy birthday." She thrusts a Sunglass Hut shopping bag at me.

"It's not my birth—"

"Knucklehead girl, hush up. Open the darned bag."

"Oh my goodness, Auntie." I open the bag and notice an eyeglass case . . . and those beautiful Gabbanas.

"Go ahead, put 'em on."

I jump up and down and squeeze Aunt Perry tight around her neck. "Thank you." I kiss her on her cheek. "I love you, I love you. You've made me so happy." My eyes glisten with tears. Inside I also tell the Lord thank you for the opportunity to spend time with my aunt and bond with her in a positive way. This makes up for every hurtful thing that happened at my daddy's birthday party.

Rachel sends me a text asking where we are. I text her back, and ten minutes later we meet in front of the skating rink. Marlene and Alita show off some matching Ed Hardy T-shirts that they bought from Macy's.

"Hmm, I didn't know you had money for that." I scowl and openly gawk at Rachel. "You didn't pay your share of the electric bill."

"Hey, hush. I got that for her," Alita says.

"Oh," I utter and avert my eyes the instant Aunt Perry gives me a you-ought-to-be-ashamed-of-yourself look.

"Okay, woo, I'm tired, ya'll," says Aunt Perry. "I'm about to pull a Marie Osmond and pass out."

"No problem, Auntie. We can leave now. It's been fun. Let's go," Rachel commands.

We find Rachel's car in the Macy's parking garage and head out going west on Westheimer. Rachel is driving. I'm sitting in the front passenger seat. Alita is sitting behind Rachel, and my aunt is behind me. We travel a few miles down the street and come to a red light.

"I have an idea," Rachel says with a mischievous grin on her face. "This is going to be a long-ass red light. Let's do the Chinese fire drill."

"What?" I ask.

"Yayyy, I'm game," Alita screams from the back.

"When I say go, everyone jump out the car and switch seats. Left to right. Ready, set. Go!"

Alita, Rachel, and even my Aunt Perry scream and jump out of the car with the keys still in the ignition. Rachel jumps out and runs in front of the car. She looks at me like I'm crazy. "Why are you sitting there? Get out and get in Perry's seat."

I swear she started to call me a dummy but thought twice about it. I roll my eyes and jump out of my seat and go take Perry's place. Seconds before the red light turns green, Alita is now in the driver's seat and Rachel is sitting in front of me.

"You all are certifiably crazy," I yell at the top of my lungs. "What have you been drinking?" I laugh so much my brand-new sunglasses begin to fog up. But I don't care. I'm having the time of my life. It's been a long time since I've felt so good. Nothing can spoil my day. No how. No way.

Many hours later, I am at home. In bed. Tossing and turning like I've been doing for the past several hours. I was this close to calling him. Telling him off. Then deleting his number from my cell phone. Why bother? I may not be the most perfect woman on earth, but what I must receive from a man is respect. He may not completely be in love with me, but he'd better respect me. Whether I cave in and give him everything he asks for or not, he'd better come correct and act like he was raised right. Enough is enough.

In my mind when you've been as humanly nice as possible to a person who doesn't deserve even two minutes of kindness, then I've done my job. I gave it my all, and if my all isn't good enough, it's time for me to do something different.

I'm lying on my side trying to get comfortable enough to fall asleep. But it's hard. He completely fills my mind. I need to go to church in the morning. Need to do a lot of things tomorrow that I've been neglecting. Attend Sunday school. Go across town to see my daddy, my mama. Normal stuff. Things I used to do that make me feel like Marlene Draper.

I turn to the other side of my bed and reach down until my hand hits the carpet. I feel around a few inches underneath the bed. My hand touches a book. I slide my fingers across the cover and rub a film of dust between my fingers. Then I grab the book and lift it up until it's lying next to me.

It's the dusty old Bible that Loretta gave me years ago. I thought it was funny at the time. Loretta giving me a Bible? What a joke. But right now nothing is funny. I need to fall asleep fast, and opening up a Bible and trying to read something from the Old Testament will put me to sleep faster than NyQuil.

Minutes after I start reading I hear a persistent knock at the front door. What the hell? It's what, almost one-thirty in the morning. Annoyed and a bit scared, I hop out of the bed and approach the door. Jeffrey's recognizable frame is visible through the tiny peep hole.

I open the door. "What the heck are you doing here this time of night?"

He smiles at me, eyes glassy. "Aww, Little Woman. Is that any way to great your man after you haven't seen him in a while?"

"Jeff, please. I'm not your woman."

"Say what?"

I angrily fold my arms under my breasts. "Why didn't you call earlier?"

"Hey, aren't you happy to see me? Don't you like surprises? I–I got you something special."

"Jeff, this isn't going to work. You've been doing things that are making me very unhappy."

"Ugh, do we have to stand outside in the cold talking about this? May I come in? Pretty please with sugar on top?"

"That is so lame." I step aside, and he smiles like he's grateful and walks in. Usually when Jeff visits, he immediately plops on the couch and reaches for the remote. But tonight he heads straight for my bedroom. He stands at the door and waits until I am in the room, then he closes the door shut and turns the lock.

Jeff peers around my room like he's inspecting it. That really irks me.

"What are you snooping around my room for, huh?" I don't wait for him to reply. I go and slip under the covers but sit back against my pillows and give him a hostile stare.

"Beautiful Girl, what's with the bad attitude? I didn't even get a hug, a kiss, nothing." He laughs to himself like something is funny.

I roll my eyes and turn over so that I'm facing the other wall. I feel his eyes boring a hole in me. Then I hear the sound of his shoes being kicked off his feet. He unzips his slacks and they crumple to the ground in a heap.

"Can I lie next to you, please?"

I don't say anything. He slides in the bed and places his arm around my waist. I feel his big lips touching the back of my neck. Small little I'm-sorry pecks that sprout tiny bumps on my skin.

"Jeff, no, stop." I scoot over and ask him to remove his arm from my waist.

"Are you sure?"

I just sigh. He removes his hand from me and turns around to face the opposite wall. Minutes later I hear him snoring. I quietly slide out of the bed and tiptoe all the way around till I reach his slacks. I pick them up and tiptoe out of the room. I go to the kitchen, turn on the stove light, and start rummaging through all his pockets. Leather wallet filled with cash, four sets of keys, and six quarters in one pocket. The other has two cell phones. One I recognize. One I don't.

I click a button so I may view the phone's call record, but there's a lock on it.

"That infuriates me," I mumble to myself. I tap on keys and punch in several four-digit combinations (his date of birth, his home address, and the last four digits of his cell number) hoping to crack his code, but none of them does the trick. Just when I'm ready to return to my bedroom, the phone starts vibrating. It feels like an electric razor is buzzing between my hands. The caller's name flashes on the display screen: Felicia.

Who the heck is Felicia?

I place his phone and other stuff back in his pocket and return to my room. I get back in bed, which causes Jeff to stir around in bed. He reaches over until his fingers come in contact with my leg. He starts making a tiny circle on my thigh with his index finger.

I stiffen and say in a steely voice, "Please don't do that. I'm tired."

"I am, too. But I can give you something that will give you a burst of energy."

"Jeff, please." I shift over in bed so that my back is facing him.

I feel him press himself against my shoulders. His body feels warm and cozy.

"Can I have some booty?"

"You have a lot of nerve."

Jeff maneuvers his body until he's sitting up in bed. He reaches over and turns on the lamp. "Why are you acting like this? You haven't been acting yourself tonight."

"I told you that I'm tired."

"Okay, I'm exhausted myself. I had a long-ass day."

I finally sit up, too. "No, I don't mean physically tired. I am tired of you, period." I hop out of bed and grab Jeff's slacks, holding them up.

"Here," I say and toss his slacks directly at him. They fall right on top of his head. "I don't want you in my bed. So go on and get dressed . . . and get out." I am so angry, it's like I don't have any other emotions. I feel so dead inside. Maybe that's what it's going to take to get him out of my life.

Jeff pulls his pants off his head and stares at me, looking hurt and confused. "Little Mama. What's gotten into you?"

"Who's Felicia?"

"What?"

"I asked, who is Felicia? Why is she calling? Why are you so secretive?"

"I–I don't know what you're talking about."

"Why do you have a second cell phone?"

"What?" He snatches up his pants and starts getting dressed. "You've been snooping in my stuff again? I told you about that insecure shit." Once he gets fully dressed he continues sitting on my bed like he's daring me to say something.

"Jeff, I don't feel comfortable with your being here right now. I think you should leave."

"You don't tell me what to do!"

"Well, I just did, Jeff." My voice is loud but calm. "This is my house and as long as you're in it, I'm going to tell you what to do."

"Marlene, you're crazy!"

"No, *you* are. You've been sneaking around behind my back—"

"Psycho bitch."

I jump in his face and point toward the door. "Get out, Jeff. Now!"

He stares at me with such dislike that I feel like pushing him out of the room until he's totally out of the apartment.

"Did you hear me?" I ask.

"Did you hear *me*? Well, in case you didn't, let me say it clear. One, you don't raise your voice at me. Two, I'm tired of you nagging me out, questioning my every move. I'm a grown-ass man, dammit. I can do whatever the hell I want to do. As far as I know I haven't put a fucking ring on your finger."

"Leave, asshole."

"That's it," he sputters. "If you don't apologize for acting like a nut, don't expect to hear from me or see me again."

"The day I apologize to you will be the day you apologize to me. You've been rude, disrespectful, lying to me, dating other women." I am so upset that I feel myself breathing unevenly.

"There she goes again, talking crazy. Oh, am I dating Felicia? For your info, Felicia is a potential tenant, okay? She lives out of town and is looking for a place to stay."

"Whatever. I don't care anymore."

"I don't care anymore, either." He gives me one last piercing look and walks out of my room. I don't exhale until I hear the front door slam shut.

RACHEL

This Situation Needs Handling

$I'm$ *deep in sleep,* comfortably resting in my bed when my bedroom lights come on and I hear Marlene screaming at me.

"Rachel, get up. Jeff just left here and my purse is missing. My wallet, credit cards, driver's license, cell phone. I know he has it."

"Girl, what happened?" I hop out of the bed and look for a shirt and some blue jeans.

"He came by, girl, trying to do some booty-call mess, and I wasn't having it."

"Oh, okay," I say, "you were actually able to resist him?"

"Girl, yes. Loretta told me that a smart woman uses sex to her advantage. That we don't have to give it up every single time to a man just because he wants it. Well, this time I didn't want it, and he definitely didn't deserve it."

"I guess he's trying to pay you back by taking your belongings, huh? That is so wrong. Jeff is such an ass. I hate to say it, but all he cares about is himself."

"Exactly. I may have looked at his cell phone a few times, but I've never thought about actually taking it. That's stealing. He's gone too far."

"Let me call your cell phone." I grab my own phone and dial Marlene's number. It rings twice, then Jeff answers. "Hello, there."

"Hi, Jeff," I say calmly, even though I want to scream. "So you *did* take my sister's phone. Why'd you do that?" I ask, trying to sound sweet and rational.

"I want her to know how it feels to be violated. She intentionally goes through my things. My pants pockets. You never did anything like that. I kind of regret hooking up with your sister. She's as lame as they come. Nothing like you, Rachel."

"I see, well, yeah, she probably shouldn't have done all that. But, um, can I meet you somewhere so you can return her purse? Where are you now?"

It's three in the morning. I'm sleepy and my eyelids are so heavy I probably look like I'm high on drugs. But he's messing with my sister, and this situation needs handling regardless of how tired I am.

"I'm around the way. But I say we let her suffer." He laughs. "What you think about that?"

"Oh, Jeff, be nice, okay. She's sorry. She didn't mean to go through your things. She's just the curious type. Now, tell me where we can meet up so I can get her purse and phone, and we can forget this ever happened."

"I'm not thinking about that girl. I'm not thinking about any girl. All y'all have issues."

I don't say a word. Let Jeff do all the talking. The more he opens up his mouth, the more I'll find out everything I need to know.

Marlene leaves the room. I am fully dressed and ready to go, but I have no idea where to start, or where he could be.

"Women play games. They're teases. Did you know that, Rach?"

"Well, every woman doesn't know how to treat a man like yourself, Jeff. You're in an altogether different league."

"Yeah, you're right. You know, I think you're the only woman who really understood me and had my back. You never nagged me about my real estate stuff."

What's he talking about? Yes, I did.

"You acted secure. Had your own thing going. I guess you just weren't ready to jump that broom with a brotha. But I would have waited for you, Rachel. As long as you wanted to wait." His voice catches. "I would have waited for you, only you, my dear Rachel."

"That's so sweet, Jeff. Maybe we can talk about this. Would you like to do that? Let's meet at our spot. Do you know the place I'm talking about?" I grab my purse and jacket and turn off my bedroom light. When I get to the living room, Marlene is pacing the floor. She sees me gesture at her, and we leave the apartment together.

The night is chilly, and I can see white clouds hovering over the early morning sky. The stars are blinking brightly in the night, and it sounds so quiet right now it's like we're deep in the country.

"Jeff, we can talk about things and take care of unfinished business—"

"What do you mean?" His voice is sharp, cautious.

"Um, I mean that this is our time to straighten out any issues we've had. Air out our differences and make sure we part as friends, good friends. No hard feelings."

"Hmm, okay. I am a bit hungry. It's been a long, stressful evening."

I keep talking to Jeff and listening to him say random things. Marlene and I get in my car, and I start the engine. Soon I'm on Highway 6. But one mile before I get to my destination, I pull over to an empty parking lot and let the car idle. I make little sounds like I'm listening to Jeff talk, but I also signal to Marlene. I open up my purse. Right on top is a Taser gun that I got at a pawn shop last night. Even though I learned a few tips through my self-defense class, I'm not sure I totally know how to use it, but that doesn't concern me. The second I get Marlene's stuff from Jeff, I'm going to try my best to use the gun on him. I want to hear him scream like he's never screamed before.

"Jeff, can I put you on hold for a second? Don't hang up. I'm almost there." I press the mute button and look at Marlene. "Okay, girl, here's our chance. I hate to do this, but we've got to make Jeff suffer for everything he's done. Don't you agree?"

"Yes, I do. I'm pissed at him, hurt by his actions. He disrespected me big time, and I won't stand for it. I've never been treated so rudely by a man in my life. Never again."

"I'm with you."

Before I can reconnect with Jeff, Marlene touches my hand and gives me a small grin, "Thanks, Sis."

"No problem. Now recline your seat all the way back so Jeff won't see you. I don't want him to know I'm up to something. You'll have to sit tight while I handle things."

I get Jeff back on the line. "Are you at Waffle House yet? Oh, I can't wait to get some coffee, some of those grits, bacon. It'll be like the good ole days."

"Yeah." He pauses. "Do you know I still have your ring in my pocket? That I never stopped loving you, Rachel?"

I wait to hear what else he has to say.

"Yeah, so, it's like I'm carrying you around with me. Not like I got anybody else to carry around with me," he says and laughs bitterly. "Yep, your sister is fucked up. She's a fat fuck, but you know, it was my first time with a big girl. Big girls need love too, ya know?"

I grit my teeth and make a right turn, slowly driving into the Waffle House parking lot. There are a few cars in the lot, and the tiny restaurant is lit up. I drive all the way to the end of the lot and back into my space so I can monitor the area. Soon Jeff's Mach 1 pulls into the lot. He flashes his lights at me. His car slowly creeps through the lot. I can tell he's about to park at an angle, something he always does.

That pisses me off. The more I think about how possessive he is over a car, the madder I get. Why am I going through this? Trying to sweet talk him into giving me my sister's purse. If it weren't for both of them, I wouldn't be in this mess. And seeing Jeff makes my stomach churn when I imagine how he put his lips on my mother. How dare he! I think about how badly he treated me and the anger I've felt lately even from the racial incidents that have happened. The lady who ignored me in the pharmacy, the waitress at the restaurant who accused me of being cheap. Who the hell does everyone think they are?

I glance at Marlene, who is leaning back in her seat. I reach in my purse and feel around until my fingers grab the Taser gun. Jeff steps out of the car. He's carrying Marlene's purse. He stands there. Looks like he's reaching for his cell phone. I place the Taser gun in my jacket pocket and get out of the car but leave the keys in the ignition. Marlene sits up slightly so she can see what's happening.

I start taking slow, measured steps toward Jeff. His cell is pressed against his ear. I see he's on the phone, and I wonder who he's talking to at this ungodly hour. He's standing next to his car. His precious car. I walk a few steps in his direction and watch him. Take another step and wait a couple minutes to see if he's going to eventually get off the phone. After a while I hear rubber burning. It sounds loud, like screeching tires. Suddenly an SUV whips out of the parking space next to my car. It rocks wildly and heads straight for Jeff.

Jeff looks up and yells, "Nooo, Felicia." He drops his phone. The driver of the SUV jumps out of the car and rolls on the ground. The SUV plunges directly into Ella, knocking it two spaces over. Soon I hear explosions. A tower of fire roars up and engulfs Jeff's car. Jeff screams, "Nooo," and runs right into the flames.

My legs hurriedly move toward the car. "No, Jeff, stay back. Noooo!" More explosions. I stop running. Bloodcurdling screams fill the air. Yelling and cursing and agony. The fire and smoke climb the air. The smell of death clogs my nose. The worst smell I've ever encountered in my life. Someone runs outside from the Waffle House. "Call the police," he yells. I can't move. I can't think. I see a figure fall to the ground, next to the car. Remnants of cash dance in the fumes. Pieces of debris fly about. I fall to my knees. Close my eyes. Think about how Jeffrey Williams just lost his money, his car, and all his women.

I beat my fists against the concrete and howl until there's nothing left in me to scream about.

RACHEL

Daughter, You Are Forgiven

It's one week later. Marlene, Aunt Perry, and I are at Solomon's Temple. We're sitting in the pews surrounded by hundreds of females and a few dozen men who are filling in as ushers and attendants so the women can enjoy this Women's Conference. I feel so numb. Yet I had to get out of the house. Jeff's funeral was yesterday. I didn't want to attend, but Blinky encouraged me to go.

Everything happened so fast that night. The fire trucks, ambulance, police cars soon surrounded the restaurant. I could barely talk intelligibly to the officers. I didn't know what to say. Couldn't understand what had happened. But Marlene explained it all to me. She saw way more than I did. She told me that while I was busy trying to get to Jeff, the SUV pulled up next to my car. A pretty but crazed-looking woman got out of the SUV and tapped on the passenger window. She knew who Marlene was. Said her name was Felicia. She and Jeff had been together the night he came to see my sister. Said they got into a fight. She was sick of his ways. Felicia told Marlene that she found out Jeff was dating other women and borrowing money from her to pay for all his hot dates. She accused him of being selfish and greedy for hoarding his own money yet sweet-talking her out of her own money so he could be a baller. Felicia was furious when she learned how she'd been used. They'd known each other three months but had been engaged only a couple of weeks. But last night Jeff took the eighteen-carat white gold engagement ring back from her. Said he was in love with another woman. She followed him to my and Marlene's place and waited outside in the car, fuming mad and plotting her revenge. Then she blankly stared at my sister and told her, "Stay away from my fiancé."

That's when Felicia got back in the SUV and sat a couple of minutes before gunning the engine and ramming her vehicle into Jeff's. Marlene never did get her purse, wallet, or cell phone. Jeff never paid her money back, either, but all that is replaceable. She has her life, her self-esteem, and more important, Marlene still has her soul.

Felicia was arrested on the spot. Jeff is now six feet in the ground. And my sister and I are trying to get our lives straight. Trying to make sense of the craziness.

So here we are. At church. Listening to speakers. Desperate for a change.

Sister Palmer is standing in front of the church. She walks and talks, stops and looks at the audience. She's bold, powerful, fiery, and honest. "I'm all about women power," she states. "Women have got to start having each other's back instead of stabbing each other in the back. Yes, you want to have the love of a man, but no, ladies, that love doesn't have to come from another sister's man. You don't have the right to flirt with, sleep with, hang out with, and follow up on some guy's attraction to you just because. Leave her man alone and happiness will spring in your direction. The things you give out are going to come back to you. You messing with someone's man? You may find your own man someday, and lo and behold, a sister ten years younger than you is going to develop a secret relationship with your guy. She will feel it is her right; she will become to your husband what you were to someone else's husband ten years ago. It's a vicious cycle, but it can be broken. Get up right now, walk across this room, and apologize to every woman who has a husband who you've flirted with, texted, posted flirty comments to on his MySpace page, or given a 'church' hug that was a little bit too tight. Go on, get up; don't act like you don't know what I'm talking about."

Sister Palmer turns around and faces everyone and says, "Watch this." She walks over to the first pew and stands before the first lady of the church, Mrs. Solomon, and hugs her. Tells her "I'm sorry. Pastor is yours, not mine, he's not mine." One by one teary-eyed women get up out of their seats and awkwardly line up in a single row to hug the pastor's wife. I can't believe all those ladies openly admit they lust after the pastor.

While I know I'm not qualified to get up and hug Mrs. Solomon, I look around and search the crowd for someone else. Sister Maria Johnson sits alone dabbing at her eyes with her closed fist. I take a deep breath and find myself purposely sitting next to her. I stare in her eyes, so afraid to talk. She looks at me, eyes enlarged. When I nod, her head drops to her chest. I place my hand on her arm, fingers trembling. I tap and nudge her, and she finally stands up and falls into my arms.

"I'm sorry, so sorry, Sister Maria."

She buries her head in my shoulders, covering her tear-streamed face with her hands, just nodding over and over again.

A flood of memories causes me to squeeze her harder. Sister Maria is a widow, but my little flirtation with her husband happened when I was almost out of my teens. He was a deacon and I was a shy girl who thought he looked cute. He started talking to me after church when no one else was around, trying to bring me out of my shell. His attention made me feel special, important, cared about. So one Sunday afternoon when we thought no one was looking, I kissed him back when I saw his lips coming toward mine. He held me tight in his arms, and I imagined that he was my first boyfriend, my first lover, my husband to be. It was the second time I had felt a man's tongue in my mouth. It felt good, yet it felt bad. I pushed him off me after the kiss lasted too long. We never touched each other again, but I could never look his wife in her face after that. She was always so sweet and kind, and I felt so guilty knowing I had this secret.

That's another reason why it became too hard for me to continue going to church with a clear conscience. I knew God was aware of what I did, and I was too afraid of being exposed. Yet right now, the feeling of being exposed along with so many other women doesn't feel as horrible as I've imagined all these years. It feels like I've stepped inside a great big shower. It's like buckets of clean water are splashing on top of me and rinsing me off from head to toe. The bad feeling is being washed away, and my heart feels much lighter, less burdened than it has felt in years.

Soon I stop concentrating so much on myself, and my ears tune in to the noise in the room. Women weeping, ladies perched on their knees, some bending over clutching their stomachs moaning and groaning, sounding like slaves wailing on a plantation. Shamefaced women crying out to God begging, "Save me, Lord. Forgive me, Lord, cleanse me, oh God." My legs start shaking uncontrollably. What's wrong with me? I thought this feeling would be over by now, yet my body can't possibly be displaying what I've tried to hide inside of me.

Suddenly a lady who I don't know walks over to me, staring at me as she walks in a circle.

"Sister, may I pray for you?"

I just nod, too scared to say anything.

She steps up to me and lays her hand on my forehead while quietly praying, which makes me feel thankful. I hear her say, "God give your daughter direction, wisdom, and guidance; oh Father, strengthen her with your peace, your joy, and your truth. Make her the strong woman you created her to be. And release her from any guilt, any age-old guilt she may feel."

Legs still shaking, I nod my head with my eyes closed tight. The lady stops praying and holds me in her arms as if I were a baby. "Daughter, you are forgiven."

Listening to her makes me feel like God is speaking directly to me.

I thank her and turn around to go back to my seat. Quietly reflecting on what just happened and what it means. If God can forgive me, I can forgive my mama. I won't forget what she did, but we're going to get past it. Plus, I need her. I still love her.

Soon the sounds of crying and wailing fall to complete silence.

You could hear a pin drop. We all wait in utter anxiety about what is to happen next.

With her hands clasped together, Sister Palmer strides to the front of the church and stands in silence for a full five minutes. When she does speak, she boldly eyes the audience.

"Ladies, I am so grateful and so encouraged by what happened here today. Do not let this moment pass; don't let it be in vain. You've gained knowledge and strength that will positively affect you for the rest of your lives, just don't get caught up anymore. Make it your business to enjoy the newness of your empowered spirit from this moment forward. But I must say that I sense that many of you have questions. I sense in the spirit that some of you wonder why woman are agreeing to be accountable for flirting with the brothers, with someone's husband or boyfriend. And you wonder why men don't have to also watch what they do with other woman. Why, you ask, is it a woman's responsibility?

"Men, you have a responsibility, too. Think about it. Every time a man lies to his woman he binds her up. It's like taking a thick rope and wrapping it around her ankles. This is what you're doing to your wife, your girlfriend, every single time you tell her a lie. And what happens to that woman? She is paralyzed, she can't move, she's not free, she is trapped. And men, the only way to reverse what you've done to her—what you keep doing to her each time you lie—is to tell the truth. When you tell the truth, you release one thread of rope that's wrapped around her ankles, that's wrapped around her mind and her heart. Never underestimate a woman's intuition. God gave us that, it is a gift, and we didn't ask for it, we don't have to pay for it. It's free to each and every woman so she can decipher a man's BS. It means that God is trying to help us wade through the BS if we want to wade through it. But some of ya'll don't want to hear the truth. You prefer to hear the lies, and that's on you. But you're living a lie, and loving a liar is no way to live. Living a lie is no way to live, either. So brothers, set your wives free and tell the truth. And if telling the truth means you're going to lose too much or that you'll be in the doghouse with the wifey, then stop doing what you're doing. Then you don't have to lie. If you're not really out with the boys but with your little girlfriend, you need to dump the girlfriend, so that when you're really out with the boys, you don't have to call up Ralph and ask him to cover for you. Because a cover is really a see-through cover when it comes to God. The eyes of the Lord are in every place beholding the evil and the good. Can I get an amen tonight?"

Not long afterward, the service comes to a close. I stand to my feet and hug Marlene with all my might. I gently tell

her, "Sister, you are forgiven." She gives me a look of grati-
tude and whispers, "Sometimes you seem like the older sister." I nod; I understand.

When we begin to leave our pew and walk out of the sanctuary, Marlene taps my shoulder and points. My mama and
Loretta are seated a few rows over. They're crying and holding
hands and are so engaged in talking that they don't notice us
slowly pass by. Marlene stops walking and I do, too. I overhear
Loretta tell my mama, "I feel compelled to counsel women
because of the guilt I feel for the scandalous things I've done,
from one woman to another. This is my way of covering my
mistakes, by being honest with women and hopefully steering
them in a better direction than the road I chose to take. Now I
realize I have to come at them with more gentle honesty. I
want something better. I want to be the best woman by having
more respectful relationships with both men and women.
With my daughter and my stepdaughter. And if it means I
have to leave Blinky to achieve something better, then so be it."

I swallow a thick, sore knot lodged in the middle of my
throat. And I can't help myself.

"Mama," I squeak. The two ladies are so busy embracing
that Marlene has to loudly clear her throat a couple of times.
Mama turns around, locks eyes with me, yelps, and wildly
gestures at me. I go sit next to her on the pew. Using the tips
of my fingers, I dab at the wet streaks that are on her face.

"I love you, Mama. I'm sorry."

Mama nods, shakes her head, too overwhelmed to get out
the words she's trying to say. But I understand. It feels so
good to understand.

After we daughters share long and tight hugs with our
mamas, we depart from the sanctuary and eventually reach

the parking lot. The brilliance of the sunny sky lifts my spirits so high I feel like I want to take flight. I am so amazed, so thrilled that deep inside, a powerful sense of happiness has overtaken my heart and completely filled it with peace. And to know my contentment has absolutely nothing to do with a man is one of the most gratifying and remarkable discoveries I've ever experienced. I feel complete without Mr. Right Now by my side. Right now, I am acceptable and fulfilled just as I am. I want to sing, I want to shout, I want to share this happiness with the world.

"So," Marlene asks me. "Did you enjoy the service?"

"It was one of the best experiences of my life. It has helped me discover who I am as a person, as a woman."

"That means a lot coming from you."

"I'm glad you invited me. I want more."

"Does that mean you may want to come back and check out the Singles Ministry?"

"I think that might be a strong possibility."

She beams at me, and I smile back. "Marlene, may I ask you a question?" We slowly start walking toward her car, which is parked way on the other side of the huge lot.

"Ask away."

"Um, do you regret getting that tat?"

She stops walking and playfully rolls her eyes. "Girl, stop tripping," she pouts. "Even though I never told you before, that M and J tattoo stands for Marlene and Jesus."

"Marlene and Jesus?" I give her a full-blown grin. "That's freaking *brilliant*. Girl, you are one of the smartest women I know. I mean that." We continue walking and chitchatting.

I take my sister's hand and raise it toward the sky.

I had so much fun writing this novel and have loads of people to thank:

GOD—Every day I still feel like I am in the midst of a wonderful dream. I am so thankful to be living the biggest dream I've ever had in my life.

FAMILY—Thanks to my family, who is very supportive and excited about my writing career. Thanks to my Aunt Janice for giving me information about her occupation.

PUBLISHER—I adore Three Rivers Press. You do your job so very well. Special thanks to Emily Lavelle, PR extraordinaire.

EDITOR—Heather Proulx. I trust your very capable editing skills. Thanks a trillion for your support and encouragement.

AGENT—The one and only Claudia Menza. Can you believe this is my fourth release? Thanks for giving me my start in the industry.

FRIENDS—You know who you are. Thanks for the conversations and the laughs.

MEDIA/REVIEWERS—*USA Today* (thanks for the wonderful feature), *Essence* (Henry Patrik Bass, thanks), *Black Expressions* (as always), all the book clubs (K.C. Girlfriends Book Club and Sistah Friend Book Club) and websites that consistently feature my novels, you are invaluable. Thanks to the Houston Public Library and Texas Library Association.

Also thanks to Ann Brown of RAWSISTAZ for a great review of MBFAMM.

AUTHOR PALS—Cheryl Robinson, Marissa Monteilh (a true gem), Margaret Johnson-Hodge, Lexi Davis, Electa Rome Parks, S. B. Redd, Aberjhani, Kole Black, Stacy Deanne, T. Styles, Desiree Day, Nancey Flowers, Joy King, Philana Marie Boles, Vanessa Davis Griggs, Marsha Jenkins Sanders, and too many others to name. Thanks for being in my corner.

UNIVERSITY OF HOUSTON—Thanks for your interest and support, for buying my book, or at least telling me you're gonna buy the book (wink). I appreciate your putting up with me! Special thanks to Mr. Irvin, Mary, and the BN bookstore.

MYSPACE BUDDIES—Haha, there are a lot of wonderful and supportive fans out there. You make me laugh, you make me smile, you make me feel so good inside.

DUANE—Babe, thanks for teaching me so many things I never knew and sharing so many special moments with me. I appreciate your earnest support of my career. And thanks for being my road dawg and having the courage to accompany me on this journey.

THE FANS—Where would I be without the readers who offer so much support, encouragement, positivity, and insight? I am so grateful to you for helping me to have a writing career. Keep buying those books! Don't forget to e-mail me at cydney@booksbycydney.com. Merci! Gracias! Danke! Asante! Cám on ! Gratia! Thanks!

Cydney Rax is the author of *My Daughter's Boyfriend, My Husband's Girlfriend,* and *My Best Friend and My Man.* Cydney is a native Detroiter and a graduate of both Cass Technical High School and Eastern Michigan University. In her spare time she loves playing Nintendo Wii, checking out the latest movies (comedies, thrillers, dramas, and action), watching *Family Guy,* and trying to keep her life in perspective. A single mother of one, she currently resides in Houston.